CHARLOTTE TOWNSEND

Dragon's Keep

Copyright © 2022 by Charlotte Townsend

All rights reserved. No part of this publication may be reproduced, stored or transmitted in any form or by any means, electronic, mechanical, photocopying, recording, scanning, or otherwise without written permission from the publisher. It is illegal to copy this book, post it to a website, or distribute it by any other means without permission.

First edition

This book was professionally typeset on Reedsy.
Find out more at reedsy.com

For Mum and Dad, who always believed.

Contents

Prologue		iii
1	Death to the Dragon	1
2	An Unexpected Summons	7
3	Bringer of Truth	15
4	Law of the King	23
5	Dungeon Dwelling	28
6	Traditional Preparations	33
7	Procession of Death	42
8	An Honourable End	52
9	No Ordinary Cave	57
10	Nivres	61
11	Of Sparring and Consequences	71
12	Return of the Knight	83
13	Aftermath and Impasse	92
14	Flight	97
15	Dunsaw	102
16	Difficult Truths	111
17	Understandings	117
18	Blossoming	122
19	Attire and Atonement	127
20	Assessments and Alterations	136
21	Infiltration	144
22	Fear Amid Flame	152
23	Purpose	160

24	Everything	168
25	Escape	172
26	Hollow Hearts	179
27	Forest Trouble	190
28	Instinctual	195
29	Protection Detail	201
30	Apart	207
31	An Unexpected Battle	212
32	Entrapment	216
33	Calm Before the Storm	222
34	Silent Death	226
35	The Arena	234
36	Standing Ground	242
37	Tracking the Dragon	252
38	At The Threshold	257
39	Lost and Found	263
40	Reunion	269
41	Declarations	280
42	Steel and Ice	286
43	United Front	295
44	Unresolved Matters	301
45	New Beginnings	312
	Epilogue	320
	Acknowledgements	323
	Coming Soon...	324
	About the Author	325
	Also by Charlotte Townsend	326

Prologue

The Palatine of Idrelas crept with trepidation through the palace, his ornate robes decorating the floors as he passed. His stomach swirled like a storm as he continued down corridors adorned with portraits of long dead royalty and tapestries of great battles. It was late in the afternoon and the glowing gold sunlight silhouetted his nervous form as he passed the large arched windows. At any other time, he might have stopped to admire the pleasing, magnificent view of the kingdom. But not now. *Why him? Why did he have to do this?* Oh yes, because he was the King's advisor, respected throughout Idrelas, the reason amidst the chaos. He grimaced. Sometimes (rarely) but *sometimes*, he could hate his position.

Being The Palatine, it was a part of his job to know the King's regular movements. In times of crisis or alarm, it was useful as the King could be reached immediately. Unfortunately, it also meant bad news reached the King's ears more swiftly. He swept down another staircase, the dread growing with each step. Almost there. The Palatine came to a stop outside a large wooden door, held together in places by black iron. Taking a deep breath, The Palatine tried calming himself before rapping on the door to announce his presence. "Enter." A voice called from beyond the door. No turning back now. The Palatine tentatively pushed open the door and stepped inside.

King Falon stood in the small circular room, carefully watering a medium sized terrarium. Various terrariums containing plants from the five kingdoms were dotted around on shelves and tables, in what The Palatine could discern, an elemental or celestial order. Plants that thrived on the moon for example, were in little terrariums high up by a large, perfect circular window, designed to maximise moonlight exposure. The river plants were generously housed in a huge fountain terrarium lower to the ground. Each was beautiful in their own way and the air here seemed peaceful. Shame he was about to ruin it.

"Viras," King Falon uttered, not taking his eyes off the little ecosystem in his hands, "I take it you didn't come all the way down here to admire my terrariums."

He swallowed. "As lovely as they are, you are correct, your majesty."

"Well out with it then Viras, you're The Palatine of Idrelas, not The Silent Tongue."

There was nothing for it now. "We've had word your highness, from Sabeline."

"Ah and does my knight tell me I can rejoice for she has finally slain the great dragon plaguing our land?" King Falon said with a tone Viras couldn't quite make out. It sounded like malice and curiosity merged into one and he wasn't sure he liked it.

"Erhm, I'm afraid not your majesty. The dragon has evaded her blade once more." Viras braced himself for the King's wrath, but Falon merely set the terrarium gently back on its table.

"I see. Sabeline is a proud Knight. Her sensibilities mean she will chase that dragon to the ends of the five kingdoms if duty called for it."

"I am glad you have such faith in the Knights of Idrelas sire, their status as capable warriors and defenders of the realm is legendary after all." Viras felt his chest become lighter. The King was a sensible man, there was no need to...

"However, just because Sabeline has the patience to spend her life hunting the dragon, it does not mean I share her sentiment."

"Sire?"

"She has had many opportunities and the dragon has outwitted her and some of our best warriors. She gets *one* more chance."

"Very good sire. One more chance and then we shall call her back to the kingdom." That didn't sound too bad, sure if she failed on her last attempt, the Knight would be restless and distraught back at the kingdom. All of the knights did not take failure well at first, but after a day or so they always retreated to their teachings, that failure makes them stronger. Another knight would be dispatched in Sabeline's place and all would be...

"Yes. For if she fails this time, the punishment will be *severe*." King Falon sneered, the shadows coating his expression in just the right menacing way.

"P-punishment?" Viras ventured. "For a Knight of Idrelas?" The very idea was unthinkable. "What kind of punishment?"

King Falon smiled. "Given the chance, she will hunt that dragon to her death. It is only fitting that she compensate for her failures in the same way."

The Palatine stared at the King aghast. "You wish to *kill* a Knight? For not taking down a *dragon*? Have you seen a dragon sire? I don't wish to talk out of turn, but they're not exactly the easiest creatures to slay."

"Don't worry Viras, I have no intention of killing a Knight. It would put me out of favour with the people, not to mention call my actions into question by the council. I could rather do without a rebellion or being overthrown."

"Oh good, because for a moment there…"

"I'll simply get someone or *something* I should say, to do it for me. And the best part? She'll walk to her death willingly due to her sense of *duty*." King Falon stated confidently and with an air of fact. "Well, I do believe it's nearly time for dinner and taking care of my little friends has left me starved. Come along Viras." The King grasped his hands and strode out of the room, the epitome of regality and with no evidence of the disconcerting change.

The Palatine, however, was rather confused and a bit pale. That side of the King had left him shaken. Surely he hadn't meant what he said? The King was probably just tired that's all, not thinking rationally. Yes that must be it.

"Oh and Viras?" King Falon's voice echoed just before he peered back round the door, "I'd appreciate it if you'd keep this conversation between us. I'd hate for you to suffer any consequences from a *loose* tongue."

The Palatine nodded his head nervously and satisfied, the King left once again. The swirling storm was back in Viras's stomach at the King's departure and he wiped his suddenly sweating palms on his expensive robes. He feared this King, the stranger he had seen take Falon's features. If the King was becoming undone, then he feared greatly for what the future may hold.

He had a feeling even the Knights of Idrelas wouldn't be able to stop it.

1

Death to the Dragon

She had this.

Sabeline remained in tense position, hidden behind an outcrop of stones. From her vantage point, she had a good view of her men, also hidden around the outcrop and in the below clearing strategically. After her last mishap, she had tracked the dragon to the Great Green Plateau. It was clever on the dragon's part, large open space and little cover for Sabeline and her team. But she was better. She had to be.

A dead cattle procured from a local village had been laid out in the centre of their arrangement. The farmer had been reluctant to give it to them at first, but as soon as Sabeline explained who she was and what it was needed for, he was all too happy to hand it over. Though she presumed the hefty gold she paid him might have also had something to do with it. The dragon would expect it to be a trap of course. What it wouldn't expect was Sabeline's surprise attack from above. The plan had been formulated for days as they travelled, every little detail had been explicitly analysed and a counter move suggested for every and any eventuality she could think of.

This time, she smirked, gripping her scabbard tighter, *the dragon will be mine.*

Some of the men shifted restlessly. They had already been out here for several hours awaiting the dragon and she could admit that even her limbs were starting to ache. But the anticipation coiled in Sabeline's gut as she trained her eyes to the sky. *Eventually it will come.* She was sure of it. The dragon had been her adversary for several months now and begrudgingly, had gained some of her hard won respect. It had been a worthy opponent, but now their little dance would be coming to an end. Sabeline felt satisfaction wash over her at the inevitable events, but there was a strange mix of sadness too. Her lip curled. *It is only because no one else has challenged me as much as this beast.*

Suddenly in the distance, the sound of steady flapping echoed across the Plateau. Detecting the loud beats, the men under her command raised their heads to the sky, trying to pinpoint the direction it was coming from. Sabeline turned to the soldier at her side, instantly making a falling motion with her fingers, imitating rain or snow. *North.* He nodded and repeated her gesture to the rest of the men. She'd know those wingbeats anywhere. The great dragon was coming and she was going to kill the creature. A dark speck slowly emerged against the clouds, gradually growing in size the closer it came. Sabeline narrowed her eyes, drawing her blade slowly. *That's it, come to me you monstrosity.* She flicked her gaze towards the men. Even though they were trained, she could still see the nervous way they clung to their swords in the face of the dragon. *Trained, but not trained enough.* She kept her stance steady and blade still as the beast flew ever nearer. She was a Knight of Idrelas after all.

With surprising speed and agility for a creature so large, it was not long before it was upon their location, circling wide several times. Gradually, the dragon decreased its distance, eventually circling to just a narrow arch. Sabeline remained motionless, though the thunderous staccato of her heart betrayed her true feelings. The dragon *needed* to land. Everything hinged on that key point. If it were to fly off now, she didn't know what she'd do (although it wouldn't be pretty, she knew that much). Barely daring to breathe, Sabeline never tore her gaze from the cautious beast. It was a good job she kept her brunette hair short, she could only imagine the long strands that would be obscuring her view and hindering her progress as the dragon agitated the airflow with its wings. Sometimes it paid to be practical.

Carefully, the dragon began to descend. Yes! The initial relief soon began to dissipate as the dragon curiously sniffed around the carcass. Silently, Sabeline held her hand up, signalling to wait. It was still being cautious. She needed the beast distracted and relaxed before her attack. A few more moments passed as the dragon continuously inspected the cattle and peered around with its searching stare. Sabeline gritted her teeth, needing to channel her itching nerves into something. *By the goddess, just eat the damned thing!* As though the creature had heard her angry thoughts, it began to settle and rip apart the meat with its long dagger-like teeth. The bloody flesh scattered into various pinkish red sized globs as the dragon began to feast. Sabeline sneered. The sight was disgusting. But, it was what she had hoped for.

Edging forward, Sabeline slowly crept from behind the rock concealing her presence. Making sure her blade was clenched securely in her fingers, she took a deep breath. This was it.

There was no room for error. Her armoured feet hurried across the grass, building up to a sprint. Coming to the end of the small cliff, she leapt off the edge. It was difficult to look dignified as she fell through the air and she had no doubt her old mentor would've had something to say about her less than elegant descent. *Who cares? Looking splendid doesn't get the work done.*

The dragon was still tearing the cattle apart as she landed solidly between its head and neck. Quickly, she raised her blade ready to plunge it into the beast's body. Just as the metal was about to slice through scales, an impact to her right side left her breathless and scrabbling on the side of the dragon, her blade balancing between the small dark red spines running down its neck. What in the five kingdoms was that? What had hit her? The thick, whip-like red-orange tail that was hurtling towards her answered the question. Releasing one hand, she managed to dodge a second impact from the limb as she flung herself backwards against the creature's side. Shouts and screams reached her ears as the men charged from their positions, forming and oval and blocking the creature. The idea was their small blows and cuts would exhaust the dragon, giving her an advantage.

Sabeline threw herself back to her previous position, sinking her hand back into the dragon's skin as she crawled up its neck. Her side was going to bruise; she could tell by the throbbing ache currently pulsating across that area of her body. Hauling herself up, she ran towards her blade. As soon as her fingers curled around the scabbard, the dragon reared up, causing her to tumble down its neck and back. Some of the spines punctured her flesh and she bit her lip to keep from crying out at the pain. The men were still valiantly attacking the creature from all sides, though it seemed the dragon had had enough. It opened its jaws and released a magnificent torrent of fire. Those with spelled fire resistant shields had been placed near the head of the beast and immediately brought them up in defence. Some unfortunate souls nearby were not so lucky as the fire caught them. Sabeline watched as they desperately tried to roll around in the grass, attempting to stop the burning. This is why the dragon had to die. The destruction it left behind devastated Idrelas.

With renewed determination, Sabeline made her agonising way towards one of the dragon's wings. Gripping her blade with both hands, she stabbed it straight down onto the joint where the wing connected to the body, feeling mildly disturbed at the squelching noise that emanated. The dragon roared furiously and Sabeline had just enough time to pull out her blade before the beast took off. When it had reached a few feet in the air, it rolled, dislodging Sabeline. There was no time to think as she careened towards the ground of the Plateau. The hand not clutching her blade flailed as she tried to grasp anything that may slow down her fall. *Come on, come on*! Her fingers eventually managed to catch a tree branch, burning with the effort. Her arm felt as though it had been pulled out it's socket with the strain of forcibly supporting the rest of her. This was no problem, all she had to do was manoeuvre herself towards the trunk and then she could climb down relatively easily. Altering her position, a deafening crack suddenly filled the air as the branch snapped.

Landing with force at the bottom of the tree, Sabeline grimaced as pain shot up her tailbone. She'd had enough of falling to her death to last a lifetime. Battered, bruised and bleeding, Sabeline surveyed the scene. Most of the soldiers appeared to have minimal injury, though there were some who looked how she felt. A glance to her left showed some charred bodies. At the sight, the despair and fury crashed in her soul and she let out an unearthly scream, throwing the tree branch she still held away from her.

The devastation of battle and failure was not the ideal time for a tidy and polished Palace Commander to come riding up to her as she sat broken by the tree. As he looked down at her from his impeccably groomed stallion (that she reasoned had probably never seen battle), the pity he was trying to hide behind a mask of professionalism made her want to scream again.

2

An Unexpected Summons

"What do you mean that was my *last* chance?" Sabeline growled at the Commander as a Healer applied a paste of tilweed to her bruised side. A second Healer was currently probing her punctured flesh from the Dragon's spikes, causing her muscles to spasm. She hoped Commander Karo realised he needed to tread *very* carefully right now. To his credit, the Commander shifted uncomfortably under her glare.

"King Falon advised me to deliver the message to you. He has decided that enough of your time has been spent trying to kill this creature and was going to offer you one more chance following your last report. However, it appeared that when I arrived, the chance had already been acted out." Commander Karo pulled out a wax sealed scroll of paper from within his messenger bag. "He wrote it down as a royal decree, if you deigned not to believe me." The Commander offered the scroll to Sabeline, holding it in his hand loosely.

Agitated, Sabeline thrust out her arm and snatched the parchment, tearing the seal apart quickly. Another prod from a Healer somewhere on her body released a hiss from her lips, following the sharp pain it caused. The Healers nodded to each other and changed to a different paste of goddess knew what. She'd stopped caring what they were doing, so long as they eliminated the protesting screaming of her flesh. Turning to the scroll, Sabeline scanned over the curving calligraphic words, carefully penned in deep black ink. It was the King's hand alright, there was no mistaking the flourish accompanying certain letters as anyone other than his.

My dear Knight of Idrelas,

By Royal Decree, should the next attempt on the Dragon's life fail following your report, you are to return to the kingdom immediately. I have had enough of failure from a Knight of your calibre and deem it best you return to...regroup.

Signed
  His Esteemed Majesty
  King Falon III

"This has to be a mistake, surely his highness knows of the destruction that *thing* has reeked across Idrelas? Why would he issue a decree commanding that I stop?" Sabeline questioned, puzzled as she crushed the scroll in her hand. The Healers shuffled around her and she raised her arms so the bandage could be wrapped around her wounds more easily.

Commander Karo shrugged, his armour clanking as he did. "Perhaps he thinks returning to the kingdom will provide a fresh perspective. I'm not a Knight, but maybe one of your Creed could provide a new solution after hearing the strategies you've used so far? That would make sense to me."

Sabeline grunted as her linen shirt was pulled back down over her stomach by the Healers. "The others must have been talking and put forward some proposals to the King. It is the only thing I can think of to justify this lunacy. Have you *seen* the aftermath of a dragon attack Commander?"

The Commander shook his head. "No m'lady."

Her eyes lost the hard glint and became softer. "I have. It is a sight one does not soon forget. I am *abhorrent* to the idea of returning and leaving Idrelas unprotected." Sabeline murmured quietly.

"I understand m'lady, but it is the King's word." The Commander stressed, though not unkindly.

A humourless smirk graced her face. "And I understand *that* more than most Commander." Her thoughts drifted briefly to the oath she'd taken when becoming a Knight of Idrelas. As much as she may despise it right now, the King's word was law. Sighing, she stretched her arms and flexed her fingers, ensuring her limbs were in working order before sliding off the long table. She still had some visible bruising marring her skin, but they would soon heal.

Carefully, Sabeline wandered over to her armour that had been placed to the side. She hated medical tents. They always smelt foul and her armour was never properly attended to. It was why she made it a point to avoid them as much as possible. *The day just goes from bad to worse, at least I'm not dead.* Slowly she redressed in the pieces that didn't require assistance to adorn. There was no way she was riding back to the kingdom in just her linen shirt and breeches. She still had some pride left after all and the Healers had assured her that wearing her armour shouldn't aggravate her wounds and injuries *too* much. The King's command was absolute. There would be more trouble to pay if she didn't adhere to the order, especially as it had been made a Royal Decree. King Falon must be extremely displeased that she hadn't slain the dragon yet. Yes, there would *definitely* be more disruption if she ignored his words. Cursing herself for even considering disregarding what was now law, Sabeline shrugged on her ornate but strong spaulders. An unpleasant feeling began to settle over her as she replayed the decree in her head. They may be King Falon's words, but some had sounded rather unlike him. Maybe the stresses of the day had affected him before he penned it. *Maybe.*

Commander Karo had said nothing as she'd become lost in her contemplations and pulled on the rest of the sections that she could manage. Sabeline gestured at the last few pieces. "Someone will need to saddle these to my horse, I'm not leaving them." Armour was damned expensive after all.

"Very well, m'lady. Does this mean you'll be returning to the kingdom?" the Commander asked, still hesitant.

Sabeline nodded. "The sooner I return, the sooner I can deal with this madness and continue hunting the dragon." Thinking better of it, she hoisted up her remaining plates of armour and shoved them into Commander Karo's arms, watching as he scrambled to accommodate them without dropping any. "Thank you for volunteering Commander. Shall we go?" Sabeline asked, striding towards the flaps of the tent. She didn't wait for an answer from the shocked Commander, but it wasn't long before she heard his measured, loud footsteps behind her.

She held her head high as she passed the me still scattered around the part of the Plateau they'd selected. Her revered war horse had thankfully already been fetched from the camp they'd set up the previous night. Sabeline stroked the horse's muzzle. "Good to see you Hylix." The horse snorted in response and stomped its front leg on the ground. Sabeline smiled. "Impatient aren't we? Well we'll be on the road soon enough." She hooked her sabaton into the saddle's stirrup, using it as leverage to mount and swing her other leg around into position. The men had begun to gather around, congregating near her horse in anticipation of her orders. *No time like the present.* "By Royal Decree, we return to Idrelas's Kingdom. We leave immediately." Sabeline called loudly to the gathered soldiers. At her orders, they instantly scattered to prepare as hastily as possible for the ride home. She noted some wore smiles on their faces and regretted she could not share their sentiment or excitement at the return. The strange feeling from the tent had remained and she could not seem to shake it.

Whatever awaited her back at the kingdom, she did not anticipate a warm reception.

***

The kingdom loomed dark and terrible before them. Well, in her imagination. In reality it appeared no different to how Sabeline had left it several months before. The grey imposing walls mixed with lighter sand coloured stone were still intact and the flags bearing the crest of Idrelas were still flying from the towers. A sigh escaped her lips as she scrutinised her home. Yes, nothing had changed but that unsettling feeling remained, curling in her stomach as though waiting for *something*. Trying to mask her body's rising tension, Sabeline urged Hylix on towards the gate.

The remainder of her men followed behind, falling into a steady rhythm. The gentle treads of their horses mixed with the pacing of the foot soldiers in a returning symphony. Commander Karo followed on his horse a few paces behind her, as was custom. No one was equal to a Knight and the only one higher than a Knight was the King.

They arrived far too soon at the gate in Sabeline's opinion, though a normal amount of time had passed. She was doing a lot of that since they had first spotted the kingdom through the trees. *Stop this nonsense,* her mind whispered as she drew herself to her full height and tried to pretend her apprehension of unknown origins did *not* exist. "Gatekeeper!" she called loudly. A portly, older man came into view, sporting a long grey beard that dragged on the floor. She got the impression the Gatekeeper had spent his youth betting how long he could grow it. "A'right A'right, I heard ye." The Gatekeeper grumbled as he stepped towards his little outhouse. "Can't even take a whizz in peace without someone demanding to be let in."

She bit her lip to stifle a smile. "I'd be most grateful if you were to let me and my men through Gatekeeper. The King is expecting me."

The Gatekeeper squinted at her face and then turned his gaze to the armour she'd managed to pull on before leaving. "Aye, a Knight eh? The Truth Bringer if I'm not mistaken?"

Sabeline nodded. "That's me." The titles bestowed upon her and the other Knights were rarely used between them, but she knew the common folk preferred to call them by their titles. She supposed a title was easier to remember than twenty or so names.

"Well Truth Bringer, it be an honour to open the gate for ye return." The Gatekeeper reached for the long wooden lever behind him, pulling it down. Instantly, a creaking groaning filled the air as the iron gate retracted upwards. She winced at the noise but nodded her thanks at the Gatekeeper, flicking the reins. The war horse trotted forward, leading them into Idrelas.

Hylix made his way around the curling cobbled streets. It was eerily quiet. Sabeline hadn't exactly expected a parade, but she did think more people would be about. Maybe it was because they were in the lower town? *It shouldn't matter though.* The lower town was a bit more ramshackle, with off centre roofs and slightly wonky brickwork, but it was still neat. After all, it was the first thing visitors and travellers would see upon entering the kingdom and it was the lower town that would form their immediate impression of the same. "Commander," she called behind her "why is it so quiet?" Commander Karo looked around, as though only just noticing the silence for the first time. "I'm not entirely sure m'lady. They may have moved up to the mid or high level town?"

Well that is a great comfort. Sabeline rolled her eyes, thankful the Commander couldn't see her face. "Perhaps." She answered with appeasement coating her tone, still keeping a wary eye on her surroundings. The quiet followed them up until the mid-town.

At least the mid-town was a bit better. People were going about daily tasks, waving at them as they passed. It was exactly as she'd expect the place to be functioning. So why was it not this way in the lower town? What was going on there? She waved back when appropriate, trying to pick out anyone that could be from the lower towns. She'd hate to admit that Karo was right, but if she could find one less thing to be worried about at this moment, she'd take it. But unless the entirety of the lower town had travelled up and purchased whole new wardrobes (unlikely), Sabeline couldn't find anyone fitting the lower town. The sun disappeared as Hylix stepped into the shadow of the castle. She was still halfway to the higher level town and not for the first time, marvelled at how big the castle actually *was* for its shadow cast over part of mid-town. From this distance, her gaze picked out the Knight's Towers easily. She couldn't be sure, but thought she saw some figures on the balcony, the only true comforting sight since she'd passed through the gate. The rest of her Creed may have answers about the lower town. With that thought, she encouraged Hylix forward. She'd had enough of disconcerting, ominous feelings. It was time to find out just what was going on.

3

Bringer of Truth

As the sound of hooves graced the fine cobbles of the upper town, Sabeline could feel the cloying luxury permeating every corner. This was where the nobles tended to remain, rarely venturing beyond their comfortable borders to the rest of the kingdom. It was fairly certain no one from the lower town would have made it this far. A handful of the nobles were kind, with morals instilled in them through generations. The majority however, were of a more spoilt nature and would detect in a heartbeat if anybody wearing less than silks and velvets was in their midst.

Sabeline continued with a frown fixed on her face. She detested the upper town. *There's more finery to be found in actions, rather than appearances.* What did how much gold you had matter if you were killed by a rampaging salamander? She could never understand the sensibilities of the noble families. Urging Hylix in, the war horse quickly trotted to the base of High Point. Sabeline's routine disgust evaporated as apprehension once again began to take root. Craning her neck back and glancing up at High Point, the ostentatious castle loomed over all. A moment of clarity came over her as a sudden thought echoed in her mind. *Whatever fate awaits me up there, I fear I will not find solace here again.* Sabeline shook her head, short brunette locks angrily scattering as she did. Surely she was being ridiculous? The failed attempt on the dragon's life was plaguing her, that was all. Her lips twisted unpleasantly. Then why did she still feel the same?

Enough! Jerking the reins, Sabeline insisted Hylix gallop forward. The sooner she arrived, the sooner she could put an end to this nonsense. Obediently, the war horse sprinted up the stone paved slope. It was a fairly long ride, the idea being that if any invading enemies made it this far, High Point was designed to be their undoing. For a Knight of Idrelas however, it was common practice.

As Sabeline rode, she kept her gaze trained on the Knights Tower. The possible figures she had seen from mid-town were more substantial now that she was getting closer. The silhouettes appeared to notice her travelling towards the castle and stepped away hurriedly from the balcony back inside the tower. *I'm going there first.* If there was anyone she trusted in this world to prepare her for what may come, it was her sisters in arms. Hylix had been bred for endurance and speed and though her ears detected some slight panting, the war horse was barely breaking a sweat. She placed a comforting hand at the base of his neck. "Almost there boy, just a little further." Securing her already tightly curled fingers around the reins, Sabeline carefully adjusted them, ensuring Hylix would follow the direction and veer to the right. She refused to chance being seen near the main gate, widely left of her position. The horse didn't fail and immediately aimed for the small courtyard laid out in front of the tower.

Shining armour greeted her vision, the sun glittering off the various types and sections adorning those who stood before her. Mariel was the first to run up to her. "Sabeline, thank the goddess you've returned! The beast is slain then?"

A confused expression crossed her face as she dismounted. "It is good to see you too Mariel, but what do you mean by asking if the dragon is dead?"

This time Mariel was puzzled. "That is why you have returned, is it not?"

The calm presence of Echoris took this moment to step forward. "We did not know of your return until moments ago, when we saw you riding. Before you left months ago, you always said you would return once the dragon was dead." Her soft but powerful voice interjected.

Unease at their earnest faces began to fill Sabeline's stomach. *They do not lie.* Why would the Knights not be told of her summons? Swallowing hard, she reached out grasping Mariel's shoulder firmly. "Call a counsel of the Knights. From what you speak, it seems there is much to discuss."

Mariel and Echoris shared a worried glance between them, but nonetheless nodded firmly.

"Go now, there is no time to lose."

The two knights did as they were bid and retreated to the tower. Once they were out of sight, a heavy sigh slowly left her. Something was amiss. She was sure that these events were not a coincidence. Receiving a strange summons, the mystery of lower town and now the Knights not knowing of her return? Gripping the reins, Sabeline made her way to the stables, Hylix dutifully following her. "Come on boy, at least you can have a nice rest. I do not think I'll get the same." She led the horse in, carefully removing the equipment gracing his form and settling him into his stall. Letting her hand pet his muzzle a few times, her thoughts drifted. Commander Karo would no doubt have made his way to the main gate, or would very soon. She'd lost him as she'd traversed the upper town, but as the man didn't seem to realise anything strange was going on, she'd lose valuable time once he made his report to the King. *Hopefully Mariel and Echoris will have gathered everyone by now.* "I'll see you later my friend," Sabeline whispered, bidding her horse farewell. Hylix huffed in return as she walked back out. Sabeline paused by the stable entrance. She'd called a counsel and now it was time to deliver. Dusting off her fears and burying the unease, she stood up straight and held her head high. By the goddess, she was the Bringer of Truth and it was time for everyone to face it, including her. Determination blazed through her as she marched towards the Knights Tower, ignoring the fading aches and twinges from her healing injuries. Rapidly, Sabeline strode towards a large set of two doors, located opposite the Tower's main entrance. The entryway was grand but modest, befitting of the Knights that lived there. Usually, Sabeline would stop and linger around the marble statue of Alondra, the very first Knight of Idrelas, who's skill and kindness had become legend over centuries. Most Knights aspired to emulate Alondra, herself included.

This time however, Sabeline stepped past it, refusing to come to a halt until she reached the large wooden doors. *Nothing is as feared as the truth.* With that thought, her eyes narrowed and she placed both hands flat on the doors, pushing them wide open.

Several heads turned in her direction.

Ignoring their stares, Sabeline calmly walked behind four

seated knights on the left side of the table and took her empty seat. Silence reigned for a moment more, then Ivetta and Jaketta, the Twin Suns, spoke in unison. "Why the need for a counsel? What has happened?"

"Things are amiss." Sabeline stated simply. "And I feel… *apprehensive* about the future."

"I, too, have sensed ill on the wind these past few days." Echoris added. Some of the Knights gathered began to lean forward at Echoris's words, giving the Counsel their full attention. Echoris was a mystery, but if she sensed something, you would do well to heed it. *At least it is not just me.*

Sabeline let out the breath she was holding. To have her fears validated by Echoris was a relief in one way, but the niggling dread that had followed since receiving the summons suddenly flooded her stomach. "Very well. Then what have you seen that is amiss?" Ascilia, seated at the head of the table, asked with curiousity.

"When I returned earlier, Mariel and Echoris asked if the dragon was dead. It is not." There were a few gasps and murmurs at this. *Perhaps I was more adamant when I left than I realised.* She held a hand up for silence. "After my last attempt on the dragon's life days ago, Commander Karo appeared with a Royal Decree from King Falon stating I was to return to the kingdom." At this, Sabeline placed the document on the table. She had procured it from her saddlebag after telling Mariel and Echoris to call this meeting. As expected, the gathered Knights immediately tried to get a better look. In the end, Mariel claimed the parchment and read it before passing it on. "Why were we not informed of this?" Kilyn frowned, passing on the scroll to the next Knight.

"I do not know. I had hoped that our Creed would have the

answers, presuming that suggestions had been given to the King on how to combat the dragon. Though now I doubt that is the case."

Ascilia nodded. "As far as I'm aware, no one has provided any strategies or plans to the King."

All Knights murmured their agreement.

"I do not like these words," Echoris interned. "There is something strange about them." She put the decree down quickly, as if the paper itself had burned her. Sabeline agreed.

"There is something else. When I arrived in Lower Town, it was deserted. There was no one to be seen. As I travelled to the castle, I kept a lookout for any Lower Town residents, but it was as if they had vanished. What has happened there?" She watched as various expressions of surprise flickered like a candle flame across each Knight.

"The Lower Town you say?" Ivetta ventured.

"Yes, it is still in good condition. Though the residents appear to be missing."

The twins shared a meaningful look. "We saw soldiers leaving the castle two nights ago. Not many, but enough. We thought they were just going on patrol but now..." Jaketta trailed off, troubled.

"We need to investigate this. First we're not told that Sabeline is to return and now the Lower Town is *abandoned*?" Mariel slammed her fist down on the table. "Something has to be done."

"Did anyone see anything else out of the ordinary? Something that they dismissed, but upon reflection could be important?" Sabeline drew her hands together, interlacing her fingers and resting her chin on her knuckles. Secrets did not sit well with her. Especially ones apparently being kept by the King himself. What could he have to gain from these events? Or perhaps, what was he trying to put in motion? If he performed the actions before revealing his plans, no one would be able to contest as it had already been carried out. *But why?* King Falon wasn't known for scheming, rather the opposite. It was an enigma they needed to solve, for the good of Idrelas if nothing else.

"I didn't see anything two nights ago, but when I was in Mid-Town this morning two Commanders went through the entrance to Lower Town. I thought there may have been a skirmish, but if Ivetta and Jaketta say soldiers went in before, do you think they were checking for something?" Kilyn offered.

"It's a possibility." Echoris spoke. "I think we are at a stage where every avenue must be explored." There were mutters and nodding from all the Knights at the table.

"I will go." Mariel said, determination lacing every sharp word.

"Then it is decided." Sabeline raised her head from where it rested on her hands, gazing around the table. "Mariel will investigate Lower Town and we will all be vigilant in *any* observations, reporting on those deemed unusual." She felt somewhat lighter as she addressed her Creed and at least provisions had been made for Lower Town. Her brow furrowed at that tendril of thought. It was just like when she had been staring up from the bottom of High Point and the ominous words had floated through her mind like wisps. *Why was she being haunted by these thoughts?* It was just a decree, wasn't it? But Echoris had sensed something sinister. This counsel was not going as she'd hoped, it seemed she was getting more questions than answers.

Ascilia broke through the swirling storm in Sabeline's head as she called "All those in favour?" All Knights raised their hands. Ascilia nodded. "Then we have an accord."

"The decree still troubles me." Bersaba uttered, the first words she'd spoken all counsel. "King Falon does not seem himself in this scripture."

"Then I must await my fate." Sabeline announced, eyes flashing like lightning. "If this decree is as perplexing to you as it is to me, then there is little more I can do."

Reluctant exchanges were made around the counsel along with discontented arguments. Sabeline snapped her gaze around, taking in each separate discussion happening around the table. Some Knights wanted to go to the King and demand answers. Some wanted to go to The Palatine instead, because if anyone held the kingdom's secrets, it was him. Others wanted her to remain in the Tower while they infiltrated the main castle on an espionage mission.

The arguments ceased when Commander Karo and another Sabeline didn't recognise entered their counsel hall.

4

Law of the King

"The King wishes to see you immediately." Commander Karo spoke with an air of authority, directing his attention towards Sabeline.

"Do not take that tone with us." Echoris replied with darkness.

The Commander suddenly seemed to remember exactly where he was and *who* he was addressing. Sabeline stifled a smirk as the entirety of the Knights shot him unimpressed looks.

"Ah yes, my apologies." Commander Karo stuttered, trying to save some grace in front of whoever was with him. Examining the newcomer more closely, she noted the sigil engraved on the left spaulder. *An apprentice. Someone just got a promotion and they sent him to us?* She didn't know whether to be insulted or honoured. The man was young, but strong. It didn't take a scholar to see that. But from his nervous glancing at them and heavy reliance on Karo's lead, whatever purpose he was to have here had clearly fled his mind.

"Very well. If the King requests an audience, then I must

comply." Sabeline rose from her seat. *Seems the debate was unnecessary after all.*

"If the King wishes to discuss the dragon, then he can do so in front of us all." Ascilia rose from her seat also. Soon the room was filled with chairs scraping across stone and armour clattering as the Knights moved.

"I hardly think that will be…" Commander Karo trailed off as Sabeline marched past him, followed by an equally agitated entourage of Knights. In the end, Karo sighed and walked out after them, motioning for the apprentice to do the same.

She stormed across the small courtyard and onto the path towards the main castle. *No more fear. No more secrets.* Sabeline would face this like the Knight she was. And after, these ridiculous feelings would disappear and she could put it down to over exaggerating for the first time in her life. It could be blamed on the failure to murder that beast and the injuries she sustained. She hadn't been thinking properly that was all. But Echoris and Bersaba's words still echoed in her head, no matter how much she tried to silence them.

The anger swirling through her (and mainly directed at herself for still entertaining these thoughts), caused the walk to be much shorter than usual. Before she knew it, Sabeline found herself charging through the main castle doors, too focused on what lay ahead to notice the guards' surprised expressions. If they were surprised at her, she could only imagine their faces at the entourage behind her.

The guards at the throne room however, were much more accommodating. Upon seeing her form heading straight for them, they quickly opened the doors for her arrival.

Her gaze immediately landed on King Falon reclining on his throne, The Palatine hovering nervously near his left.

Sabeline halted a respectful distance from the dais and bowed before him. "My dear Sabeline, the Bringer of Truth." King Falon started, taking a sip of wine before continuing. "You stand before me, after *months* away, without the dragon's head."

Sabeline flinched at the reminder of her failure. "Yes my lord, but if I could just have more time…"

"*Time,*" King Falon spat the word as though it tasted foul upon his tongue, then composed himself. "Time is why we're here Sabeline. You've already had adequate time to destroy the creature for a warrior of your calibre. And each *time* you fail to stick your blade through that thing's heart, it's destruction grows until villages are blackened and charred." Though the King did not shout, Sabeline's ears noted the barely contained fury. Fear for the people is something she understood. Protecting them was her most sworn duty.

"I understand your majesty. A Knight's duty is to the people of Idrelas and I have failed in that duty. But please, I beg of you, let me put this right. If you believe I have lost sight of my duty, then let me prove to you that I am a Knight of Idrelas in every respect." Sabeline pleaded, eyes blazing as a satisfied smile grew on the King's face. The Palatine rubbed the pads of his fingers over his mouth in a repetitive motion, while glancing between her and the King. The movement drew her gaze and Sabeline's brow furrowed slightly. While The Palatine was a cowardly sort of man, he was never this out of sorts. She quickly smoothed out her expression.

"Indeed, a Knight's duty is to the people." King Falon placed the goblet back down and calmly stood from the throne. "And it is with a heavy heart that I have come to this decision."

He does not mean to strip me of my knighthood does he? Is that why The Palatine is so concerned?

"As the dragon takes more and more lives, it seems we must return to more drastic measures to combat this. And so, I have come to the decision that one life must be sacrificed to save the many. In order to save the people, I, King Falon, decree that Sabeline, The Bringer of Truth, be sacrificed to the dragon."

Her jaw fell open. *What?* "Sire please, there must be another way…"

"I have considered a great deal of possibilities. When Idrelas was young, maidens were sacrificed to dragons to stop their reign of terror. I am bringing back this tradition for the good of the kingdom."

Sabeline stood still, every muscle had turned to ice as the King continued with his proclamation. The Palatine covered his face, refusing to watch the situation. An explosion of protests erupted from behind her and idly Sabeline wondered how long the rest of the Knights and Commanders had been standing there.

"You can't…"

"Sire!"

"This is madness!"

"Take her to the dungeon." The King cried, his voice rising above the angry shouts and shocked yells.

Her mouth moved, but not even a whisper emerged. Even when her statuesque limbs were yanked by some complying guards, she couldn't tear her vision away from King Falon. The outcry from her sisters in arms and Commanders had faded in her ears, replaced by the loud pounding of her own heart as it pumped blood frantically. As Sabeline was dragged across the throne room (her limbs were still struggling to adhere to the forced movement), she watched as King Falon tried to reason with everyone present.

She would never forget the malicious grin that slipped through his façade for just a moment before it was masked once more.

5

Dungeon Dwelling

The dank air hung with heaviness in the shadowed cell she'd been unceremoniously thrown in. Sabeline imagined the guards had wanted to get her incarceration over with as quickly as possible, uncomfortable like everyone else at the turn of events. All the scenarios that had run through her head, the apprehension on what awaited her, she never in her wildest nightmares thought it would be *this*.

Death. He had sentenced her to death. A chill coated her skin as the reality began to sink into her being. *She wasn't going to live.* She conceded the King's order might have been easier to process, if she had at least been granted an honourable death. Instead she was to be sacrificed to that goddess damned *monster.* The world was cruel indeed, she knew this, but today had shown her just how torturous it could be.

A constant dripping echoed around her dishevelled form. Her eyes traced the sound to a crack in the stone wall, watching as droplets of water fell and splashed to the ground in a rhythmic pattern. It created the kind of noise that once heard, would be difficult to ignore. *Maybe insanity will get me before the dragon does.*

How had it come to this? She'd had a distinguished career as a Knight with a reputation that spoke for itself across Idrelas (and maybe some of the other five kingdoms, she wasn't too sure). She'd killed the dark manticore of Plyhaven for goddess sake! Did all her achievements count for nothing? Did this one failure eclipse all that she had done? *It wouldn't be a failure if she had been given more time.* But despite her reasoning, the King had been unwilling to listen. He had already decided the outcome before her audience and was not going to be swayed by anything or anyone.

Sabeline turned her attention to the thick blackened metal bars, preventing her from escaping. They made up a grated door, typical of most dungeon cells and the only way in or out. There was the usual large, imposing lock merged into the metal, a glaring reminder of "prisoner" status. It was a damned shame they'd stripped her of all her gear, otherwise she could have picked the lock. She threw her head back against the wall. Of course that's why they had procured the equipment that she kept on her person. Knights were legendary for their skillset. That reputation was only earnt by being prepared for every situation, *including* the opportune moment to escape an enemy dungeon should capture occur.

I'm going to die. No matter how she tried to distract herself, the reoccurring thought slammed into her mind. Nausea boiled in her stomach each time her brain kindly reminded her. Sabeline had known being a Knight could result in her death each time she faced a monster, a battle or departed on a mission. She'd accepted that. The fact her own King had offered her freely up to slaughter? *That* was something she couldn't accept and she never would.

When the dragon came for her, Sabeline would be ready. She'd stare down at King Falon with defiance, the man she'd once respected and show that a Knight could not be broken. *She* could not be broken. Even at the end. Clenching her fist, she let the anger flow through her blood. She needed something to hold onto in this disgusting cell and anger was as good as anything right now.

Hurried footsteps sounded eerily in the air, coming closer with each step. Clanging accompanied the sounds as squeaking, rusted metal was opened. Her position obscured her view of the dungeon as a whole, but Sabeline knew someone was entering this place via the main gate. Once through, the footsteps continued at a slower pace and Sabeline imagined whoever had entered was peering into each cell. Were they trying to find her?

A silhouetted figure appeared in front of her cell, the lingering shadows making it difficult to see the person clearly. The figure crouched, becoming level with Sabeline's sitting form. From the new angle, the vague murky light illuminated their face just enough for her to determine it was Bersaba.

"Sabeline?"

"Who else?" she replied back grimly, shuffling closer to the other Knight.

"By the goddess...this is not right." Bersaba whispered, properly taking in the conditions Sabeline had been forced to endure for the last several hours. Or had it been a day? Time had become irrelevant down here.

"Trust me, I'm very much aware of that." Sabeline sighed. "What are you doing down here Bersaba? I have no doubt in light of current events that if you're caught down here, you could end up on the other side of the bars with me."

"It was worth the risk." Bersaba stated. "The others continued to protest fiercely against the King's decision, but he could not be swayed. Since your imprisonment, he has ordered them to remain in the tower until your execution. Each in their own rooms. Under guard."

"*What?* Has he lost *all* reason?!" Sabeline voiced aghast.

"I managed to slip away while being escorted to the Tower, but they'd already stripped us of our gear. We can have it back *after* your execution." Bersaba spat with disgust.

"He's methodically removing any possibility of my escape." The realisation came to her. From a practical perspective, she would have done the same when faced with a gang of criminals. From a personal perspective, they were the kingdom's best warriors and were currently being treated like horse dung. She knew of no Knight that would stand for it, but they were smart and not adverse to playing the long strategic game if need be.

Bersaba nodded. "It appears so. But I had to come. King Falon refused to say anymore after his decision, but I heard The Palatine whispering about "dusk", "reconsidering" and "it was too soon." The King merely replied "the sooner the better." I think that is when they will come for you. Whatever death he's planning for you, it will be tonight."

Great. She swallowed hard. "Thank you for telling me, Bersaba." She let out a sad chuckle. "I don't know what's worse, the knowing or the not knowing."

Bersaba didn't say anything but reached a hand through the bars. Sabeline grasped it with firmness.

"We will stand with you until the end. It is the least we can do in this madness."

She ignored the fact her eyes were developing a glossy sheen at the words. "Thank you Bersaba." She gave her hand one last squeeze and released it. "Now go, before they find you and throw you in here too."

The Knight was reluctant, but after a moment nodded and dashed away, leaving her with her tormented thoughts. Once she knew Bersaba had gone, Sabeline threw her head back against the wall for the second time. Suddenly she released a blood curdling scream, pouring all her anger, rage and sadness into it.

The scream continued to resonate through the castle as she descended into choked sobs.

6

Traditional Preparations

She didn't know how long it had been since her heaving, ragged breaths had returned to normal. She *did* know that her throat was still raw and her chest ached. But the cathartic release, while curing some of her despair, was not a practical solution to her upcoming...*problem.*

The rest of her Creed were as imprisoned as she, with their equipment to be returned after her death. So the King must be storing the gear somewhere safe and hers would likely be included. She had no way of searching the castle and no idea where the items would be held. It was more likely she'd be re-captured before she could even begin to find it. No doubt the Commanders, while in disagreement with her sentence, would not want to do anything to compromise their own positions. They were as likely to drag her before the King or throw her back in this grimy, filth stained cell than help.

Maybe Bersaba is searching. Sabeline scoffed. If she was, then she was a fool. King Falon was unpredictable now, Bersaba would not escape his wrath if caught. Not when he'd apparently gone to such extreme measures to ensure her death by the dragon. She could only hope Bersaba would not wind up next to her, in another forgotten cell.

Her mind continued to race through logic and reasoning, but a solution? It evaded her with each new thought and situation she conjured. *Perhaps there really is no way out of this.* If that was the case, then she would go proudly. She wouldn't give anyone or *anything* the satisfaction of seeing her cower. No, she would march with her back straight, head up and the defiant glare she'd already decided to adorn her face with. *I'm finally ready.*

It had been hours (she deduced) of tumultuous thoughts, sickness, shock and horror. Each thing rolling over her like a great wave of the Eastern Sea, before retreating similarly to the tide, only to wash over her again with the same force moments later. *No more. I will decide how my last hours upon Idrelas will be.* Despite the fate coming for her, Sabeline felt more like herself than she had since the King's proclamation.

Footsteps greeted her ears for the second time, though her hearing detected more than one set. Both were not as hurried as Bersaba's had been, they were slower and had a more cautionary edge. Even the goddess damned noise from the gate seemed to be lingering, hanging in the mould ridden air longer than it had a right to. Sabeline rolled her eyes, setting her sights on the left side of the entrance to her cell. *Of course they're here for me. I wish they'd move it.* It was strange how her fear had evaporated with her decision. Maybe that awful persistent dripping had driven her mad after all.

Eventually, shadow obscured figures shuffled in front of her cell, avoiding looking at her directly. They were guards that much she could tell from their willowy shapes and legs a war horse would be envious of. Guards were used more for chasing intruders or criminals, rather than capturing them. *That* part was usually left to the Commanders or Knights.

"What is it?" Sabeline asked, tired of their silence. Each guard jumped shocked, as if remembering the reason they'd been sent down to this goddess forsaken part of the castle. One of them cleared his throat, standing up a bit taller.

"Bringer of Truth, we have been tasked with escorting you to the bathing chamber. There you will be prepared for your noble duty and with great honour, protect the people of Idrelas following this."

So King Falon is portraying the same line of thinking to the people as he did to me. Does he really believe that, or is he working toward some other purpose?

Sabeline hauled herself up from the dirt infested floor with surprising agility. "Well in that case," she responded to the guard who had spoken, crossing her arms confidently in front of her. "We'd better not keep the beast waiting then." *The King or the Dragon?* Whispered her thoughts.

The female guard approached the bars, not as confident as the other to address her and reached out to grab Sabeline's wrists through the metal. Securing them in one hand, the guard quickly and far more effectively than Sabeline would have given her credit for, brought heavy iron shackles down over her wrists, clipping them into place. A thick chain connected the two in the middle, adding even more weight.

Now suitably restrained, the guards adopted a new but still nervous confidence. The male guard who'd spoken procured a haggard key from the thin silver loop affixed to his belt and slid it carefully into the lock. She stood in silence, watching as the key screeched with the full turn being forced upon it. The guards pulled the barred door open and wrapped their hands around each or her arms, hauling her forcibly out of the cell. Sabeline stumbled slightly from the unexpected force, but quickly regained her footing, walking steadily ahead. The guards fell into step either side of her, casting worried looks at each other.

"I'm not going to hurt either of you." Sabeline sighed, their behaviour putting her on edge. It had been a *long* day and she could do without any more emotional distress, especially as she'd just *dealt* with the bulk of her own.

"Oh erhm we know that Bringer of Truth." The female guard uttered, using her voice for the first time since Sabeline had set eyes on her.

"It's just that…" the male guard carried on "If you escape on our watch…"

"Well it doesn't look very good…on us." The female guard continued sheepishly.

Goddess save me. "I understand. Do not worry, I won't do anything to compromise your positions." Sabeline answered them, unable to help the dry tone. Not that she could anyway, the negatives of trying to escape already outweighed the positives. Mainly for the reasons she'd run through her head earlier, but now she was heavily shackled. The weight would slow her down and she'd have to break them on something to escape effectively, costing more time. Time she'd likely get caught in with the whole castle searching for her. Then she'd end up getting forcibly prepared for her own death surrounded by armed guards watching her in the *damned* bath. No thank you.

"Oh you are most gracious Bringer of Truth." The male guard murmured, relief coating his words.

"Yes, so gracious." The female guard nodded emphatically

with the same tone. Sabeline was surprised the guard's helmet didn't fall off with the force of the movement.

"So now that's been established, shall we go?" She motioned towards the stairwell entrance with her manacled hands, the thick chain connecting them rattling as she did. The guards, now seemingly much more comfortable knowing she wasn't going to bolt the second she was out of the dungeons, escorted her towards the main entrance. In haste, they opened up the doorway and wrapped her arms in their grip again, "for appearances."

As she was led up the stairwell and into the upper corridors, Sabeline turned her head towards a small unremarkable arched window that captured her attention. From this angle, her eyes latched onto the golden sun descending slowly behind one of the distant hills of the Great Green Plateau.

They had come for her at dusk, just as Bersaba said.

***

The specially warmed water had long since accrued a thin layer of grime floating on its surface, though thankfully, neck deep in perfumed bubbles as she was, it was easy for Sabeline to ignore. A vast array of hair potions and skin lotions surrounded her, each in various size, shape and coloured bottles. There were ones that smelled of moon lotus, ones that smelled of fruits and ones that claimed to smell of things like "morning mist." Sabeline sank deeper into the water. She doubted very much the dragon would care what she smelled like as his fangs dragged through her flesh in a few short hours.

At least the soak was soothing on her wounds. They'd had time to heal and partially close since her last encounter with the dragon, the tilweed wrapped around her side had already worked wonders on her battered muscles and skin. She stretched her arms and back upwards, relishing the gentle lap of heated water running over her. She would make the most of this while she could. Her logical half screamed that it made no sense to heal up, but the part of her in touch with her own morality told logic to take a hike back to the dungeons. Facing death clean and in less pain gave her some dignity, rather than being coated in dirt and leaking from her injuries, people would remember her last moments the most and she would be as strong as she was able in those moments.

A few more minutes, just a few more and then I'll get out. Her wishful thinking was interrupted by a gentle knock on the door and the entrance of a rather timid handmaiden. "Excuse me ma'am?" she uttered weakly.

"Yes?" Sabeline answered with a sigh. Was nothing sacred anymore? *Just a bit longer was all I wanted.*

"I'm here to help you prepare for the ceremony."

"Ceremony?" She questioned, confused. She was going to die, there was no ceremony about it, no matter how King Falon dressed his ludicrous decree up.

"Yes ma'am. I'm to help you dress and appear presentable in accordance with the old tradition." The handmaiden murmured. Idly, Sabeline wondered what family she served, the King had no daughters after all and the Queen had long since passed. *Probably some wretched nobles from Upper Town.*

"I'll be wearing my armour and my hair is too short to be displayed in a fancy style. I understand you've been sent here, but I'm afraid your service is not required." She answered as evenly as she could. She didn't want to scare the poor woman who looked delicate enough as it was, but she was having difficulty keeping calm. She was the one being forced to meet her end by the beast she despised. Why did no one in the castle understand that!

The handmaiden's face was aghast. "You cannot wear your armour; it is against the old tradition."

By the goddess, that's it. "Listen, I am being forced to die because for whatever reason, the King wants me dead and has turned this murder into me voluntarily sacrificing myself so no one can speak against it. If I want to wear my armour in my final moments then by the goddess I'm going to, no matter what you, the King or the bloody dragon prefer!" Her voice has risen steadily as she spoke and she found she didn't care. Funny how impending doom could do that to a person.

The handmaiden let out a little squeak at the end of her tirade. "I'll have to check your attire with his majesty." She stuttered, "but you will have to wear this." The handmaiden gently placed a woven crown of flowers and other flora down on the floor.

"Check it if you need to, but either way I *will* be wearing my armour." Sabeline's eyes blazed and she turned them towards the hand crafted crown. It was rather exquisite, though she noticed some of the flowers interlaced were known to glow under starlight. That was one way to make sure the dragon detected her from the sky. She also caught sight of small and medium sized berries scattered across the thick leaves forced into this thing. While bright and almost ornamental in appearance, Sabeline couldn't help but wonder if they were an attempt to provide the dragon with a balanced diet. The whole adornment was a carefully constructed instrument to call the creature to her.

"And don't think for one second that flower headdress has fooled me. It's a beacon designed from pretty things to maximise the chances of my death." She spat at the uncomfortably shifting handmaiden. Maybe she was being too harsh, after all, she didn't know if the handmaiden had made it, she might just be following orders and was just as surprised with the revelation. She seemed the type to blindly follow what she'd been told and from the unsure glancing around and silence emanating from the handmaiden, Sabeline believed she'd made the correct conclusion. Eventually the handmaiden found her voice and with a "I'll go get approval for your attire now" she scampered off.

As her shoes disappeared behind the closing door, Sabeline released a loud groan. Her brief tranquillity had been ruined and with the arrival of that handmaiden, it meant that events were progressing. In other words, the King expected her to be done with bathing by now. Resigned to the fact that if she didn't emerge from the basin at once, someone else would be knocking on the door shortly, Sabeline hauled herself out of the water. She grabbed the towels that had been left aside for her, scrubbing her short dark locks with the cloth to dry them and wrapping the longer towel carefully around her body. She didn't want to aggravate the wounds she'd spent blissfully easing for the past however long.

Her bare feet padded over to where the flower crown had been placed. Bending down, her fingers clutched part of the branches making up the base and lifted it to her face for inspection. *All the hidden little secrets this thing has...* It was apparent there was a lot more than berries and glowing flowers wrapped in it. Plants that released a particular fragrance in the right conditions, plants that resembled shiny treasure, all of which would pique the interest of a dragon.

It was beautiful, no doubt about that. But like most beautiful things, it would only reveal how deadly it was when it was too late.

7

Procession of Death

She had been permitted to wear her armour in a "gracious" act by King Falon but of course, they were insistent she wear the flora headdress. Sabeline imagined her appearance was in contrast, but her attire was all for practicality (well, both her and the King's idea of practicality). She had been reunited with her old friend, the iron shackles, though this time they were restraining her arms behind her back. By the time they arrived at wherever they were going, her arms and wrists would be in agony. Another ploy to ensure she didn't make a dash for it the moment she was un-cuffed.

The night air was cool on her face as she stood on High Point, surrounded by a small plethora of guards. She noticed the two who had dragged her from the cell had been drafted in for escort duty as well. A humourless smirk crossed her face before she hid it. *Looks like those two are having quite the day.* Commander Karo was there too, situated on top of his horse and casting his gaze around at everything but her. Whenever he did accidentally make brief eye contact, he dropped his eyes with haste before turning his sight towards something else he pretended to find fascinating. A soft sigh escaped her lips, leaving a little mist of breath in the air. This was going to be a *delightful* journey.

To some extent, she understood why Karo was acting that way. Nothing had been able to change the King's mind and now they were here. The vague notion Karo could be feeling responsible for all this suddenly struck her. He'd delivered the decree and insisted on them returning home effective immediately. If she was able, she'd try and remedy that before her heart stopped beating. Of course, she could be wrong and the Commander was only acting awkwardly because of *him.*

King Falon was perched on his white steed, his regal status emanating from his elegant posture and manner with which he held himself. Occasionally a confused expression wandered across his face, as if he couldn't quite recall what they were all doing here, before it smoothed out again. The Palatine was also here, hovering on an older horse next to the King and watching him, wariness dancing in his eyes. *Now that was interesting.* The Palatine had been doing the same thing during her audience with the King. It was also The Palatine's occupation to know everything about Idrelas, including every depraved secret lingering in the walls and histories of the place. *Something is being kept from everyone. Something even The Palatine is unsure about.*

Before her thoughts had chance to explore this avenue further, the King's joyous call of "Ah they're here!" interrupted all those gathered. Each and every Knight of Idrelas was being led under armed guard to where Sabeline stood waiting and each one had a face like thunder in the sky. It was *not* a good move to anger one Knight, let alone the whole creed of them.

"I do not appreciate being treated like a dog!" Ascilia snapped at a guard, causing them to spring away in fear.

"Now, now," King Falon spoke, "No one would ever treat you like that Ascilia."

Ascilia just glared in response, but Echoris let loose what they were all thinking. "Just as no one would divest us of our equipment and lock us in our own tower until summoned. Isn't that right *your majesty?*" Echoris's strange voice wrapped around the last two words as if they were a threat, but Sabeline had no idea how that could be.

The King adopted a puzzled frown at Echoris's words. "Yes, no one would do that..." he trailed off and suddenly his face appeared brighter "Unless it was for the good of the realm. It would not do any of our people any favours for Sabeline to have escaped and the dragon to destroy more villages, when we can put a stop to it tonight."

Contempt was evident in their faces, but they said no more. *Probably dawning on them this is a battle they cannot win...yet.* While the others were stewing in rage, Sabeline had heard the odd intonation of King Falon's voice. Coupled with his shifting expressions, there was definitely something *wrong.* It wouldn't save her now, she knew that, but if she could just voice her suspicions to her creed without being noticed...

"Well, now everyone is in attendance, perhaps we should press on your highness?" The Palatine uttered nervously.

"Splendid idea Viras! We must make haste." The King ordered. "Keep the Knights under separate escort to the Bringer of Truth. I don't want any conspiracies or plans being made."

There were a few shouts from her creed in response, including Bersaba's distinct grumblings. *So she made it back after all.* The nervous guards tried shushing them, but soon gave up. Sabeline was already being pushed forward, remaining under the watchful eye of King Falon, The Palatine and if he'd ever look at her, Commander Karo. Guards closed in behind her, sealing her off from the rest of the Knights. As they marched down, the steady realisation she was going to be paraded through each of the towns flooded her being. The glowing lamp lights in the darkness of Upper Town below already told her word had gotten around and fast. The people she protected, the people she cared about, were going to see her bound like a criminal in a procession of death, populated with *lies* from the King. There was no guarantee this insane course of action was going to work, (unless someone could secure an oath from the dragon that after killing her, it wouldn't devastate a village).

She refused to be beaten. Not now. Taking a deep breath, Sabeline braced herself. She stood taller, prouder, with all the honour and courage she could summon. She was a Knight of Idrelas. She was the Bringer of Truth.

And despite the humiliation the King was trying to force upon her with this unhappy spectacle, she *always* would be.

The first pale faces appeared amongst the gloom as the macabre procession stepped into Upper Town and from the corner of her eye, Sabeline noted movement closer to her from both the King and Commander. Ah. Penning her in. They feared her trying to escape. While she had a feeling Commander Karo might be relieved if she did make a dash for freedom, the King would certainly be furious that his finely crafted deception would be ruined. And she was above being killed in the street like a criminal by the guards. No, they need not fear. She retained some choice as to her fate, no matter how little it was.

Glancing to Falon, his expression had become indifferent, as though his face had turned to stone. No longer did his features flit between strange confusion and certainty. A kind of resoluteness had overcome him, causing Sabeline to grit her teeth. How could he? How could he do this when they were surrounded by distraught faces illuminated by the lamps? Ripping her gaze away from the betrayer, she caught sight of a few residents staring at her with a mixture of pity and fear. But after the child who watched her with abject horror and then clung to his mother's skirts in tears, Sabeline vowed to remain staring ahead.

It seemed the King had also noticed, for a loud speech suddenly erupted from his mouth. "Do not weep, good people. It is with true regret that we carry out this course of action. The Bringer or Truth vowed to destroy the beast desecrating our lands by any means necessary and as you can see, she is fulfilling that vow to the very end. This is the only choice left to us. Rejoice, for soon the dragon will be gone and the Bringer of Truth will have protected us all."

Fury ricocheted through her blood like a wayward arrow as the lies continued and were repeated to reassure the people as the sombre parade stepped into mid-town. She wanted to scream, to shout the truth over Falon's lies and damn the consequences. With every ounce of strength she possessed, Sabeline swallowed the words and bit her tongue. There were worse fates than death and if she spoke out, she feared the King would do much more than give her over to be massacred by her nemesis. The very idea would have been preposterous only a few moons ago, but now…Now the King she had respected for his firm but fair rule and same wish to protect the people was a malevolent stranger to her.

The Lower Town remained quiet and eerie, as though any loud noise would be wrong within its boundary. At least here, Falon finally ceased with his traitorous speech. There was no one to reassure after all. She could only imagine what her sisters in arms were thinking and feeling as they observed the absent Lower Town, making their way through with ease.

The darkness had grown since leaving the relative safety of the kingdom and she didn't just mean the sky. Now they were trudging through wide open spaces, not quite the Great Green Plateau but, Sabeline admitted, it was greatly similar. Every time the clouds moved and her head was caught in starlight, the damned flower abomination affixed to her hair glowed silvery white until the clouds covered the sky once more. There had been several intervals of this during their trek and she was secretly hoping the stars remained hidden forever. But with her luck today, that seemed unlikely.

Gazing ahead, she could just about detect a tall silhouette appearing on the horizon, darker than the night surrounding them. The King's eyes lit up at the sight of it. *Oh dear.* Whatever was good for the King, she had come to realise in the past day, was bad for her. No matter what that structure was, Sabeline was overcome with a desire *not* to step another foot near it. Of course, being the one about to be sacrificed, she had no say in the matter.

They were in an old part of the kingdom, that much she could gather. A part potentially disused since Alondra's day, if the decrepit and dilapidated ruins sticking out at odd angles from the grass gave any indication. While The Palatine took great interest in them, King Falon's focus never wavered from the larger structure ahead.

Sabeline had been correct in her assumption about her arms. It felt as if the muscles were ripping under the weight of iron and the contorted, uncomfortable way she was forced to hold them. Her armour added an extra complication, with the metal sections scraping against each other in ways they weren't designed to. *Between the grating and the pain, the dragon may as well kill me now.*

As they stepped ever closer, the odd architecture gradually became more discernible against the shadows. A large crumbling wall formed a partial crescent shape around where a cracked and broken obsidian pillar stood. At its base, was a slightly raised stone circle, with carvings in a long dead language etched in the slabs around the middle where the pillar stood. The stillness in the air surprised her. Sabeline was sure there had been a cool breeze accompanying the macabre parade, but within these ruins, *nothing.* Her flowers lit up again, giving her enough light to detect much darker stains and splashes against the glistening pillar and stonework. Their presence brought every emotion she was trying to contain rushing to the surface, her heart missing a beat as the reality of her situation sunk deep into every single fibre of her being. She was going to die here and it would not be peaceful. The copious amounts of blood still coating the ruins after all this time was enough evidence of that.

The King, despite lording over them all on his stallion, must have noticed the horror she attempted to mask. "This is where maidens of old were brought to dragons in offering."

"So you have brought me here too. As an *offering.*" Sabeline spat.

"Of course my dear, Idrelas needs to be protected from the monsters of the realm and your sacrifice in a place of historical tradition and significance will do that."

Monsters like you? The thought came unbidden to her mind. "It is not *my* sacrifice is it though sire. It's *yours*." Before he could say anything more, Sabeline turned to the King, matching his calm expression with furious eyes. "Something has happened to you sire. I may be the first casualty of what's going on, but I give you my word my death here tonight will begin your downfall. The Knights of Idrelas *will* find out the truth and they *will* expose it. You have sealed your own fate as well as my own." It felt good to give the King a piece of her mind. *It isn't as though I have anything to lose.*

An arrogant smirk crossed King Falon's lips at her words. "We shall see about that. Either way, you won't be around for the outcome." He nodded to Commander Karo as the rest of her sisters in arms were assembled in an orderly fashion by the guard trope.

Karo grimaced as he advanced towards her, gripping the shackles in his hands, pushing against her back and forcing her forwards. Muttering protests arose from the Knights again, some louder and pointedly for the King's ears, though he gave no impression he heard them as Karo pressed her against the pillar. He held her there securely, summoning two guards to unlock the cuffs. Each took one of her chained wrists and as the weight of the shackles lifted, Sabeline had a brief moment to flex her fingers and roll her shoulders in an attempt to alleviate the scorching pain shooting down her limbs. The moment quickly ended when the goddess cursed guards took both arms, locking them back in the shackles behind the pillar. The minute the guards and Karo took a step back, she tried moving only to be held steadfast by the restraints. It had been worth a try.

"I am sorry." Karo whispered regretfully, meeting her gaze for the first time all night. Before she could formulate a response, he walked away, as though the mere sight of her was too much for him to take. Suddenly remembering her promise, she called out to Karo's retreating back. "You are not to blame for this." He paused for a second, but did not turn back to face her, then continued on to re-join the large gathering.

Sabeline's shout had awoken something within the Knights and in return, they began to call things out to her. They were restricted by coming any closer to her (in case of an escape attempt she imagined) but that didn't stop them vowing things in her name.

"I swear to you I will unravel the mystery of the Lower Town!" Mariel yelled with passion in her tone, though Sabeline noticed the Knight cast a suspicious glance over the King as she sealed her promise.

"We will avenge you." Ascilia swore, with so much conviction Sabeline had no doubt she would. Echoris was chanting prayers to the old gods. Sabeline and the others had no care who she worshipped, Echoris had always been mysterious and it was a part of who she was. She had never really displayed the fact around Idrelas however, knowing of the prejudice against the old gods. Sabeline was sure Echoris was saying these prayers with deliberation and defiance in the face of King Falon. Kilyn, Bersaba, Ivetta and Jaketta along with many others also shouted out vows of vengeance and they would honour her name and principals. *At least my mantle of Bringer of Truth will be continued.* It was a small comfort, but Sabeline would take anything she could get tied to this hard and cold beacon of death.

Trying to regain some order, Sabeline imagined, the King launched into a speech with deafening loudness, drowning out the angry grumblings of the Knights. "Oh great dragon! We offer you no mere maiden, but a noble warrior. In return we ask that the devastation to Idrelas by your claw cease. Here be Sabeline, the Bringer of Truth and your failed murderer."

Sabeline bit back a growl. *That thing is a monster! How dare he make out like I'm some common criminal!* The King sensing her fury, carried on. "And now I shall say farewell to my dear knight."

Keeping a wary eye on him as he approached, Sabeline struggled against her bindings to no avail. King Falon smiled, leaning down to whisper goddess knew what convoluted nonsense he'd come up with. Sabeline doubted it would be a farewell of any kind. She felt his breath fanning across strands of her hair. *"I will destroy you all."*

The phrase caused her to recoil as much as she was able. King Falon just leaned back with a malicious smile on his face. His demeanour sent a chill flying like an arrow down her spine.

But the sudden dominating roar cutting through the night sky did worse.

8

An Honourable End

She snapped her head towards the sound, keeping her eyes trained on the sky. It was a mocking turn of events that all the skill she'd acquired in hunting the beast was now being used to brace herself for death. The others gathered also cast their gazes towards the sky, wildly glancing around to try and detect the creature. But Sabeline knew where it was. She knew the direction it was coming from. She would face the monster as an equal. The King noticed her preoccupation with a point in the sky and turned away from her towards her fixation. She could almost sense the smirk on his face as he proceeded to walk away. "Get everyone to a safe distance! The dragon is coming!"

Sabeline watched with resentment as the guards herded the Knights in attendance further back from the ruins, escorted by the King, The Palatine and Commander Karo. They were far enough away that meant they wouldn't be harmed, but still had a full view of what was going to happen to her. *They shouldn't have to see this. None of them should.* But she knew her sisters in arms would watch until the end. Honour was not taken lightly among her creed.

Another roar shook the sky and Sabeline felt it reverberate through the pillar, even from this distance. Snapping her face away from the Knights, her gaze soon relocated the dragon. She had to admit, it made a graceful sight. It's large leathery wings reminiscent of a lesser bat's moved in perfect synchronisation, the sounds of their beats thundering across the stars. Its long reptilian body took on a darker, omniscient shade of red amidst the consuming night. And encased within were teeth, claws, spines and fire. *An array of built in weaponry.* Perhaps if things had been different, she'd have marvelled at dragon biology a little more. Or maybe it was because she was in this position that she found herself marvelling at all. There were worse things she could be thinking in her last moments she supposed.

The beast was becoming closer. Sabeline could now make out hints of golden eyes soaring towards her. No doubt those keen orbs would detect her goddess damned flower monstrosity in a heartbeat. She hoped she lived long enough to see it get torn to shreds in the crossfire. Small mercies she hoped. She really hated that thing. *The dragon or the flowers?* Both.

It seemed her mind was on the verge of hysteria by the way her thoughts were going. It was only reasonable considering the rest of it was screaming at her *"I'm going to die!"* Sabeline supposed that's what happened before the end. Not that she'd been in a position to compare the experience to. She'd run with the possible hysteria. It was nicer than the constant reminder of death, a death she could do nothing about.

Struggling with what else to do in the face of a swift encroaching creature designed from its fangs to the tip of its tail to kill, Sabeline parted her lips and took a deep, shuddering breath of cool night air. *It's nearly here.* The centring breath quietened the chaos of her mind and she stood up straighter. She refused to close her eyes in the face of her end. No, she'd watch it, just as her sisters in arms were watching. She would not show any weakness before King Falon.

The dragon had dipped, descending until it was level with her position, but still able to fly. She noted it had adjusted its wings slightly due to the lower position. *Goodbye my friends.* Sabeline would not cry. Not now. There was no reason to. The creature advanced its speed.

The whooshing air stirred up by her proximity to the dragon drowned out any other sound. Unfortunately, she could just about hear the King yelling something. At least she couldn't hear the words, though she'd rather not hear him at all. *It's only a few feet away.* Time was running out. In a well-practised motion, her body on instinct, braced for the impact.

And then there was screaming in the distance, a great cacophony of loud shrieking that sounded like her creed. There was shooting pain down her sides, idly she looked down to see long dagger-like claws tucked under her armour plates and piercing her flesh. The force of impact had yanked her arms so forcefully; the shackles were cracked in pieces around her wrists and the chain broken. Her muscles burned in furious agony. She discreetly checked if the dragon had just decided to set her arms ablaze. It would have been preferable. Alas, no luck.

The claws dug in tighter to her flesh as the dragon gripped her harder. Sabeline gasped at the sensation. *Maybe it'll just squeeze the life right out of me.* She was bleeding again. She could feel it crawling down her sides in thick, congealing rivulets. So she was either going to bleed out or be asphyxiated, neither options she'd considered at the hands of the dragon.

For the first time, it occurred to her that the dragon was carrying her and they were still above the ground. Another very real possibility struck her. *What if it drops me instead?* The beast had dropped her before, but she'd survived. This time, it would see the matter through, she was sure. Sabeline tried desperately writhing in the dragon's hold. It was immediately a bad idea. The scores in her flesh dragged and sliced deeper across. Her arms were practically useless, tortuous pain radiating down in each one. She was prolonging the inevitable, she knew that. Perhaps it was time to stop.

Her pathetic wriggling had drawn the attention of the dragon. An unpleasant, twisting growl rumbled through its chest. *It doesn't need to worry. Not anymore.* Her body went limp. It had been a very distressing day (to put it mildly) and she was tired of being in several different variations of pain over the course of it. She hoped her mother and father were proud of her. Even if her death was going to be a mockery. She'd vowed that day as she rose covered in ash amongst still burning flames she would protect Idrelas from monsters. And she had. She just hadn't been able to protect herself.

The growling still continued, though Sabeline thought she detected a frustrated edge to it. For some reason, she found the fact the dragon would possibly be annoyed at being summoned here to kill her incredibly hilarious. To her amazement, she started to laugh. It was completely illogical, this reaction, but she continued giggling as though Kilyn had told one of her bad jokes that had (for once) turned out to be a good one. *The hysteria again.* The beast cocked its head, peering down at her like she was some kind of mystery.

Her laughing ceased however, as the beast lowered its jaws down over her head. Sabeline pressed her eyes together, expecting fangs to detach her head from her body. A second passed. Two seconds. She dared to crack one eye open. The beast had that goddess damned floral headdress between its teeth and was snapping the thing into oblivion with one bite. Thank the goddess and all the gods Echoris worshipped for the destruction of that awful adornment.

As the dragon's mouth descended towards her again, shadows crept across the edge of her vision. She felt its hot breath pour over her hair and face.

As a pale, thin tongue reached out to her, the shadows consumed her sight.

9

No Ordinary Cave

Blurred shapes greeted her vision as Sabeline flickered her eyes partially open. She was lying on a hard surface; she knew that much. The prickling, digging sensation across her cheek indicated she was against grit or stones of some description. Where was she? She tried shuffling around, attempting to at least sit up, but her arms wouldn't cooperate and not just because of the lingering pain still throbbing throughout. It felt as if they were *sealed* by something. Determining that her wrists were where the sensation was strongest, Sabeline tried prying them apart. Only to be met with firm resistance. By the goddess, her wrists were bound *again*. If she wasn't supposed to be dead, she'd have been filled with a lot more rage. At least these weren't iron shackles anymore. Wriggling her wrists a little more, the texture of hemp rubbed against them. Rope. Someone had bound her with rope.

Her eyes adjusted to the environment and she cracked them open fully. The indistinct shapes she'd first seen were stalagmites and other strange paraphernalia. Bits of coloured fabric here, a rusted sword there. Things that were very out of place in a cave. Well, that's what she assumed she was in. There was no light filtering down from above and a distinct chill was present in the air. It was also fairly dark, but glowing across the walls was an orange light. Craning her head as much as she was able from the ground, Sabeline traced the origin of the glow to a tunnel, presumably leading further back into the cave. *A fire.* She'd had to make a fire in some strange places in her time, the light from it always reacting differently depending on where she was. Though this one in particular had to be a large fire if the glow was dancing across the rock way out here.

She wasn't alone. Unless she'd set a fire and tied herself up while unconscious (very unlikely) someone else was in this cave with her. A hermit maybe? Or a soothsayer? Searching her memories, the last thing she remembered careened to the forefront of her mind. *The dragon and its jaws.* Had someone saved her before the beast had a chance to devour her form? That too, seemed highly unlikely. Her and her men had been trying for months to bring the creature down, it was difficult to accept a random stranger had been able to accomplish what she had not. *And by difficult, I mean impossible.*

The cold surrounding the room was starting to seep into her skin and she felt it more acutely. It was either stay out here and possibly become sick (or worse) or make her way towards the fire. The decision was easy, the execution of it however, could be problematic.

Having a better idea of why her movement was restricted, Sabeline tried again to arrange herself in a sitting position. This time, it was easier as she used her bound hands to her advantage, shuffling around and leaning a little weight on them. Using her arms as leverage, she hauled the rest of her body upright. *Now to do the next part.* Using her legs to push, Sabeline hobbled across the floor until her arms and back were pressed against a towering stalagmite. Utilising her hands, she pushed against the stalagmite while balancing and slowly unbending her legs, finally managing to stand.

Taking a moment, she orientated herself to the new environment. If she'd hoped she could just run out the cave entrance, she was sadly mistaken. Now that she could see a lot more from her better vantage, it was clear the room she was in had various passageways and tunnels leading from it. She could take a chance she reasoned, but she had no idea what was waiting at the end of each one. *There may be worse things than a chill down there.* The implication of all these paths alluded to the fact this was no simple cave. No, whatever lived here had made great effort in turning this place into a labyrinth. Strategically, she understood. However, the fact she was with something that very clearly didn't want to be found caused unease to echo through her.

Turning her head back towards the glowing passageway and filled with new resolve, Sabeline stepped towards it. She wasn't dead yet, thank the goddess, and she intended to keep it that way. As she walked carefully down the tunnel, following the light, it became apparent that something was shifting under her armour. It definitely didn't feel right, but it also wasn't too bad. Sabeline likened it to stalks or leaves brushing against her skin in a hefty quantity. The sensation was mainly focused down each of her sides. Looking down, for the first time she saw some of the clasps and straps of her armour left undone around those areas. Thankfully, all her other armour remained securely in place.

The end of the route was just ahead. Cautiously, Sabeline altered her position, stepping from the middle and leaning against one of the walls. She was still out in the open, but at least less obvious than before. Slowly, she edged forward, peering her head around the exit.

A large burning fire immediately greeted her vision, with flames as tall as houses twisting and twirling in a magnificent, warm display. The fire was in the middle of a grand space, a few stalactites and stalagmites littered the corners and edges, if it wasn't for them, Sabeline would never have believed she was still in a cave. The ground and walls were polished and shiny, as though made out of rough marble. The firelight reflected off a pile of glittering gold coins and chalices stacked in one of the corners. Ornate furniture was arranged precisely around the room, from high backed chairs and long settees that could easily fit her entire creed, to a table big enough for a banquet and…

Sabeline's breath hitched. A tail of scarlet scales flicked lazily near the fire. Sudden movement caught her attention and she swallowed hard as the head of the dragon emerged through the flames, golden eyes locking onto her without hesitation.

A deep, grumbling voice cut through the crackling and spitting of the fire. "Ah good. You are awake."

10

Nivres

"Y*ou!...*You can talk?" Sabeline spluttered as the dragon gazed down at her with unimpressed golden eyes.

"Yes, I have always been able to do so." The beast answered, as if this fact should have been obvious to her.

Her eyes narrowed. "Did you do this?" She moved her arms as well as she was able, hoping the monster could grasp what she meant.

"If you mean, did I restrain you with rope then yes, yes I did."

"Why? Why bring me here and tie me up? Why not just kill me when you had the chance? It would have been easier for you surely?" Sabeline spat. If this creature planned on torturing her or other such unpleasantness, it was going to be very surprised.

The dragon turned his head through the flames, drawing back out before wandering around the side of the fire and coming much closer to her. Familiar tension filled her abused limbs as her body braced for an assault. The dragon however, just stood there, continuing to look down on her with a certain wariness. "I have a question, one that only you can answer."

Sabeline's brow furrowed. "I don't know what answer you think I have, but it might not be one you want to hear."

The dragon chuckled. "Yes, I am prepared for that. I have heard rumours of you Bringer of Truth, whispers on the wind across Idrelas. It is nice to know they do not disappoint."

She remained quiet, not sure if that was some kind of backhanded compliment or just an observation the dragon was happy with.

"Now, let's get straight to it." The dragon's head leaned forward until he was inches away. She dare not move, lest his jaws snapped her up out of instinct. She could smell the smoke in his breath. *"Why do you want to kill me?"* The oddly menacing and curious question rumbled out of the dragon's mouth. Sabeline was getting the distinct impression that rumbling and growling meant the beast was *not* happy.

What a ridiculous query! Is it not obvious? She said as much back to the beast, who seemed rather perplexed. An irritated sigh blew past her lips. Was he being deliberately obtuse? "You are destroying villages, towns and other settlements across Idrelas! Why would I *not* want to put a blade in your belly?"

The dragon withdrew his head slowly and almost looked as though he was considering her answer. There wasn't any *considering* as far as she was concerned. It was plain and simple. To stop his reign of terror (a brief flash of King Falon echoed in her mind at the term before it disappeared) and the death of innocent people, the dragon had to meet its end. It was the only practical solution and the discovery that the beast could talk didn't change that. No doubt it was just as unlikely to be reasoned with as before.

"That seems a fair reason." The dragon uttered carefully, apparently still thinking it over.

Her cheeks grew warm at the beast's indifference and Sabeline knew they would be as red with rage as the dragon's scales. "Of course it's a fair reason!" She exploded. "You. Are. *Killing*. People. Desecrating families. Leaving them with nothing but half a scorched shack and dead relatives! How many more times must I repeat that until you get the point? Unwarranted murder and annihilation from *monsters* like you is something we don't stand for! Of course I'm going to stop you by any means possible!" Her chest heaved at the outpouring of her anger before her voice dropped to a deadly threat. "I'll kill you in your sleep if I get the chance."

"Then I suppose it's in my best interest to leave you in that rope." The creature stated calmly, beginning to turn its back on her.

"Where are you going beast?"

"To bed. You've slept for nearly a day little Knight. I have not. Sleep sounds perfect and with you safely bound in here, I won't have to worry about my impending demise will I?"

The rage was still rolling around in her blood, waiting for the chance to bubble and burst again, though from a practical perspective she could see the dragon's point. And Sabeline was nothing if not practical. She was still going to try and get out of these bindings though. The dragon was a fool if he thought otherwise.

"Very well dragon. Get your rest. I'll be waiting." She glared at its retreating form.

"It's Nivres actually." The dragon called back over its shoulder.

"What is? What does that mean?"

"My name. I have one you know. It's Nivres. I'm already tired of you calling me dragon, beast, monster and various other names. Nivres from now on, if you please." And without any further word, the dragon continued lumbering towards an archway carved out of the rock, large enough for his form to fit through.

Once the last red scale was enveloped by the darkness, Sabeline whispered to the air. "You underestimate me, dragon."

Quietly she stepped across the room, assessing the various objects. While the fire would burn the rope, there was no feasible way she could accomplish it without burning both hands badly. She valued those more than being unbound at this moment. The gold hoarded in the corner was useless for her purpose, along with the various furniture. Turning her head, her eyes latched onto the stalagmites. If she could somehow loop her wrists over, a sharp piece of the rock formation may cut through or at least wear part of the rope away, making it weaker and thus easier for her to break.

Anticipation thrumming in her veins, Sabeline carefully selected a decent looking one from the cluster near the edge of a chair. Glancing towards where the dragon disappeared, she slowly manoeuvred her arms towards where she wanted. It was not the best angle, but it would have to do. Still no sign of the dragon. She moved her wrists up, digging them against the crevices of the rock. With the first motion successful and leaving her flesh intact, Sabeline began furiously raking the rope up and down the stalagmite.

Her movement was so vigorous, that strange green clumps started to spill out and fall from underneath her armour. The precise sections where she had felt something was off. Pausing in her attempt at freedom, Sabeline bent down curiously examining the odd shapes. They gave off a subtle fresh scent, one that couldn't really be named other than the fact it smelt *clean.* Awkwardly, Sabeline brushed her fingers over them, rubbing the mystery substance between her fingers. There was a grainy quality to it, but also… smooth? Her brow furrowed again. It was as though someone had given up trying to make a paste halfway through the process. *A paste.* The identity of the material filled her head in sudden, perfect clarity. After all, she'd used it enough times in the past.

It was Tilweed. The healing herb.

Why in the goddess's name would the dragon do this? Sabeline peeled back her armour, revealing green tinged bandages, packed with crudely mashed Tilweed. Carefully, she grasped the ragged fabric and pried it away from her skin, ignoring yet more of the herb that spilled to the cavern floor. Her flesh was puckered with raised pinkish white marks, though the holes and blood that had once graced her skin were now sealed and clean. Her wounds were almost healed, meaning the Tilweed must have been applied as soon as she had arrived in this beastly lair. The dragon had only needed her alive as long as she answered his question theoretically, why ensure she continued to live?

It made no difference. During her examination of the plant, the hemp rope had frayed enough so that a little movement had weakened the restraints further and they now lay in pieces around her. Free of these bindings, she'd enact the promise she'd made. If the dragon thought she dealt in empty threats, Sabeline was going to make it his last regret. *For the good of Idrelas, that monster is still a danger.*

Moving away from the stalagmite and ensuring her motions

made as little noise as possible, Sabeline shifted into a defensive position, creeping towards where the dragon had sauntered away. The tunnel *appeared* normal. There were scores in the ground from heavy claws and a few more marks on the walls, which was to be expected considering what resided here. Sabeline wasn't going to risk charging straight down after the beast, it was darker here despite the flickering remnant light from the ridiculously sized fire in the other room. Experience had taught her that *anything* could be lurking in the darkness, dragon's lair or not.

She took a few more steps forward, biting the inside of her cheek as her foot accidentally knocked a stone. The sound of it bouncing off other rocks echoed loudly in the deafening quiet. She held her breath, keeping still as a shrine statue. A moment passed. Then another. No dragon came sprinting out in a rage, spewing fire and smoke. Sabeline took another tentative step.

Before she could blink, a wall of flames sprouted from the ground, singeing the tips of her fingers. With a muffled cry, she hobbled backwards waving her right hand frantically so that the cool cavern air could soothe the sore skin. It had become smooth and a vivid pink where the fire had lapped at her. Sabeline threw a vicious glare at the dancing orange and yellow blaze. That damned beast! There were no doubt traps similar to this scattered throughout the cave, more than likely to guard sentimental or important areas. There was no way she would be able to discern how the dragon felt about various caverns. It would be foolhardy to even attempt it, lest she end up a charred husk.

Defiance bubbled within her and she allowed herself the rash action of spitting at the flames. *I will honour my threat.*

Though small this time, the defeat again by the dragon's claws left a bitter taste in her mouth. Growling, she wandered back to the main chamber (as she had come to think of it) finding the Tilweed remnants and smashing them between her burnt fingers. The relief was instant.

She drifted over to one of the couches that had all the characteristics of being from a lord's house, taking a seat and assessing the situation. She could not kill, nor escape. *But I can use this time to make preparations.* With renewed determination, she examined the chamber, her eyes landing on the pile of gold. If she was going to find anything of use, it would most likely be found there. Sabeline walked over to the mound of shining coins, goblets, jewels and other pretty artefacts. If nothing else, she had at least discovered the legends of dragons hoarding gold and other trinkets held some truth. She directed a scowl at the opulent pile as a well of disgust flooded within her. *The beast is just like the spoilt nobles of Upper Town, gathering coin just to sit on it and say they have riches.*

Fury sang in her blood and with force, Sabeline shoved her arms into the pile, digging through the treasure and throwing it behind, uncaring of where it landed. The tinkling sound of precious metal falling or colliding with other precious material reverberated throughout the cavern, but it only encouraged Sabeline to rummage faster. She tore apart the mound with her hands. Finally, her fingers grazed something long and thinner than the other trinkets and baubles. *This could be promising.* Gripping it tightly, Sabeline yanked it free and more gold trickled down in rivulets to conceal the gap she had made.

Holding up her find, a small smile crossed her face. It was a dagger, a more slender blade than she would have liked but it was in good condition. Not like the rusted and rotting blades that had greeted her when she'd first awoken. She guessed this one was ceremonial in nature, the hilt was far too garish for battle. Probably just used for a quick slash or stab. *As long as it's sharp, it will do.* Clutching her prize, Sabeline trudged back to the couch, kicking a few gold pieces out of the way as she did.

With great care, she wrapped the blade in torn bandages and artfully slipped it in behind her right greave. Experimentally, she wriggled her leg, satisfied the dagger was secure and would not pierce her flesh as she moved. The security of the blade resting there gave rise to a more practical thought. *I probably should have done this before following the beast.* She blamed emotional fatigue for the lack of planning on her part. With nothing more to do, she reclined on the chair. It was better than lying on the cave floor. She had no concept of time, but apparently she had slept for a day. By that logic, she estimated it to be evening or night. Sabeline was unsure whether she would sleep again so soon, but even if she did not, the pretence might give her an opportunity to attack if the dragon came sniffing around. Assured, she let her eyes close.

***

"I see you are out of your bindings." The rumbling voice of what could only be the dragon reached her ears.

"You really thought they would hold a Knight of Idrelas?" she countered, flicking her eyes open. Strangely, no scaly visage met her sight.

"I suppose not, though fire holds all things." The words

were coated with pride, which meant only one thing. *The creature knew.*

"I commend you for your precautions." Sabeline spat, rising from the cushions. She had been awake for a while, hoping the dragon would mistake her defenceless form. *Alas, no luck.*

She turned her head towards the ever blazing mountainous pyre, expecting the dragon's head to be bobbing around in the flames like the previous night. She searched avidly, but no fang, claw, wing, horn or even tail could be detected. "What trickery are you playing dragon?" she snarled unnerved.

"I thought I told you before Bringer of Truth, my name is Nivres."

A shadow of movement caught the corner of her eye.

"And this is no trick."

The glimpsed movement became more pronounced until the figure of a man emerged from the flames. His skin was pale, but his ears were pointed and emerged from deep crimson hair that fell to his waist in a loose braid secured with leather. He wore a silken black robe, covering his modesty. As she looked at the stranger, Sabeline noticed more unnatural features, fingernails ending in sharp tips like claws, a glint of a fang as he smirked. The most prominent were the eyes. Still glowing a vivid gold with a pupil slit into a diamond shaped line, rather than a normal circle. *The dragon.*

"You say this is no trick, but I see an illusion before me." Sabeline folded her arms across her chest. *A trap, just like the wall of fire.*

The mirage shrugged, before stepping closer to her. "Believe what you will Knight, but tell me I am still an illusion after this." As fast as the lightning of a storm, the illusion grabbed her right wrist and blew across her nearly healed fingertips.

She could *feel* the warm touch where his flesh met her own and no illusion could produce breath, for they did not need it. Whatever was before her was *alive*. She jerked her wrist free. "What *are* you?"

"You already know. I am Nivres, the great dragon. For one who hunts monsters, I would expect better knowledge."

Sabeline narrowed her eyes. She would add his attitude to the other reasons to kill him.

11

Of Sparring and Consequences

"I had thought this form might be more amenable to you." The dragon uttered, following the silence that had reigned since his insult. Sabeline had not seen it fit to say anything further, but now she felt it was time to put the dragon back in its place.

"Why? You are still a beast, only now you wear the face of a man. Changing your form does not change who or *what* you are." She countered, though truthfully her thoughts at this new found knowledge were whipping through her mind like the wind before the weather turned. It had not been recorded that dragons could shift their shape, each tome and scrap of paper portrayed them as gigantic destruction loving lizards, who once upon a time, had a penchant for taking maiden sacrifices.

The implications of what this could mean troubled her greatly. Could courtiers be dragons masquerading as men? Were noblewomen or townsfolk disguised beings infiltrating Idrelas and pilfering to learn and trade in its secrets? The dragon's voice pulled her from these worries.

"You speak with wisdom. I see now why they call you the Bringer of Truth."

"Your new shape does not erase what you've done. It just makes it easier for me to kill you. You have left yourself vulnerable *Nivres.*" It was the first time she had used his name and she sneered it, as if talking about an unpleasant bog.

"Perhaps this shape *does* calm you more, considering you have used my name." Nivres idly examined his clawed fingernails, as though this fact mattered little to him but Sabeline noted how his chest puffed with pride. *He has won again! No longer.*

"Your shape is nothing to me. But to you, it is no good unless you can utilise it properly. I am this form all of the time. Now there is an even match." Sabeline spoke, her eyes dancing with fierceness as a risky but delightful idea grew as she sharply uttered the words. She snapped her gaze at the dragon, fixing him in place with her expression. "I propose a contest. With you in this form, sparring would be easy."

Nivres appeared weary but his interest was piqued. "You wish to spar with me?"

Sabeline nodded.

"You are still recovering from your injuries."

"I've fought before with worse than this." She pointed out with barely constrained glee. *So close to getting an agreement...*

She could see the war raging in Nivres's otherworldly eyes before coming to a conclusion.

"I accept, though on certain conditions."

"Which would be?"

"If I win, you cease trying to murder me in my sleep. If you win, you may leave here on the proviso you stop trying to kill me."

"So," Sabeline uttered, standing from the chair and stretching her limbs, "both conditions end with you keeping your life."

Nivres nodded.

The very suggestion of letting the beast go free rebelled fiercely against every sensibility and principle she lived by, every oath and promise she'd sworn to the land and herself. Here she was, in the perfect location to end the dragon once and for all, with ample opportunity to enact the deed and he was forcing her hand, stealing the chance away from her. She was a woman of honour and he knew it. He knew that she would keep her word no matter who won. But at the same time, the chance to prove herself against him, win against Nivres after all the defeats at his hand was lapping temptingly at the back of her mind, contrasting sharply with her other thoughts. To finally regain her pride…the lapping became a tidal wave, washing away the rest.

"Alright dragon, I accept your terms."

Nivres inclined his head. "How do you wish to spar? Hand to hand combat? Or with training weaponry?"

"Hand to hand is acceptable." Sabeline advised, already shifting into a fighting stance. Now that she had him, she didn't want to waste any time or have him try and back out. No, she was ready to put her skills into practice here and now. The dragon sensed the change in her demeanour and seemed to sigh before matching her stance.

A second passed, then another. Sabeline struck, jabbing Nivres in the shoulder. The blow caused him to stumble back, giving her an opening but she had to move fast before he recovered. She adjusted, preparing to kick his legs out from underneath him when Nivres sidestepped the move at the last minute.

He countered, grabbing her leg and pushing her off balance, but using it to her advantage, Sabeline spun and landed a hit across Nivres's stomach. The impact caused involuntary fire to erupt from his mouth and he threw his head back. *An odd sight* Sabeline noted, watching warily as the flames and smoke came to an end. Nivres coughed and deeming it safe enough, Sabeline went in for a punch.

The dragon dodged but not as smoothly as before. Perhaps she was wearing him down already? Suddenly two hands gripped her lower and upper arm, hauling her up and flipping her over. Lying on her back, Sabeline let out a groan before gasping at the sight of a foot about to slam down on her body. She rolled quickly, rising to her feet and assuming a defensive stance. Nivres threw a punch, but she blocked it by raising both arms together in front of her chest and face. Her mouth still twisted at the hit. That was going to bruise.

Keeping her arms together, she threw them down, landing with force across Nivres's shoulder and part of his torso. The dragon winced and she imagined it was because the shoulder was the same one she'd hit earlier. He reacted by striking out with his other hand, the sharpened talons managing to catch her flesh through the armour plates and she winced at the brief stinging sensation. Brushing it aside, she used the same arm to quickly elbow jab Nires's other shoulder. The dragon hadn't been expecting her to retaliate so soon and a displeased snarl passed through his lips as he grasped where she'd hit.

She had to be wearing him down now. Sabeline reasoned she'd managed to land a strike to both shoulder joints and part of the chest area. That *had* to be affecting Nivres's reaction speed. By her logic, there had to be at least some straining or pain emanating from the nerves or muscles she'd managed to land blows on. He'd also snarled and everyone knew that anger and desperation would cloud judgement in a fight. If she could keep him enraged, then her victory was most assuredly guaranteed.

A confident smirk crossed her lips and she made a mocking "come on" motion with her fingers. He charged towards her, an expected tactic and giveaway sign the dragon was losing his composure. *Right into my trap.* As he ran towards her, she ducked just as he was about to reach her and she flew up into an uppercut. The momentum and shock of her move knocked Nivres firmly to the ground.

Sabeline waited a few seconds, but the dragon made no motion towards her. She stepped over, towering above him. He seemed relatively uninjured for the most part, but a look of surprise was plastered onto his face and he seemed to be getting his breath back. *Perhaps he was not as used to fighting in this form as he thought.* His reptilian eyes flickered over to her face when her shadow covered him.

"I am a dragon of my word Bringer of Truth. You may go. No traps or harm will befall you as you leave this cave. You have my promise."

Sabeline inclined her head. "It was an honourable fight." She said calmly, though inside it was as though a thousand giddy butterflies had been released. She had done it! Finally, the dragon bowed to *her* and it was more than satisfying to watch.

"I shall tell you the way to the entrance and then you are free, but remember your word Knight."

"Of course, a vow is a vow and we do not take such things

lightly."

Appeased, the dragon raised himself from the ground. Sabeline took another moment to savour her victory. He muttered a few directions, describing some of the caverns so she would know she was in the right place. When he was done, all he muttered was "Now go."

And so she did.

***

The cool, crisp air of the morning blew across her face as she stood at the lair entrance. While it was light, the thick tall trees surrounding her prevented much light coming through, thus giving the little sunlight a dim and gloomy feel. It was clear she was in a forest, but as for which one and where in the kingdom, Sabeline could not tell. Though the area did look intimidating, another clever ploy by the dragon no doubt. Many would keep away from this type of forest, purely on the unease they'd feel gazing upon it. She had to hand it to the dragon, he had his own security here and didn't even have to lift a claw to maintain it. To a Knight however, it was more of a challenge. She could think of worse places she'd been in. King Falon's dungeons for one.

Sabeline carefully wandered away from the entrance, across the bracken and grass, crunching them underfoot. The odd bird call echoing across the trees at least showed there was life in this place. She couldn't decide if that was a good thing or not. On the one hand, she could at least rustle up some meat if needed, on the other, she probably wouldn't be the only thing in this forest searching for its next meal.

She trudged deeper into the foliage and thickets, hoping to come across some monument or landmark that she recognised either from her travels or texts. Alas there was nothing.

Well, if all else fails, I can continue straight and eventually come out the other side. Feeling marginally better about her current course, she pressed on. The possibility she may have to make camp at some point entered her mind. With no supplies, other than the dagger she'd secreted away, a fire would be the only thing she'd be able to put together. *But a fire is the most important thing.* It would ward off whatever else lurked in this goddess forsaken place, at least for the night if she was still stuck here.

Hours passed and she was no closer to finding her way out of here than she'd been when first setting off from Nivres's lair. Sabeline could just about see the luminous sun, trying it's hardest to shed more light through the dappled trees. The position informed her it was late in the day, by her best guess either luncheon or a little after that. The thought of food caused her stomach to react instantly and she was sure the grumbling reverberations would signal her location to something.

It was decided then. She would have to procure edible sustenance. Reaching down, her fingers slipped between the greave and pulled out the stolen dagger. At least the dragon had had something of use in his stash. Birdsong continued to drift merrily through the forest, at odds with its ominous and dark atmosphere. Birds would be too difficult without a crossbow, they were startled easily and very flighty. Throwing her dagger would only end in failure after failure. No, she needed simple prey, on the slower side preferably, if the goddess took pity on her.

She'd seen the odd rodent running around, squirrels, rats, even a weasel. She'd had experience with catching them before, during a particularly lengthy assignment when she'd first become a knight. They hadn't tasted great then either. *It's that and survive or eat nothing and die,* Sabeline's mind reminded her, a lesson that had been imposed upon all Knights. She thought it strange how in the most desperate of times, even nobles could concede their picky habits and dine on a nice juicy rodent skewer with the rest of them. The memory of watching a smug noble they were escorting *demean* himself by eating a crispy rat after realising no one was going to get him anything else still brought a smirk to her face. It was almost as satisfying as the dragon defeated by her hand at last. *Almost.*

The undergrowth trembled to her right and immediately she froze. Food was about to appear, she could *feel* it and she'd be damned if it got away. An umber squirrel leapt out, sniffing the air before scurrying over to another tree. It stayed around the base of the trunk, digging around. Sabeline dropped to a crouch. If she had her supplies, it would be over by now. She could have set a successful trap or used an arrow. *Curse the King.* The monster had seen fit to keep her weaponry and survival pack, considering she was supposed to die. A pang blazed in her chest. She would never see her things again. The sword that had been her faithful companion, the battered pack from all her times on the road, each mark with its own story to tell. Shaking her head sharply, Sabeline tossed the thoughts from her mind. She could afford to mourn her situation if she survived.

With lack of her usual arrows and with no time to craft anything, she slowly reached out towards a large rock, gripping it tightly. This would have a more accurate trajectory than the dagger. *Well, here goes nothing.* The stone forcefully flew through the air, aiming straight for the squirrel. Sabeline's stomach murmured in anticipation. It grumbled even more when the squirrel evaded the projectile at the last moment, hurrying up the tree and high into the branches until she could see it no longer.

***

Darkness had descended and the sun had long since disappeared. Sabeline's stomach had grown more and more demanding. Since the failure with the squirrel, she'd scarcely come across anything else. To distract herself from the insistent hunger, she'd managed to put together a fire and though not a grand blaze like the dragon's, it was enough to provide some kind of protection.

As well as building the fire, she'd found herself with more time and had attempted to build a crude trap. It was a dismal thing and she doubted it would do much or catch anything, but even if a creature came to investigate, some quick movements and luck might mean she'd eat today after all. Was this to be her life? Sabeline hadn't really considered where she would go. If she set foot in the kingdom, King Falon would come up with some concoction to kill her and absolve himself of blame. His descending behaviour gave her enough reason to believe he would try it. She could perhaps return to the village of her youth but what would be the point? Even if it had been rebuilt, everyone she knew was already gone and there would be nothing there for her except nightmares and troubled memories.

The sound of the trap going off pulled her from that depressing line of thought. Springing to her feet, she dashed over, moving the hedge leaves aside. A large, fat rat flitted about. She wasted no time in giving it a quick, clean death.

Her stomach gurgled rapidly in excitement as she took it over to the flames, skewering the rat so it could be roasted. A change of fortunes indeed.

The smell of the rodent cooking was like a symphony to her senses. She could survive out here she supposed, but should she have to? Each day hunting for scraps of meat or vegetation? Sure, she could build herself a small hut in this forest but how long could she sustain it for? She would think more on it later, when her mind wasn't addled by an all-consuming need to eat. With one side of the meat looking fairly crispy, she reached out to turn the stick so the other side could cook.

A hollow noise that sounded somewhere between a grunting yowl and piercing scream broke through the night. Sabeline tightened her grip on the dagger. Another similar answering call echoed somewhere near the trees on her left. Twigs loudly crunching and snapping underfoot reached her ears, the sounds trailing closer and closer.

Suddenly, a creature emerged, sniffing the air as if it was being led by its nose. It was approximately the size of a human, with mottled leathery skin covered in patches of flaking tree bark and moss with long arms ending in pointed claws. The creature had oversized slit nostrils that were currently flaring and great bat –like ears. Where its eyes should have been, there was nothing but unusually smooth skin. *A bracken troll. Great.*

Another bracken troll stumbled out from the opposite side, again nostrils flaring as it scented the air. Both of them followed their noses and with startling clarity, Sabeline realised with a mixture of horror and disbelief what they were after. Her rat roast. By the goddess, could she not have a reprieve just *once?* There was no way she was going to let them take her rat without a fight. Rising to her feet, the bracken trolls twitched their massive ears, letting out brutal growls.

Without another thought, Sabeline charged at the closest one, thrusting the dagger into the troll's chest. She didn't expect the hollow-ish *thump* and what looked like tree sap to leak out of the wound. The troll still moving and becoming enraged was also unexpected. Yanking her dagger free, a long limb side swiped her straight to the ground. The other troll, hearing the commotion, turned towards her and screeched.

The shrill noise was deafening and Sabeline gritted her teeth, unsure whether the troll was still screaming or if her ears were ringing. Clambering to her feet, she went after the one bleeding sap again. This one already had a good idea where she was, the other might take a while to get its bearings. If she could take down the already wounded one first, it would be an easier fight. Brandishing her dagger, she ran again at the bracken troll. Sensing her footsteps, the troll charged straight at her. Once again, it swiped at her with long flailing limbs. She managed to evade one, but the troll's other uncoordinated hand slammed across her face, the force of it sending her careening to meet the forest floor for a second time.

Fury filled her body and a wrathful snarl of Sabeline's own left her lips. She threw herself back up, but two sharp, quick barks erupted behind her. In response, the bracken troll turned its back on her and lumbered back into the trees, disappearing back into the forest as suddenly as it had appeared. Confusion came over her features. Why would it just leave? *The other troll.*

Sabeline swung round, but the troll that had been behind her was also gone. That was even more odd. Why would they both just leave? She cast her eyes back over to the fire. There was a noticeable absence of stick and rat. *The goddess damned trolls had taken it.*

The remaining anger left her as despair took its place. She'd lost her hard won meal to bracken trolls of all things! Creatures she should have been able to take down without much problem. Sabeline put her hand over her face. If she'd had this much of an issue with damned *bracken trolls* who was to say she wouldn't have bigger problems with anything else? The trolls' presence alone had given good indication that other large beasts could be about. After all, there were things that preyed on trolls as much as they preyed on *her* rat.

She wouldn't survive this way on a long term basis. No one was coming to get her. Everyone thought she was already dead. She wasn't going to get out of here without a map or equipment. It could be days, weeks or even *months* before she found her way out of the forest and even then, as she'd contemplated earlier, where would she go? Or a better question, *what* would she do? She'd been a Knight for years, it had become an integral part of *who* she was. It couldn't be extinguished like a candle.

There is one place you have a chance, her traitorous mind suggested. She dragged her hand down her face until it fell by her side. Realistically, it was her best chance of continued survival. The only other option would be to stick the dagger in herself now and be done with it. With those choices the decision was easily made, but it didn't mean she had to like it.

She'd stay by the fire tonight. In the morning, she'd make her way back to Nivres's lair.

12

Return of the Knight

The look of shock upon Nivres's face as she casually sat by the mountainous blazing fire, holding a nicely roasting rodent on a skewer caused a smirk to appear on her face. "What? Do you want some weasel?" She asked, keeping the smirk in place. There was no way she was going to up the meagre meal she'd managed to catch (by some miracle of the goddess) on the way back to the lair, but teasing Nivres, especially after her victory against him, was just too good to pass up.

Nivres blinked, then took a moment to compose himself. "Why are you here, Bringer of Truth? You were free to leave and not return."

Sabeline took a large bite out of the now crisp weasel, crunching it loudly and a shiver of delight ran through her as Nivres winced at the sound. "You failed to tell me dragon, exactly where I am. The forest is not of the normal kind, the perfect place for setting up a lair. People naturally feel uneasy and stay away. The problem with that line of thinking means it's also problematic for *me* to get *out*." She threw a glare his way for good measure.

"Yes, well, I assumed a knight of your calibre..."

"Could manage to locate a way out and back to civilisation with no map, defensive equipment or anything else that might be useful for survival?" She pointed out, raising an eyebrow. She wasn't going to tell him about the dagger she still possessed. The small blade may still come in useful, so she'd secreted it away once more behind her greave.

Nivres, at least, appeared abashed at her words. "I apologise Bringer of Truth."

"Good." She nodded with sharpness at him. "This arrangement works out better in your favour anyway."

Puzzlement came over his features. "What do you mean by that?"

She swallowed, a big portion of the weasel sliding down her throat. It was something she'd thought of on her weary way back. Something that she hoped would secure her stay here. "Well if you had won, I would be unable to kill you in your sleep. In our waking moments, I would have free reign on your life. As I won, by terms agreed, I am unable to make *any* attempts on your life." She bit another chunk out of her meal. There wasn't much left and her belly, while grateful, was still woefully under satiated.

The dragon's otherworldly eyes widened, as though he'd only considered this for the first time. "I shall have to word my terms more carefully in future," he murmured, contemplation clear in his tone. Sabeline polished off the remnants of her weasel, her stomach letting out a grumble as she did. Immediately, she dug her fingers into the flesh in an attempt to get her body to be quiet. She would not show the dragon exactly how hard the previous day had been. She wouldn't give him the satisfaction.

Sabeline felt the weight of his gaze on her and defiantly narrowed her own at him in response. "Something I can help you with dragon?" By the goddess, she wished he would just spit out whatever he wanted to say already, instead of looking at her with something akin to pity. She didn't need his pity. She didn't need *anyone's* pity.

"No, but perhaps I may be able to help you." Nivres uttered mysteriously. "Wait here."

"Did you not listen to the conversation? Where else am I going to go? This goddess damned lair is the best chance of survival I've got." She huffed at his stupid remark.

"Ah yes of course," the dragon muttered, as though distracted. "I'll be right back." And with that he swept out of the room, off to goddess knew where, black robe dragging across the cave floor as he did. Though Sabeline noted peculiarly that the material didn't snag on any rock or uneven ground. He was still in human form, which was of interest. Did it take more effort or energy to alter between forms than she'd first thought? She had assumed he would be back to his scaly origins upon her return. Perhaps she would find out, it would at the very least, give her some research to keep herself occupied. *What exactly is he doing?* If he'd gone off to fight something, then she didn't hold much hope after their sparring. Then again, maybe he wasn't used to an opponent of her skill if the bracken trolls were anything to go by.

Glancing around the lair, Sabeline again reminded herself she'd made the correct choice. The cave system would provide shelter much better than anything she'd be able to cobble together or find and with this fire, there would always be a place of warmth, something she wouldn't be able to guarantee herself night after night in whatever woodland awaited out there. From her miserable time traipsing around the trees, she'd also deduced that little, if any creatures came this close to the dragon's den. Whether that was because they knew what lurked here or their instincts simply told them to avoid the area, she couldn't be sure. But she knew she'd have no such luck in keeping beasts away. Everything would probably try and eat the human before long. *Or let me do all the hard work and steal from under me*, the resentful thought echoed through her head. Next time she came across a damned bracken troll; she was going to slice its head off.

She certainly hadn't come back for the dragon. He was just as infuriating as ever. Survival was a skill, one she was proficient in and this had been the only logical solution. Until she could figure out her next move, she'd have to remain here. Maybe she could convince the dragon to provide her with her own section of the cave. *Yes and manticores weren't poisonous*. Sabeline scoffed. Honour dictated she keep her sparring oath. The dragon might feel relieved at the fact she wasn't going to kill him every few minutes, but it didn't necessarily mean he fully trusted her.

A heavy swiping noise, as though something was being dragged against the floor suddenly broke through the silence. Each time it filled the air, it grew closer and closer to her position. Had she been wrong in her assumption about the forest creatures? Had they tried their luck after all with what she imagined to be quite a desirable residence for them? She hadn't been here long enough to know if the dragon had to do pest control. Flying to her feet, Sabeline immediately adopted a defensive stance, ready to attack whatever beast was gradually making its way to her. Keeping her gaze trained on the entrance, she bent her knees, preparing to pounce.

A figure dressed in a black robe with loosely braided red locks which were swinging with effort walked in, pulling what appeared to be at first glance, a deer. Nivres dragged the carcass towards the fire, releasing it when he was close.

He grinned at her, flashing sharpened teeth and said in a way that mirrored her earlier tone about the weasel, "Well, do you want food or not?"

***

The deer had been skewered on a rather large pole the dragon had procured from somewhere in the cave. She watched as he idly turned it with one hand on the roasting spit he'd managed to set up at the bottom of the blaze. With a fire such as that, it wouldn't take long for the deer to be cooked. The smell of roasting meat reached her nose. She could hardly wait to sink her teeth into some more food, though Sabeline eyed Nivres carefully.

What were his motives for bringing her food? He had let her go, she had been the one to return and assert quite clearly she was staying. He did not have to bring her anything, especially as she had been his would-be murderer for the past several months. Had her time in the woodland the previous day really made her so pathetic? She did not think so.

Her gaze turned towards the slowly rotating deer, the meat crisping as she stared. Didn't dragons eat their kill raw? She had seen it, more than she cared to admit. It would still be a little while before the food was done and there was nothing else to do besides wait. Perhaps asking the dragon would make the time pass quicker.

Without preamble, Sabeline spoke cutting through the silence like a blade. "Why would you bring me sustenance?"

Nivres paused in turning the spit "You were hungry." He said simply.

"Yes, but I had eaten something, meagre as it was. You saw me chewing on it. Why gather more for me?"

"I know what it is like to not have enough to eat. Dragons have a simple philosophy. If we are hungry, we eat. If we are still hungry, we will eat again. If a hunt does not go well, we can also find ourselves eating, as you put it, meagre meals frequently until we are satisfied."

His words resonated with her logical mind. It was an unpretentious albeit practical principle of survival. Dragons were wild creatures, predators in the grand scheme of things. The same ideal could easily be applied to the castle hounds. They were fed by servants, but if they were hungry, the dogs still rummaged around the fields seeing what they could rustle up. Nivres had obviously applied the same principle to her when she'd failed to silence her stomach, Sabeline concluded with embarrassment. *Well that's one question out of the way.*

"Very well. Then why are you cooking it?" she asked.

Nivres appeared confused at her question. "I understand humans cook their food before consumption. You did it with the weasel if I'm not mistaken. Is a deer different?"

Sabeline shook her head. "No. perhaps I was not clear. I am not going to eat a full deer by myself. *My* understanding is that dragons feast on meat raw. I have seen it. Therefore why not have halved the creature? A raw portion for you and roasted for myself."

"Ah I see." Nivres returned. "I can eat meat either way. An acquired taste perhaps, but I find it adds more variety to my palate. On cold nights for example, I'd much rather consume a warm steaming hide than cool raw cattle."

His explanation seemed reminiscent of something a chef or cook might have said. Indeed, he spoke in a similar way to Yavid, the palace chef when he was preparing a banquet. Her and the other knights often listened (without much choice) as he had prattled on about flavour palates and complementing foods. A small sting echoed through her heart as she realised she would never hear Yavid talk about his recipes again. Dismissing the thought fast, she tried bringing her focus back to the matter at hand. Could a dragon really be so cultured? They were nothing more than murderous, destructive beasts that delighted in causing pain and misery. One of them just so happened to be experimenting with its food. That's all.

"I see." Sabeline eventually responded, though the disbelief coated her tone.

"You are sceptical. I can sense it in your words." Nivres uttered back, though his attention was mainly taken by the deer.

"It is strange to me, a dragon choosing to consume cooked food."

The dragon shrugged. "Well I am about to cure you of your disbelief. The deer is done."

He yanked the pole up, bringing it away from the fire. Though the meal was burning hot, Nivres handled it without effort or injury, expertly slicing it with his claws into manageable chunks. He grabbed a silken cloth from another smaller stash of treasures in the room, piling some meat into it before handing it over to her. She took it gratefully. She supposed the dragon had no need for objects such as plates and cutlery. In his world, you either ate or you didn't. With that dictating his life, Sabeline understood he wouldn't waste time tucking in. Not when there was no guarantee where or when the next meal would come from. She plucked a piece of the meat from her pile, popping it into her mouth. *Oh that was delicious.* She had no clue how he'd done it, but the deer had been roasted to perfection. Yavid would have been impressed.

Her chewing slowed as thoughts of her home once again crossed her mind. She wondered how the rest of the knights were in the aftermath of her "death". Knowing her creed, they would mourn and then they would come back stronger than before. She hoped they would be able to do something and by the goddess, that they would stay safe. She refused to imagine what else the King might do to her brethren.

Swallowing the morsel, she picked up another, chewing it plaintively.

"What troubles you?" The question stirred her from her dark thoughts. She glanced over to find Nivres watching her with curious eyes. A sigh slipped out of her lips as she gulped down the meat. What did she have to lose by answering?

"I worry for my sisters in arms." Sabeline admitted.

"Why? They are more than proficient in battle from the whisperings I've heard."

She snorted. "It is not their skills in battle I fear. I worry that the King will do something terrible to them. Find an excuse and dress it up like an honour, hurting or even *killing* them."

"Is that what he did to you? I must admit, it did puzzle me when I felt a summoning to the ruins and found high ranking members of Idrelas there."

"Yes." She whispered, turning her gaze away. She had no desire to elaborate any further and she hoped the dragon would not ask any further. Alas, the goddess was not on her side.

"The King would kill you if you returned to the city." He summarised, as if finally making sense of the strange events that had led her here.

She nodded, reaching for more deer meat.

"If you could not return there, why not return to your family? Your place of origin? Surely your people would not inform the King and you could be protected."

The memory of ash scattered along the breeze, the scent of charred flesh and burning wood, devastation everywhere and hearing a scream only to realise it was being ripped from her own throat slammed into the forefront of her mind.

"I can't." Sabeline spat with ferocity, willing the memory to be buried once again.

"Is it because of the forest? I may be able to procure…"

"No." She interrupted, fury from the memory long past bubbling within her blood. "It is because there is *nothing* left. My village was destroyed, family and friends all dead. I was the only one to survive."

"I am sorry Bringer of Truth; I did not mean…"

The anger still dictating her soul, she disregarded what Nivres was saying, ploughing forward. "Would you like to know what caused it? It wasn't bandits or marauders or an accident."

Wisely, Nivres remained silent.

In a voice akin to a hiss, she continued. *"It was a dragon."*

13

Aftermath and Impasse

Nivres merely blinked his wide yellow eyes at her. "So that was your true motivation to murder me. Vengeance for your lost village and people."

Sabeline sneered at his dispassionate response. "I swore that day I would protect the land and prevent this from happening to other folk. I did everything I could to make it happen and became the Bringer of Truth. I should thank your kind. You made me into a weapon capable of destroying your tyranny."

"I cannot speak for the dragon that destroyed your home, Bringer of Truth. But I am sorry for what they did to you."

"You don't know what remorse feels like. You apologise to me, but destroy land and villages yourself." She picked up more deer meat, chewing it ferociously as the anger sang through her soul. Why had she agreed to those stupid terms? Sticking the dagger through the dragon's eye would do a lot more to quell her fury.

"You are correct. I do destroy and everything else you claim. But my reasons are my own."

"I care not for your reasoning. You still commit the act.

That is all I need to know."

"Then you may judge too harshly, Knight of Idrelas."

"How else am I to perceive such blatant acts of destruction? Only monsters destroy without purpose, ignorant of the lives they ruin."

Her fingers itched to retrieve the dagger from its hiding place and throw it squarely into the dragon's chest. She clenched them into a tight fist instead. Just because the beast had no morals or sense of honour didn't mean she had forfeited hers.

"Perhaps there is more to the monsters than you realise." Nivres said with an ominous tone, tucking vigorously into his own hunks of meat.

"I doubt that very much." She uttered back.

The dragon shrugged. "Maybe one day you will see that the world is not as clean cut as you think. What constitutes your perception of order and laws may only be the surface of what is really going on in the overall situation."

There was no getting through to him. What did she expect? Sure, she had received an apology but it didn't mean much when the dragon continued to do the same. "We are at an impasse dragon. Let us agree to disagree with each other. I believe nothing is going to change our minds about how the other behaves."

"Very well." Nivres conceded, tearing apart another chunk of meat. Those two words hung in the air as nothing more was said. In the quiet, Sabeline's fury ebbed as she turned to watch the flames dance, her fist finally relaxing. The dragon would not understand avenging fallen kin, no matter what explanation she gave. And in return, she could not fathom how the desecration of lives and land was an acceptable action in not just the dragon's, but any monster's eyes. It was inconceivable.

"I will be gone tomorrow." The sudden words interrupted her contemplation, but she refused to turn away from the fire and meet his gaze.

"Why tell me? You may do as you wish."

"I did not want you to be concerned that someone else succeeded in ending my life." The sentence had a note of humour to it, causing her to shift around.

"That would indeed be a cause for concern." She responded.

"I could take you with me. Drop you in a village or near civilisation somewhere. You could start a new life."

For one moment, Sabeline allowed herself to indulge in the idea. She could be a tavern owner, serving drinks and putting rowdy drunk folk in their place with her fighting skills. Or she could end up a farmer, rearing cattle, chicken and sheep. It would be a simple life, far removed from everything she had known. Maybe a merchant? She could travel all over Idrelas, selling wares and sleeping in inns. But even if she did, how long would it be before someone let something slip to the wrong person? How long would it be before the guards came and hauled her back before the King? A week? A month? A year? Did she deserve a life where she would never stop looking over her shoulder, never able to trust anyone, lest they get suspicious? She knew the answer. It would not be a peaceful one. No matter what she did or where she went, the shadow of the king would follow her. But the possibility of leaving the cave and the forest, to see a vaguely familiar sight, was too good an opportunity to pass up.

"I accept your offer, dragon." She held her hand up before he could answer. "But I will not be starting a new life. I merely wish to determine what news has spread across Idrelas following my supposed death."

Nivres tilted his head in confusion. "I do not understand."

Sabeline sighed. "Give me a day in a village so I can determine the lay of the land so to speak. Then bring me back here at nightfall. You are the only being in Idrelas that knows I am still alive. Unfortunately, it is a necessity for my survival to keep it that way. A new life will not erase who and what I am. The eyes of the people do not forget and tongues will wag for the right coin."

The dragon seemed to contemplate this. "If that is what you wish, our sparring terms are still in effect so there is no issue for me. But I will say this, be prepared for things you would rather not hear or wish to see." His golden eyes became downcast as he finished speaking. *Something is afoot, is he referencing himself or the people?*

Slightly perplexed, she nodded her agreement. What was he hiding? One moment he suggests she start a new life for herself and the next he warns her of…what exactly? Rumours? Crime? Destruction? With the dragon any and all of those possibilities could come to fruition. Well whatever he was alluding to, she hoped she could keep her identity secret and resist the ingrained instinct to get involved, restoring peace and truth. *By the goddess, that's going to be difficult.*

"I will find some things for you. You cannot go as you are."

She glanced down at her armour. That would be problematic indeed.

"Afterwards, we should rest. We will both need to be at our best." With that enigmatic statement, Nivres rose to his feet, disappearing down one of the cave tunnels and leaving Sabeline alone by the fire.

A disturbing thought crossed her mind as he vanished into the darkness. Why was a beast, a monster with no regard for life, actively trying to help *her*?

# 14

Flight

It was the next morning when Sabeline stood there inspecting the dress she'd been garbed in with a wary eye. It was a simple garment, cheaply made and deep brown in colour, with some white linen lining the chest area. She'd blend in with the folk of any village Nivres deigned to drop her in, but by the goddess was this thing prickly. She'd never felt the urge to scratch so much in her life. Even her poor armour, abandoned in a neat careful pile, was not this uncomfortable.

"Are you ready?" Nivres came lumbering out from a separate cavern, once again in his natural form.

"Yes," She answered, dropping the hem of the dress from her fingertips.

The dragon nodded and moved forward, stepping down another tunnel branching off from the main room. Flicking his tail, he motioned for Sabeline to follow. At least she was in boots rather than useless pumps. Her feet would have been ripped to shreds before she'd even made it out of the cave. She liked boots, they were faithful, sturdy things. They didn't itch either.

She continued behind the beast, keeping to his pace. The last time she'd taken this route was after their sparring match, but it was still a marvel to navigate. There were enough twists, turns and short cuts through a few other rooms that she truly felt as if she were in a labyrinth. She wondered how much was natural structure and how much the dragon had carved out. It definitely wouldn't have been a quick task, that was certain.

A bright glare of light suddenly streamed through the gaps either side of the dragon's form. Sabeline raised a hand to her face in an effort to reduce the glow. The morning light was particularly strong today. She wasn't sure whether that was a good omen or not.

Emerging from the mouth of the cave, she watched as the dragon stretched his limbs and shook out his large, leathery wings. Despite her simmering dislike for his kind, Sabeline could admit it was a glorious sight, observing such a creature prepare for flight with early morning sunlight glinting off of every crimson scale. After a few more moments of shaking and stretching, Nivres huffed out some smoke through his nostrils and seeming satisfied, turned his reptilian head towards her.

"Sit just above the middle, hold tightly to one of my spines." He instructed, the voice again taking on an underlying rumble now it was back in a lizard-like throat.

Sabeline nodded and he lowered his bulk for her to climb up his side. It didn't escape her notice that this was the strangest and most unlikely situation she would have ever pictured herself to be in. *Well, here goes everything.* Sinking her fingers into the beast's flesh, she managed to crawl up the scales without much effort, though she begrudgingly conceded the lightweight dress could have helped. Carefully, she sat in the position Nivres had advised, gripping one of the thicker spines until the palms of both hands hurt. The dragon shuffled a bit underneath her, adjusting to the new weight.

"Ready?" He uttered.

"As much as I'll ever be." The unclear confirmation spilled from her lips. His attitude this morning had been strange. He had not spoken much to her and from their previous interactions, he had never had an issue with talking to her before. Perhaps he was upset he would not be rid of her just yet. Maybe she was finally making him as miserable as he'd made her.

Before she could explore this avenue of thought further, the dragon broke into a slight run, thundering across the grassy outcrop by the cave. *It's not so bad, it's like riding a massive horse.* Sabeline assured herself. His wings extended to the full length and with an almighty downward thrust of them, he launched into the air. The wind whipped unrelenting around her short locks as they ascended further and further into the sky. She clenched the spine until her knuckles were white with the effort and as the dragon continued to rise, she dug her knees into his flesh for good measure. The lurching of her stomach and slipping sensation (which could have been real or her imagination, she wasn't sure but the fact it was there was enough) gave her the motivation to keep hold.

Nivres suddenly altered position, straightening out and finally saving her stomach from doing acrobatics again. The heavy wingbeats adopted a steady rhythm that was almost calming. After a few minutes of stable flying, Sabeline dared to gaze around. She could see the landscape below, a patchwork of fields, farms, plateaus and woodland, occasionally broken up by clusters of villages or the odd secluded house. It was much more pleasant than the last two times she'd ended up in the air with the beast.

Just as she was becoming accustomed to the flight, Nivres made a sudden downward swoop, sending her poor stomach back into her throat again. The descent was fast, much faster than the ascent. *Is this speed normal?* Immediately, she hunkered down, clinging to the spine with everything she had and digging in not just her knees, but as much of her legs as she could. Even her ankles embedded themselves in fleshy scales.

With a fury of wind that ricocheted through the tree branches and a deafening slam, the dragon landed on another grassy outcrop, jarring her bones.

He paced a bit before murmuring, "You can get off now."

Pulling her shaking legs up, Sabeline slid down the same side she'd climbed, landing with an inelegant thump. She couldn't help picture her old mentor's seething face at her poor landing, but Sabeline could bet the taskmaster had never ridden a dragon before. The unmistakable heat of breath gushed over the back of her neck and every nerve fired into alert as teeth brushed against her skin. They sunk into the collar of the dress, gently pulling her up until she was standing (albeit a little unsteadily) on her feet.

"Thank you." She gritted out, her frantic heart finally starting to settle after all the events of the morning thus far.

Nivres nodded, pulling his head back from her and gesturing west of their location. "The village of Dunsaw is along that road. I am sure you'll find what you seek, even in a village as remote as this. I will meet you back here at nightfall, should you still wish to return with me."

"I've already explained, *repeatedly*, why it is necessary for me to return with you." Her irritated voice pointed out. By the goddess, did dragons have problems with short term memory? Or did they just not listen?

He didn't look at her. "I have a task to complete. One a knight such as you may perhaps come to understand, but would not accept. As I said, if you still wish to return with me at nightfall, I will be here, but I will understand if you do not arrive." So, it appeared he was talking in riddles now.

"What is this task?" She asked, the beginnings of apprehension appearing on her face.

"It is complicated." Nivres stated, but did not expand any further. He still would not look at her, causing her apprehension to grow.

"What are you going to do?" Her eyes narrowed. *Something* was going to happen, the beast had been acting off and secretive since she'd insisted on him taking her to a village. She'd be a fool if she couldn't read the signs. And the signs pointed towards whatever plan being wrong, but wrong to her or the dragon, she did not know.

"Dunsaw is that way." Nivres grumbled out instead, taking to the air without even a backward glance, the wind from his wings dancing over her.

Sabeline was alone. Again. But this time, she was going to solve the mysteries plaguing her thoughts once and for all.

15

Dunsaw

The thatched roofs of Dunsaw loomed against the horizon as she made her way down the path. By the goddess, when she next saw Nivres she was going to strangle him, agreement be damned. Leaving her without so much as a goodbye. She didn't know why she cared. Maybe it was because he'd openly admitted he was planning to do… something. She nodded to herself, continuing to match at a furious pace towards the village. That had to be it.

Passing under the timber arch indicating the village entrance, Sabeline assessed Dunsaw. There was nothing remarkable or interesting to set it apart from any other farming village. The ground was hard mud and it had turned to sludge in some places. There were no constructed pathways like Upper Town, though delight crept through her as she imagined the nobles trying to navigate this place. She particularly enjoyed the image she conjured of them getting stuck in the sludge. Villagers in ragged clothing were merrily traipsing about, conducting their daily business. Carts of grain, fruit, vegetables and meats were being pulled in every direction by strong, broad work horses. A sharp pang hit her chest as thoughts of her own loyal steed filled her mind. She hoped her sisters in arms were taking care of him. Sabeline brushed the thoughts away regretfully. Now was not the time to mourn her losses. She was here for information, that was all. A rusted squealing noise echoed above her and she turned to see the rickety sign of the tavern swinging overhead. *Well, information and a drink.* Goddess knew she deserved one.

Pushing open the tavern door, she entered the surprisingly large establishment. There were simple tables and chairs scattered across a dark hardwood floor. It looked like someone had tried to put a rug down, maybe to make the place a bit more welcoming, but the filth from many a farmer's boot had rendered it flat and the same colour as the wood. Sabeline stalked up towards the bar, finding a space far down from the drunkards at the top end. The barkeep gave her an appraising glance, but continued to clean out the tankard in his hands with a dirty rag.

"Ale." She directed the demand at him.

He nodded, finally putting the rag down. He kept hold of the tankard and turned to a keg behind him, twisting the tap and filling it with her request. The barkeep pushed it at her and Sabeline tossed a few of the less conspicuous coins she'd taken from the dragon's hoard (with his consent) the barkeep's way. He inspected them carefully, before shoving them into the noisy till.

"Not from round here are ye?" He asked, picking up another tankard.

"Just passing through." She answered, picking up her own and taking a swig. By the goddess, that was some good stuff.

The barkeep nodded. "So where you headed?"

"Wherever the wind takes me I suppose," She answered carefully. "This is some fine ale." She drank again, waiting. In her experience, compliments, no matter how small, had an excellent way of encouraging people to spill rumours or secrets they knew.

The barkeep puffed his chest a little. "It's a homebrew. We make it right out back with the crops grown around here."

"Well, you do an excellent job." Sabeline continued, taking another gulp. The barkeep seemed pleased. Seizing an opportunity, she carried on nonchalantly "Though someone along the road told me to avoid the kingdom. Didn't say why. I have relatives there, thought I'd drop by some time on my travels, but now I'm worried for them." The best lies always had a grain of truth to them. The Knights may not be relation by blood, but they were still family. And she was indeed worried for them.

The barkeep glanced around, then filled up another tankard, passing it over to one of the soberer drunkards. "Cannae say about your relatives, but rumour has it the King killed one of his own knights."

Sabeline played along, adopting a wide eyed surprised expression. "Really? The Knights are legendary; why would he want to do something like that?" She resisted the urge to grit her teeth.

The barkeep sighed. "I dunno lass. From what I heard, it was the Bringer of Truth. She couldn't kill a dragon and when she got back to the castle, King said he'd found the solution. I heard she agreed to enact the King's plan but they're knights ain't they? Anything to protect the kingdom. I guess she was desperate to stop the beast. Don't change the fact the King killed 'er."

Interesting. Even though Falon had dressed her execution up as an honour, this man clearly still held him to blame. She sipped her ale before digging a little deeper. "She agreed to go along with it though." *She most certainly did not.*

"Aye, but it weren't 'er that suggested sacrificing herself. It was the King. She'd have probably found some other way if he didn't convince 'er to jump on the pyre. Knights ain't stupid, they're resourceful, skilled warriors. King played on her sense of duty, that's all there is to it. Now we got one less Knight in the world and for what? Dragon's don't stop just because they get offered a maiden." The barkeep huffed and rolled his eyes. It was heart-warming to hear that at least one person, far removed from the influence of the King in this little farming village, believed in her.

"Branston's grandson is a guard at the castle." Another man who'd recently settled himself near her at the bar chimed in. "I heard they kept 'er in a cage until the night she was taken to the mourning fields."

"A cage?" She asked the newcomer, eyebrow raised. What in goddess's name were folk writing home about her incarceration?

"Aye lass. Branston's grandson says the Bringer of Truth was caged right up until her death. That don't sound too much like agreement to me."

"Maybe it was just for show." She murmured. So far, whichever guard was Branston's grandson, had just gone up in her estimation.

"Nah," the man said, waving a dirt stained hand dismissively. "If it were for show, they wouldn't have kept the locks locked. If she'd agreed, she weren't gonna run were she? No need to lock 'em."

"Very true." Sabeline answered, downing the last of her ale. If she ever had the chance to speak to her sisters in arms again, she'd ensure they'd arrange for Branston's grandson to get a hefty pay rise. "So, I'm probably best to avoid the Kingdom for a while then."

"Aye lass, till things settle down again. It only happened recent you see." The barkeep assured her.

"Well, thanks for your help." She smiled, leaving a few more coins on the counter as she exited the tavern. He'd never know it, but the barkeep deserved more coin than she could give for his faith in her and her Creed. She stepped out into the village, deciding to head for the market. Meat was delectable, but she couldn't live off of deer and weasel alone, like Nivres. Markets were also just as good a place to pick up gossip as a tavern.

As Sabeline walked, it wasn't long before she realised some footsteps were matching her footfall exactly. When she stopped, so did they. When she moved or sped up, so did they. *They've picked the wrong target.* Steeling herself, she turned abruptly. Two of the drunkards she'd seen at the bar were trailing behind her. "What do you want? Stop following me." She growled.

"Come on darlin', don't be like that." One of them slurred.

"Like what? You're the ones following me and I do not care for it. At all." She glared.

"We can show you some hospitality." The other one garbled at her.

"No thank you, you've already shown me enough of that. Now stop following me or I will ensure your lands won't have any heirs."

Just as the threat left her mouth, a sudden boom ricocheted

deafeningly through the air and a large column of fire rose in a glorious upward burst along an area of the distant hilled horizon on Dunsaw's outskirts.

She vaguely made out the fleeing footsteps of the drunkards as she gazed upon the scene. Other villagers of Dunsaw had come to a halt and were staring at the blaze with fear in their eyes while whimpers and cries filled the air. Nausea crawled up Sabeline's stomach. Whatever that was, she had no doubt Nivres had caused it. Directly or indirectly, that remained to be seen.

Snapping into action, she turned, running up to a villager who was trying to get as far away as possible. "What's over there? Tell me quickly!" Sabeline shouted over the panicked racket surrounding them.

The woman looked at her as though she was mad, but answered anyway. "A settlement I think."

Sabeline kept pace with her. "A village?"

"No, a ramshackle set up with a few people. Now get lost!" The woman barked, picking up her pace. Sabeline had a feeling the woman would have reacted the same way, even if she had been wearing her armour. *If the settlement has been attacked...* Sabeline abruptly altered her course, heading to where she'd seen a few horses corralled together. They may be work horses, but right now, any horse was better than none. Her feet sped easily over the mud and dirt. She thanked the goddess again for the boots strapped securely to them.

It wasn't long before she found the horses tethered to a wooden bar, waiting for their owners to return from their errands. Fingers working rapidly, she set about untying the first one her eyes laid sight on. The horse was tacked up which was a relief. She'd hate to ride bareback in this goddess forsaken dress. With swift expertise, she mounted the horse without effort. An angry cry of "Hey!" reached her and her eyes swept over a man sprinting up to her.

"I'll bring him right back; I just need to borrow him for a bit!" Sabeline shouted back, pulling on the reins.

The horse immediately moved following her motion. She shook the leather sharply, hunkering down against the creature. A whinny erupted from the horse's mouth before it broke into a gallop, leaving the enraged man behind. Guilt began to settle within the crevices of her mind, after all the man she'd stolen from probably relied heavily on his horse. *I'm returning him,* she consoled herself, *and right now, needs must.* She propelled the horse faster, steering him in the direction of the flickering orange glow. She didn't know how long it would take to get there, even with the horse moving at full speed.

By the goddess, what had Nivres done? Had he really destroyed an entire settlement? She couldn't imagine what the reasoning would be. *Monsters don't need a reason to destroy.* Was it instinct? Could dragons just not help themselves? As if it was an inane need they were required to sate? As much as she wanted to believe it, her more practical side chimed in. If they couldn't help it, why not attack the first place he came across? Why travel all the way out here, in the middle of nowhere to attack a random settlement? Why not go for Dunsaw itself? The wind whipped her short locks across her face and she shook her head in an attempt to keep them out of her eyes. There were too many conflicting questions resonating through her mind. Nivres had planned this, that was for certain, otherwise he wouldn't have been acting so secretive earlier. But for what purpose? She had to find out.

But what if she was right? What if there was no good reason? The answer came forcefully, slamming into her heart. His life would be forfeit, sparring agreement be damned. Why did that thought not give her as much pleasure as before? Perhaps because despite everything, Nivres was her only ally right now and she'd never killed an ally of hers. That had to be it. Sabeline spurred the horse on. No matter what awaited her, she would stand strong. She was still a Knight and a Knight of Idrelas never cowered. Not even in the face of difficult, potentially soul shattering decisions.

***

The flames still licked at the skeletons of haphazardly built huts as she approached. The horse had slowed to a usual walking pace and cautiously, Sabeline edged the beast forward. It was quiet, except for the odd crackle as the fires consumed as much as they could. The stench of various burnt items reached her nose, including…Oh goddess. That was burning flesh. The smell almost caused her to gag.

The horse slowly made its way around. There was no life, nothing left anywhere. The sight caused the memory of *that* day to surge to the forefront of her mind. A child, surrounded by the burning death and decay, screaming for someone, anyone…Sabeline shook her head, dispelling the image. *Later.* She could deal with the memory later.

Charred remains of buildings and other wooden structures crunched under hoof, becoming nothing more than a black stain of soot across the landscape. This place had truly been purged from any map. The fire grew warmer as she headed towards the main part of the settlement. While the flames were only caressing the bare outer structures, they were still ravaging these main buildings in full force. *This may be where the fire column first originated,* she mused, glancing over the settlement. Coiling dark smoke also hung thick in the air here. Bringing the horse to a halt, Sabeline dismounted, leading him back out towards an area with less smog.

Pulling her dress up over her nose, she headed back in. She stepped deeper and deeper into the main area, ensuring the flames didn't find her dress an attractive alternative. Turning another corner, she stopped at the sight greeting her. Nivres had returned to human form, but instead of a silk robe like in the cave, he appeared to be wearing some kind of simplified armour, the type used by bandits and other un-savoury groups.

He stood on a large burning pile and Sabeline had the distinct impression a good portion of it was comprised of bodies. The fire didn't bother him, wrapping around him and dancing over his form without leaving so much as a mark. Suddenly, her throat burned and she couldn't help but let out a few retching coughs.

Immediately, Nivres swung around, fixing those golden eyes directly on her.

16

Difficult Truths

She didn't know if he recognised her from his position but those eyes…She had never seen them like that before. They were cold, uncaring and filled with a simmering malice. Her gaze dropped to Nivres's hand and her own eyes widened. Was that…a head? A *person's* head? He tossed it to the side as if it was rubbish, letting it roll over the flaming pile. *This is more than simple destruction.* She stayed rooted to the spot as Nivres slid down the pile and walked at a steady pace towards her. She didn't dare breathe as he stopped in front of her.

"I told you I'd be back for you at nightfall." He stated with gruffness.

"Yes well, plans changed when an explosion of fire suddenly went off." Sabeline countered, though her dress muffled her voice somewhat.

"You didn't need to come towards it."

"How could I not? People were panicking in Dunsaw and with your attitude today practically admitting you were going to do something, of course I was going to come!"

"A Knight through and through." Nivres uttered, but his eyes had not changed.

"I want answers Nivres, why do this? Why here?" Her voice a mixture between form and imploring as she vaguely gestured her right hand at the desecrated surroundings. She hoped by using his name, he'd be more inclined to tell her.

He remained silent, unwavering. Anger pounded through her blood as he continued to say nothing.

"Answer me for goddess sake! Or are you really just a mindless monster, destroying lives on instinct despite your claims of being better than that? Because that's what you're proving to me here. Do you even have an answer huh?" She spat, erupting into coughs again. At her coughing fit, Nivres actually turned his head upwards, as if just noticing the thick smoke polluting the air. She narrowed her eyes at him.

"You shouldn't linger here, Bringer of Truth."

"Oh no, you are not getting rid of me that easily. Tell me dragon! They call me Bringer of Truth because I always get to the truth eventually. I just watched you throw a goddess damned *head* into the fire! That alone deserves some explaining, if nothing else!" Her passionate plea was ruined by another round of coughs. Strange how Nivres seemed unaffected by the smog.

"I will tell you if you leave." He growled, reaching out and gripping her forearm. He tried to pull her away, but she dug her heels in.

"Tell me and then I'll leave." She countered.

He growled again and Sabeline detected an edge of frustration. "It is too long for me to tell of now. Leave and I promise you Bringer of Truth, I will explain."

"You swear it?"

DIFFICULT TRUTHS

"Yes!" Nivres roared, "Now for Draconis sake, go before…"

Sabeline doubled over as coughs racked her frame, but panic gripped her as she realised she couldn't stop. The coughs devolved further into retching bursts, throat straining to expel something that wasn't quite there. She dropped to the floor, dress slipping from over her nose. Nivres growled words under his breath but she couldn't understand what he was muttering. All of a sudden, it felt like she was flying before being deposited over a hard, sturdy surface. Her watery eyes cracked open to reveal Nivres was carrying her over his shoulder, moving hurriedly away from the main area of the settlement. More coughs pounded through her chest and she closed her scratchy eyes against the imposing view, gently drifting off to the rhythm of Nivres's movements.

***

"Bringer of Truth?" the question echoed in her unconscious mind. Yes, that was her. A sharp jab hit her shoulder and her eyelids flew open with a start. Nivres was sitting beside her on blades of grass, she followed his arm, realising his hand was still on her shoulder. She shuffled up into a sitting position and the hand withdrew. In silence, Nivres offered her a flask of water. Goddess only knew where he'd procured it from, but she accepted it greedily. Her throat was screeching in dry agony.

"What happened?" Sabeline gasped out. "Why am I on the ground?"

Nivres shuffled around. "The smoke was thick, it affected your body. I tried to tell you…" He trailed off and Sabeline nodded. The dragon had indeed tried to warn her, but she had been insistent on retrieving the truth from him. She still was.

"Do not think I have completely forgotten everything that has happened." She murmured with severity. "You vowed to tell me your reasons if I left. Though you ended up helping me, I still retreated from the area."

A low, heavy sigh spilled from Nivres. She waited patiently, still grasping the flask. Whatever he said, she would listen. Then she would pass judgement. The conflict bubbled within her again and she found herself simultaneously wanting the answer but being fearful of it.

"I understand your need to avenge your people." Nivres rumbled. A sudden movement and chewing noise caught her attention and Sabeline realised the horse she'd borrowed was with them. Nivres must have brought it along.

"How so?" She prompted, turning her attention away from the horse.

"This place," The dragon waved a hand to the left of his position, towards the smoking remnants of the settlement. "It belonged to members of The Chaos Convocation."

The Chaos Convocation. She'd heard of that name. It was an organisation of bandits or marauders; she wasn't completely sure. She was fairly certain another knight had begun investigations into the group, but didn't know much beyond that. "They are criminals if I understand correctly."

Nivres nodded. "The worst kind of human scum. Gambling, theft, murder, nothing is beyond their repertoire. They feel no regret. No remorse. They delight in suffering. They are nothing like me and my kind." He levelled her with a stare so fierce, that any counter argument she was going to make died in her throat.

Instead, Sabeline jerked her head in a nod, to show she

understood.

Satisfied at her reaction, Nivres continued. "My sister, Myvanna, she had crossed into territory they proclaimed was theirs. Despite her protests that she was just passing through, that she didn't know, they kidnapped and tortured her. Just for something to do." He snarled, fury lacing his form.

"But she was a dragon was she not? Surely she fought and escaped?" If Myvanna's strength had been anything like the kind she'd witnessed today, surely Nivres's sister had been victorious?

The dragon looked at her with a sad smile etched across his mouth. "Your faith in her is reassuring. But alas, she was in human form. Myvanna did put up a fight, but she was already in a weakened state from another brawl. With their numbers, The Chaos Convocation overpowered her with ease. Hours had passed before I'd tracked her location. By then, it was too late."

Sabeline remained quiet. She sensed Nivres wanted to tell her and she wasn't going to interrupt.

"I found her in one of their barns. Covered in blood. Greatly injured. Her throat was covered in bruises. They punched it so she couldn't breathe fire. They laughed when she choked on it." He spat. "She died of the injuries they'd given her."

"I'm sorry." Sabeline uttered softly, but with sincerity. No one should have to go through something like that, not even a dragon. "So these people in this settlement, they are responsible for Myvanna's death?"

"After her passing, I ensured their territory was barren of life. It is custom for a dragon to avenge their fallen kin. But after I had destroyed every last piece of their presence, the rage was still strong within me. I knew to truly avenge my sister; I would have to wipe their organisation from the face of Idrelas. All of it."

It was beginning to dawn on her where his story was leading. "So the places you've been destroying across Idrelas, they are The Chaos Convocation's camps, settlements or villages?"

The dragon nodded. The horse pulled up some grass, the sound of ripped vegetation settling between them. "I can only assume reports of dragon attacks reached King Falon. To be seen doing something, he then dispatched a Knight to kill me and put an end to my terror." He raised an eyebrow at her as the words buried themselves in her mind.

"It was not reported that you were attacking Chaos Convocation sites. Another knight is investigating the organisation." Sabeline pointed out.

"That was evident. But tell me Bringer of Truth, if you had known from the beginning what types of locations I was targeting, would it have made a difference to your cause?"

Would it have? If she had known the truth, the full truth, would she still have relentlessly hunted down Nivres? She honestly did not know. Her main focus had always been that he was a dragon and dragons destroyed without reason. But he *had* a reason. A very good one. One she found herself empathising with and understanding.

And if he had a reason, then what did she have to justify her hunt?

17

Understandings

Silence as thick as the smoke hung in the air as thoughts continued to race through Sabeline's mind. She did not think her vocation was rendered meaningless at the dragon's revelations. After all, she had done a lot of good for the people of Idrelas. She had protected them, not just from monsters, but the dredges of humanity. People like The Chaos Convocation, who cared not for the pain and suffering of others.

Could she have investigated the situations further? Yes, she conceded. Their investigations were usually compiled of witness accounts from the people. It had never occurred to her to ask the monster why they might be destroying the crops or attacking the town in a rage. Maybe in some of those cases, the people she had defended had been in the wrong. She would never know now.

But what if she had the chance to right those wrongs now? The Chaos Convocation was a threat, that was something both her and the dragon agreed on. If she could aid in taking them down, it would benefit both of them. Nivres would still get his vengeance for Myvanna and she would regain some of the honour she'd just lost.

It was the duty of a Knight to protect Idrelas and by the goddess, she was going to do her duty. This time with all the facts and thorough investigations. And with a dragon. It was clear Nivres already had more knowledge on the subject than her. She would need to convince him to share it with her and also take her along.

"I've been thinking." Sabeline began, causing Nivres to snap his attention back to her. "In truth, I do not know whether your cause would have made a difference to my hunt if I had known in advance. But I do understand and empathise with your reason."

"I thank you for your honesty." Nivres murmured.

"But, your reasons have given me cause to contemplate methods used in the past to assess the situation at hand. They are perhaps not as inclusive as they could be."

Nivres remained quiet as she spoke, as if both dreading and anticipating her next words. Sabeline almost smiled at the irony of it.

"The world believes me to be dead and therefore I cannot introduce new measures. However, despite this, I am still a Knight. It is my sworn duty to protect the land and its people from danger and other threats. The Chaos Convocation fits this category perfectly."

"What are you saying?" Nivres rumbled.

"That I want to help you take them down." She gazed at him with all the determination she possessed.

Nivres was silent for a few moments, watching the breeze sweep across the grass. "I do not think I have a choice. Even if I left to pursue them, you would find a way to follow regardless. I would rather know where you are when facing these villains, lest I accidentally set you on fire." He fixed her with a disapproving stare, no doubt imagining the situation he'd painted, despite the fact she hadn't done anything.

"Then we have an accord?" Sabeline asked, shuffling to face him better. "You will let me help you take down the organisation?"

Nivres nodded. "You have already proven to be a capable warrior. I believe you would be able to handle them in a fight." Sabeline was practically giddy at the prospect. Nivres had been easier to convince of this than she'd thought. "But," he continued.

By the goddess, so close.

"Would you be able to remain collected if I had need to burn down whatever hole we find them in?"

She cast her mind back to when she'd been walking through the settlement, smothering the images of her past down as far as she could. What if she saw something that reminded her of that day and the hesitation got her killed? Sabeline swallowed. She'd just have to keep a tighter rein on her memories. "It will get easier. I will not be a liability to you."

Nivres nodded. "Very well. I will hold you to your word."

"Haven't you always?" She quipped back.

Nivres allowed a smirk to cross his face. "Only because you are the Bringer of Truth."

Sabeline smiled back. However, the use of her title caused her to think. If he needed her while they were in a Chaos Convocation camp, settlement or whatever, Nivres shouting *Bringer of Truth* would be a sure fire way for her identity to be revealed. After that, how long would word take to get back to the King and for him to realise he'd failed? She couldn't take the risk, but the alternative…Could she do it? Could she really give a dragon this part of her?

Her heart hammered against her chest. *I refuse to be a liability.* "S-Sabeline." She stuttered out, the word full of hesitation. Nivres looked at her with surprise etched on his features. "If we're going to do this, calling me by my title in front of Chaos Convocation members is probably not the best idea." She blurted out her reasoning.

"Indeed." Nivres agreed. "Then I shall call you by your name."

Sabeline nodded. A Knight's name was mainly known by other Knights, The Palatine, The King and whatever family and friends the Knight in question had. She had the strange advantage of no one outside the castle knowing her name. Except for now. It was an odd feeling, but not entirely unwelcome.

"Night is falling." Nivres suddenly remarked. "And you are still here."

"Of course I am. I came searching for you well before time due to your escapade." She huffed back.

"Then I presume you would still like to return with me?" Nivres smirked at her, already knowing the answer. *Stupid dragons.*

"I think that would be obvious." She muttered, rolling her eyes.

"I am just being certain, Sabeline." He grinned, showing off a nice set of fangs, which were strange in a human mouth.

Why in all the land were her cheeks warm? Was she *blushing?!* No. She couldn't be. She didn't blush. She was a Knight. It was just her damned name. She could not have this reaction every time he uttered it for goddess's sake!

"Er, yes, very good." She said, trying to regain some composure.

"I will need to change in order to take us back." Nivres rose, searching for a suitable area. Sabeline presumed he was looking for a secluded spot to shift into his true form. Though a loud whinny soon interrupted that plan.

"The horse!" Sabeline cried. She'd completely forgotten about its presence. "I gave my word to return him." She clambered to her feet, getting ready to mount. "I'll take him back to Dunsaw and meet you in the original clearing. That will give you enough time, will it not?"

Nivres agreed. "I will await you there."

Sabeline nodded once and urged the horse forward. The hooves galloped rapidly across the ground, kicking up loose patches of earth and grass. Despite the rhythmic pounding as the horse ran, she almost thought she heard the words "Be safe Sabeline," carried to her by the wind.

18

Blossoming

Sabeline traipsed down the path that had brought her to Dunsaw in the first place. She had secured the horse as quickly and as discreetly as possible. Now all she needed to do was return to Nivres. More than enough time had passed to change form and fly to the meeting place by her reckoning.

As she walked, Sabeline couldn't help but think of the words uttered softly as she galloped away. She had not imagined them, that was for certain. The only other being near her capable of speech at the time was Nivres, so they had to have been spoken by him. It was an odd sensation to have someone worry about her safety. No doubt her long deceased family had, but Knights were independent, self-sufficient people. Yes, they worried for each other, but not in terms of safety. A remark of "Sabeline's fighting a warlord," would barely cause them to bat an eyelid.

Still, a warm feeling filled her chest as she stepped along the path. To be concerned for her safety meant that Nivres had to at least somewhat care about her. Perhaps they could grow to be friends. It would be pleasant to have someone she could consider a friend outside of her sisters in arms.

Sabeline diverted from the path and headed towards the clearing. She brushed past some of the trees and bushes, dress snagging on needle-like branches. She huffed. This was why she wore armour. Armour broke through the spindly foliage. Pretty dresses did not. Wrapping her fingers around the fabric, Sabeline tugged and a harsh ripping sound filled the air. A good chunk of fabric was embedded into the bush's spines, leaving her left shin exposed up to the knee at the front. By the goddess, why her? No doubt she was going to get scale burn or something on the journey back. She was never going to wear a dress again if she could help it.

Nivres was back in dragon form, sitting on the grass waiting for her. His position reminded her of a cat when it tucked its legs under itself. His eyes widened slightly when he saw the jagged fabric and the pale skin of her leg illuminated by the starlight.

"Please tell me this dress didn't belong to anyone important." It had occurred to her on the horse ride back to Dunsaw that it could have belonged to Myvanna. If that was the case, she could wave goodbye at the chance of a blossoming friendship.

Nivres shook his crimson reptilian head." It didn't. I found it in the forest one day, along with a broken trunk and other items. Never did find out how it had gotten there or who it belonged to."

Strange. Maybe someone had been either desperate or brave enough to venture into those woods. Sabeline was betting it had been the former."That's a relief."

"Were you attacked? Is that why the dress is torn? I confess, I did not hear anything. " Nivres rumbled, both with a hint of anger and undertone of concern. It restored some of her hope anyway.

"No. It was the stupid foliage. This is why I need armour. Armour is reliable. It doesn't betray your trust with a hedge."

She could tell Nivres was trying not to laugh at her. "I will remember that."

"Good. Now let's get back to the cave. We have planning to do and a dress to burn." Sabeline grumbled while climbing up the side of the dragon.

"Indeed." Nivres agreed, as she adjusted herself into the correct position, once more digging her knees into the scales and gripping onto one of Nivres's spines. He raised himself from the ground, stretching out his wings.

As they soared high in the darkened sky, Sabeline realised that for the first time in her life, she could almost touch the stars.

***

As Nivres touched down by the familiar cave, a sense of forlornness overtook her and Sabeline found herself sad that she was no longer a part of the shimmering stars, opulent moon and wispy dusk coloured clouds. It seemed she was more at ease with night flying than any other previous flight. Or maybe it was because so much had happened since the morning.

Sabeline swung her legs, dismounting the dragon as gracefully as she could manage. She had to be getting better, at least she didn't fall flat on the grass this time. Once her feet met solid ground, Nivres lumbered towards the cave entrance and she followed. The flesh of her exposed leg stung a little as wind and breeze no longer berated it at great speed. It was irritating, but hopefully it would soothe quickly once she was able to settle inside.

"So when is our next attack?" She asked Nivres, as they travelled towards the room with the large, crackling fire.

"You do not wish to rest first?" Nivres questioned.

Sabeline shook her head, though the dragon could not see her motion from his position. "No. I am far too excited! Planning an upcoming battle, laying out strategy, it is something that makes my heart race. There is no greater thrill. I have been denied the opportunity for too long." She breathed out. Already she felt her blood singing beneath her skin at the anticipation. No, she was in no mood to rest.

"Very well. We shall plan. " Nivres agreed, as they entered the large chamber that was becoming easily recognisable to her.

The moment she was able to cross the entryway, Sabeline sprinted for her armour. *By the goddess, I can't wait to be out of this thing!* Her fingers clutched the metal plates as if her life depended on it.

"For these assaults, we will have to obtain new armour for you." Nivres said solemnly, no doubt in response to her desperate action.

She glanced down at the spaulder she was holding. Ornate, engraved and with an edging of gold. It was the only armour she'd ever known, but Sabeline didn't need Nivres to explain why. It was the armour of the Bringer of Truth. Armour that would make her easily identifiable.

"For the assaults yes, but right now in this cave where it is just you and me? Just try and stop me."

Seeming to accept her threat, Nivres turned, so he was no longer facing her. Immediately, Sabeline divested herself of the goddess damned dress and expertly adorned herself in the different parts and components.

"I am done." She called to Nivres, buckling the last plate in place. The dragon turned, eyes roving over her form.

"Armour does indeed suit you well."

A smile etched its way across her face. "All the better to plan an attack with. Shall we get started?"

The dragon nodded, picking up a stick with his pointed jaws and creating a crude image in the dust and dirt on the floor. "This is a settlement on the outskirts of Malwey village, it is closer than Dunsaw but…."

As Nivres continued to provide an outline and details of the target settlement, renewal burned within her. This is what she was born to do. Protect people. Fight for those who could not.

And if that meant wiping the Chaos Convocation from the face of Idrelas, so be it.

19

Attire and Atonement

She had slept sparingly; the notion of bringing down the Chaos Convocation bit by bit, of doing some good again had swirled through her mind like a cleansing storm. It seemed odd that only mere days ago, she was ready to run a sword through the dragon's throat. Now the very idea of that seemed to pain her. Sabeline had been forced to do a lot of reflection, following her noble sacrifice. Nivres had saved her life and had not kept her prisoner. Even now, she had the freedom to wander as she pleased, though next time she ventured into the woodlands, she hoped she'd be able to bring back something more than weasel for them.

Still, strange circumstances had brought them together. She had even given the beast her name. He seemed content to let her join him in his crusade. Were all monsters as bad as she feared? Or were they more like Nivres, keeping hidden, personal agendas secret, knowing no mortal would help them? Her gaze wandered over the etchings in dust on the ground, the plan they had settled on before finally turning in for the night. So far, Nivres had given her no reason not to trust him. But she didn't want to make the same mistake twice. Lumbering footsteps reached her ears, ones she was slowly coming to associate with Nivres's dragon form.

Nivres stepped through one of the tunnels into the main room, opening his jaws wide in a yawn.

"Good morning." He mumbled, noticing she was awake and sitting up.

"Good morning." She responded. *No time like the present.* "I know you've not been awake long but I need to talk to you about something."

"Oh?" Nivres uttered, moving closer to the fire. She wondered if dragons needed to warm up before they started their day, or if it was just comforting for them to be near fire.

"Yes, it has been playing on my mind throughout the night and this morning. I do not want to make the same mistake as I did before. Blindly hunting without finding the reason why. I refuse to kill innocents. It is the way of the Knight."

"What are you asking?" Nivres grumbled, sounding more alert.

Sabeline sucked in a breath. "When we do this, I want proof that the people in the settlements are part of the Chaos Convocation. I want to bring them down, but I don't want the wrong people to be mistakenly caught in our need for vengeance or honour. Can you understand that?"

The dragon stared at her for a few moments, to the point she shifted uncomfortably under his reptilian gaze. Was it really that awful of a request? *Damned dragon, say something!*

"I can understand your reasons. I assure you Sabeline, it will be easy enough to procure the evidence you seek before an attack." The dragon finally said, reassurance echoing through his words.

"Excellent. That is all I ask." Sabeline responded with a slight smile. Perhaps progressing to a friendship would be easier than she'd anticipated.

Nivres nodded. "There is much to do before our attack at dusk. Which reminds me, I have some armour for you to try. I found a few sets while rummaging through my hoard. Hopefully one will be a good, less conspicuous fit."

"Thank you." Sabeline stood, peering round Nivres. "Where is it?"

"Ah forgive me; I have laid them out in a small cavern, down this tunnel and to the left." Nivres inclined his head towards the archway where he'd emerged. "While you try them, I will see about finding us some breakfast. We will need our strength."

He stood, ready to pad off towards the cave entrance, crimson scales glinting gloriously as the firelight caught his motion. Sabeline nodded in acknowledgement. The sooner she tried them on, the sooner she could tinker or make adjustments to the armour. She needed to break it in, ensuring it was easy to manoeuvre while wearing it, as well as ironing out any uncomfortable points. *It has been a long time since I have tried new armour.*

"I will be back shortly. Do not worry." The dragon said in parting, his bulk disappearing down another tunnel.

Well, with Nivres gone there was no time to lose. Sabeline stepped through the archway, slowly making her way down. She peered into each cavern on the left, searching for any signs of armour. She thought "Small" was a subjective term compared to the difference in size between her and Nivres. *This is not small.* Armour greeted her vision as she glanced into another decidedly large cavern.

Assuming this was the correct room, Sabeline wandered inside. There were three sets of armour laid out before her. One set was similar to what she had found Nivres wearing at the settlement. It was of a lesser quality, but he had been able to move around with ease while adorned in his set. Perhaps she should give it a chance instead of dismissing it outright like her head was telling her to do. After all, there was no better attire to blend in with bandits than the one favoured by them.

The second set was more in line with what she was used to. It was comprised of more metal plating and pieces than the other, with none of the usual fancy embellishments or etchings found on Idrelas Knight armour. It had probably belonged to a Commander or foot soldier once.

The last set almost called to her. Again it had more metal pieces than the first set, but the design of this one... She had never seen such smooth curving of the material. There were scarlet dashes across the shins and arms, which reminded her of blood, though on closer inspection, turned out to be carved lines that had been filled with melted rubies. A golden dragon rested in the centre of the breastplate.

Before she knew what she was doing, her fingers had reached out and grasped the armour. It was both lightweight and strong in her hands. She felt her heart pound and the blood thrum beneath her skin.

No matter what it took, by the goddess, she would wear this armour. The golden dragon would be the last thing her enemy saw before she annihilated them.

Exhilarating flooded her being at the thought, within moments, the armour components adorned her form. The fit was almost right. She would have to do a bit of hammering out here and there around the knees and elbows so the metal stopped sharply digging into her skin, but overall the armour looked and felt good. For the first time in several days, Sabeline felt like a warrior again. It was as though her purpose in life had been restored to her and she certainly wasn't going to waste it.

She walked out of the cavern and back in again, taking note of any other issues the armour might have, no matter how small. It had been something most of the knights had learned one way or another. The slightest thing could grow to be a great issue later on. Mariel had learnt it when she didn't take care of a little scratch in her arrow. During the next battle she was in, the arrow had snapped. Bersaba had not taken her usual healing potion for simple aches and pains after a fight. The following morning, she had woken in agony and had downed at least three bottles of the stuff in one go. A sad smile crossed Sabeline's lips at the memories. *I wonder what they're doing now?*

It was best not to linger on the thought. Shaking her head, she turned her attention back to the matter at hand. Luckily, apart from the problems she'd noticed straight away, there was nothing else to do to the attire apart from give it a thorough clean. Carefully, Sabeline removed the armour piece by piece, redressing in her old, familiar gear. It was dirty and dented, with scratches and fragments missing. She hadn't had the chance to restore it to its former glory with everything that had happened, but it was the only thing she had retained from her old life, before Falon had decided she'd be better serving Idrelas as a sacrifice. *I'll fix this one up*, she vowed, gazing at the damaged vambrace on her forearm, *and wipe away the stain of his actions.*

Gathering the new armour in her arms, Sabeline traversed back towards the main room where the smell of roasting meat greeted her nose. Nivres was turning the spit with one clawed hand, rotating a sizeable grebe fish. It crackled as it cooked, juices breaking through the skin and covering the fish in a succulent coating. Nivres turned at her footsteps, focusing on the pile in her arms.

"I see you have decided." He inclined his head towards the stack.

"Yes, they were all very suitable, but it is this one that called to me the most. I will just need to hammer out some pieces and clean down the metal."

"Very good. I am glad to hear not much work needs to be done." Nivres turned the fish again, before turning back to her. "Which one did you choose?" He asked, curiosity lacing his tone.

Sabeline shifted the pile in her arms, before raising the breastplate to him.

The dragon was silent for a moment, eyes widening before softening at her. "A very fine choice." He murmured appreciatively. "A fine choice indeed."

Was there more to this armour than she knew? Sabeline lowered the breastplate back down. "Is my decision alright?" She asked with care, both puzzled and intrigued by Nivres's reaction.

"It's perfect." He responded with sincerity.

She could tell he was still keeping some secret about the armour from her, but Sabeline decided she wouldn't push for more details just yet. After all, breakfast was almost ready and her stomach was clawing at her from the inside. The dragon pulled the spit out of the ever blazing fire and slashed up the fish with his claws, just as he had done with the deer. He offered a pile to Sabeline, which she took gratefully before sitting down.

Sabeline plopped a piece into her mouth, the fish so juicy that it almost melted on her tongue. *By the goddess, that's delicious.* She devoured several more pieces, watching as across from her, Nivres did the same. For the first time she noticed the difference in his chunks compared to hers. He'd cut hers into finer, smaller bits while his reptilian jaws engulfed sizes that even a snake would give up on.

As she chewed, an idea crossed her mind. Perhaps he would tell her more about the attire if she told him something. After all, they were moving forward together weren't they? *The dagger*, her practical side reasoned. Telling him about the dagger would show that her mistrust of him had finally disappeared. Sabeline swallowed and sucked in a breath. *No time like now.*

"Nivres?" She asked, breaking the silence that usually accompanied consuming food.

The dragon swallowed. "Yes Sabeline?"

"I feel that I should tell you something." She began, moving the leg where she usually had the dagger secreted out a bit more.

"Oh?" Nivres murmured.

Sabeline sighed. "When you first bought me here, I raided the piles of stuff around the room. I took this." She stuck her hand down the spaulder, pulling out the dagger she'd been carrying most of the time. Except for when she had to wear that atrocious dress. "I carried it around with me, thinking I could use it to end you. After our sparring match, I used it to hunt in the forest."

"And still you kept it?" Nivres questioned, though Sabeline noted he didn't seem angry.

"Yes. My experience in the forest only reinforced that I keep a weapon on me, no matter how small. I am a Knight; I am not used to being without my blade. But it has been some time since I have longed to use it on you. Initially, it was our terms that prevented me, but now... Now I do not wish you harm. " Her heart echoed in her ears as Sabeline realised just how true that statement was. She did not wish him injured and she herself did not wish to hurt him. Not anymore. She tossed the dagger a few paces in front of her, so it was out of her reach.

Nivres was quiet for several minutes. She hoped he was thinking things over and wasn't going to scream at her. Finally, he spoke "Thank you for telling me this. I know it was not easy for you. Though I must admit, I am glad you no longer desire to kill me of your own violation." He grinned, showing all his sharp, pointed teeth, putting Sabeline slightly at ease. Wait, at ease? The sight of all those lethal teeth should inspire the opposite. There had to be something wrong with her.

"I understand your reasoning for taking it, however I would not throw aside that dagger just yet."

"No?" Sabeline queried, reaching out to pick it back up out of the dust.

"You will need it for the battle ahead and perhaps something else as well. It is said the Knights of Idrelas are proficient in most weapons, though each has a signature one they are skilled in."

"That is correct." Sabeline responded, wondering if Nivres had a secret weapon cache hidden somewhere within this labyrinth of a cave.

"The Bringer of Truth is an expert in swordsmanship, so it is said."

"Why do you think I took the dagger? It is essentially a miniature blade." She said haughtily.

Nivres grinned again. "Iron out your armour Sabeline and I shall return."

She clocked her head to the side "Return from where?"

Nivres hauled himself up, "From another cavern of course." He wandered off, disappearing before she could say another word. Considering how big a dragon he was, she was impressed at how fast he could be. His behaviour was also giving her weapon hoard theory some weight.

No matter what he returned with, their preparations were well and truly underway. Sabeline stood, rubbing her hands together and arranging the new armour across the floor, dividing it into parts that needed adjusting and parts that didn't.

She could hardly wait for dusk to fall.

20

Assessments and Alterations

The sun was low in the sky when Sabeline emerged from the cave with Nivres in tow. She had perfected the armour and it now moulded to her form, allowing her to move with the fluidity she was used to. Her fingers latched around the hilt of the new blade secured on her hip and she drew it from the scabbard. Her hand guided it through the air in a few simple movements, testing out the weight and balance. While she couldn't say for sure whether Nivres had a steady supply of weapons somewhere in the cave, the fact he had presented her with this a few hours ago made her believe it.

The hilt was gold, inlaid with lines of red, as if made to pair with the armour she wore. The blade was crafted from the usual folded steel, light but strong. The name of the sword had been etched in runes down the length of the blade, but Sabeline could not read them. It was a language lost to her, but she had a feeling Echoris would be able to translate. *As if I would ever be able to show her.* Sabeline sighed, shoving the sword back into the scabbard with a flourish. She couldn't get distracted by thoughts of what once was. She had a battle to win.

Nivres had been silently watching her, but now he spoke. "I take it the blade is to your liking?"

"It is a fine blade. It will look better painted in the blood of the Chaos Convocation." She smirked back at him, grateful for the distraction as she shook off thoughts of her fellow Knight.

The dragon huffed a strange sort of laugh. She had not heard him make that sound before and it was oddly pleasant to hear. "That would improve its appearance greatly." He agreed.

"Well then, we best not keep my weapon waiting." She said in good spirits. Sabeline walked closer to the dragon, climbing up his side and taking her usual place. *This is getting easier each time; I am sure of it.*

"Are you ready?" Nivres asked, craning his long neck to glance at her.

"Do the stars shine?" She retorted, causing a fang revealing grin to stretch across his face.

Nivres's crimson wings shifted and for the first time, Sabeline found herself fascinated that such a thin membrane of skin (compared to the rest of him), could support the dragon's size. She did not have a chance to ponder long before Nivres took flight, the wings she'd been examining pounding in a steady rhythm as they rose further and further into a sky painted orange and red by the slowly descending sun.

***

Nivres settled behind a rocky outcrop as Sabeline dismounted. He gestured with his reptilian head towards the top of the stones. It wasn't hard to ascertain what he wanted her to do. Complying, Sabeline climbed up before lying on her front against the smooth surface. "Do you see the settlement?" Nivres asked, his voice soft.

She could just make out some huts that looked as though they'd been cobbled together from scrap wood. There was a fence around the huts made of sharpened stakes. *A crude defence*. Due to the darkness gently creeping across the land, the odd flame sprang to life and bobbed wildly as someone went round the settlement lighting lamps. "I see it." Sabeline confirmed just as softly.

"It appears this will be easier than before. Those lamps give us the advantage, though they do not know it yet. We can use them to burn down the fence, while simultaneously causing a distraction."

Sabeline considered the change of plan. Originally, she was going to be the distraction, allowing Nivres to sneak in the gate. However, this seemed more advantageous. *If they want chaos, we will give them chaos.*

"I am not opposed to such a change. " She agreed.

Nivres nodded. "Excellent. Now, I must shift form before we get close."

"Why do you shift to take on the Chaos Convocation?" Sabeline questioned, curiosity lacing her tone. She knew there was probably a better time to ask such a thing, but she could not help but wonder.

Nivres moved away from her carefully. *He is not going to answer.* He did not have to of course, but Sabeline felt that somehow, if they were going to be fighting side by side, she should at least know why he opted for his human shape. "Because of Myvanna. She was in her human form when they took everything from her. Those monsters need to know that a dragon in human form is still a dragon." He whispered with both sadness and rage.

Her heart panged sharply. She knew a thing or two about proving her worth. It seemed in his grief, Nivres was trying to prove the same thing to his sister.

"I am sure though weakened, your sister would have fought them until the last breath left her body." Sabeline offered in comfort.

Nivres said nothing, but nodded at her words. The next thing she knew, the dragon had lowered his head and a grimace appeared on his face. A shudder ran under his scales and it almost looked as though the muscles were spasming or cramping beneath his flesh. Sabeline tried to turn her gaze away, but her eyes refused to move. They remained fixed on Nivres's form as convulsions ricocheted through his limbs, stretching and altering them. By the goddess, it had to be the most fascinating but painful things she had ever seen.

Finally, he resembled a human shape and Nivres's signature scarlet scales receded into the now mortal skin. Sabeline remained transfixed as her mind comprehended the alteration that had taken place before her. Nivres's heaving, panting breaths reached her ears while he stayed crouched on all fours for several seconds.

"Nivres? Are you alright?" She whispered concerned. She did not know if this was usual, or whether the forced change had had some adverse effect.

"I am fine Bringer of Truth; this is but a brief resting period." Nivres called to her, still keeping his voice low.

That is a relief, she thought as the faint worry left her.

She watched as Nivres rose to his feet and he turned to her

unashamed. Her eyes widened and she was sure her face was glowing as brightly as the settlement lamps as she continued to take in the vision in front of her. *By the goddess.*

"Let us advance." Nivres stated, stretching his arms.

She hated to hold up their attack, she really did, but the pressing matter needed to be addressed.

"Perhaps it would be prudent to adorn your armour first?"

Nivres gazed down at himself. "You make a good point, Sabeline."

How can you forget something like adorning clothes? Though she supposed being in dragon form much of the time, Nivres probably had little need for attire, other than the black robe and armour she'd seen. Perhaps he had been too distracted by the thrill of the hunt to remember such a thing as getting dressed. "Does this happen often?" She wondered. It would be useful to know for future assaults whether she'd need to remind him to dress.

"No," Nivres answered, fastening the armour he'd retrieved from a knapsack they'd brought with them, as she finally turned her gaze away. "But from time to time, I forget the need for such mortal things."

"Even though you have brought the armour with you?" Sabeline asked, puzzled. How could one remember the clothing, then forget to wear it?

"Just because I remember to bring it with me, does not necessarily mean I remember it needs to be worn."

She nodded as though she understood, but in truth, he had just confused her further. *Dragon logic.* Eager to direct attention towards another topic and regain focus, she uttered "So, how will we reach the lamps? Using them to burn down the fence is a good idea, but we will still need to navigate the fence to reach them. That and you promised me proof these people are part of the Chaos Convocation." She refused to let him forget that part of the bargain.

The sound of armour being slotted into place and fastened reached her ears, while she kept her eyes resolutely to the side. After all, she didn't know which half the armour was currently covering. "It will be easy enough to prove, I promise you that." Nivres replied. "As for the fence, it may be lacking in architectural skill, but it is stronger than it looks. I can pull one of the stakes out of the ground, allowing us to sneak through and unhook the lamps."

A sudden thought occurred to Sabeline, one she had not initially questioned, but should have been obvious to ask from the beginning." Why must we do this, if you can breathe fire?"

Nivres sighed. "I wondered how soon it would take you to ask. While breathing fire is a natural trait for dragons, it does expend some energy. Personally, I would like to keep as much energy in reserve as possible for slaughtering the bastards."

That was a reason Sabeline could support. Both the sword and the dagger she still carried sang a song of bloodshed.

"I have finished enrobing." Nivres said, though Sabeline detected a hint of humour in his voice. She turned her head back, vision settling on the warrior before her. *Because that's what he is*, her mind whispered, *a warrior in every sense of the word*. "Let us begin." He smiled with malice, sharp teeth glinting in the starlight.

She knew that grin. She'd seen it enough times on the faces of her sisters in arms before battle as the excitement and anticipation reached its crux. Sabeline found herself responding with one of her own. "Indeed, let us begin."

They crept carefully from their rocky outpost, sticking

to where the shadows laid thickest, advancing closer to the settlement. Just as Sabeline was about to scuttle further forwards, she felt a sturdy grip on her arm, holding her back. Nivres's hand was enclosed around her armour, holding her in place. She looked up, raising an eyebrow at him.

"Do you see the flag just there?" He jutted his chin in the direction of the settlement.

Near one of the lamps, illuminated by the firelight, a ripped and battered flag blew slightly in the wind from a pole attached to the roof corner of one of the buildings. A symbol painted in white decorated the middle. Sabeline narrowed her eyes. From what she could make out, the bright symbol consisted of Idrelas being consumed by... something. Whether it was a monster, a representation of darkness or chaos, she could not tell.

"I see it. It has some kind of emblem of the land." She whispered.

"That is how you know the settlement belongs to the Chaos Convocation. Each of their *bases*, for lack of a better word, will have a flag or banner somewhere with that symbol."

A strange feeling thrummed in her heart. *He did not forget.* The feeling intensified as she realised his fingers were still curled around her arm. Gently, she shook it, causing him to let go. "Thank you." She murmured with sincerity, trying to disregard the strange feeling. They were here on a mission. By the goddess, she couldn't afford to be distracted, it could cost her her head.

Nivres nodded, then shuffled forward. Following his lead, Sabeline emerged after him, keeping one hand on the hilt of her blade. They darted out, reaching the fence. Nivres immediately went to work, encasing his hands around one of the stakes. A motion to the side caught Sabeline's attention as a dark figure wandered towards them from the other side of the fence. Without wasting time, Sabeline ducked down, grabbing Nivres by the chest plate and dragging him down too.

They sat on the ground, looking up as the figure passed by, caution in his gait. *A patrol.* It was something Sabeline had expected, but from her and Nivres's observations earlier, she had thought they had forgone any extra security measures. *Maybe they only initiate it at a certain time. For saying they enjoy chaos, they seem remarkably organised.*

The figure lingered far too long for Sabeline's liking. Had they given themselves away? Why would the figure stay this long for no discernible reason? Beside her, Nivres was barely daring to breathe. It reminded her to release his chest plate. The figure finally drifted away, but she remained still for several seconds more. She wanted to be sure the Chaos Convocation patrol were as far away as possible from them.

Slowly she turned, rising to her feet and peeking in a gap between the top of two sharpened stake points.

Only to see a large group gathered round a table on the other side.

21

Infiltration

"We should move further down." Sabeline whispered, carefully dropping back behind the stake pole and more importantly, out of the line of sight.

"What is the situation?" Nivres murmured back.

Crouching, she quickly explained about the group just on the other side, only to receive a grin in response. *Why is he so happy about this? If they catch sight of us, the plan is forfeit!*

"Do you not see Sabeline? This is just what we need. A group of them will come running straight for our distraction, especially if it is only a few feet away from them. Naturally, more numbers attract more attention. Other members of the Chaos Convocation will see a hoard running for the fire and will follow suit. We could end up with half the settlement on their way here."

She had to admit, it sounded good. Excellent in fact for their purposes. Half the settlement combating the fires of their own lamps would gain them extra time and less chance of being noticed. But there was still one issue niggling at the back of her mind. "But what if we're seen by the group? That was the reason for my suggestion. Moving further down to set the lamp off will mean a better chance of slipping through unnoticed."

Nivres leaned up a little, craning his head to just above the gap between the stakes. He was only there for a few seconds before resuming his normal position opposite her. He nodded his head in her direction and began shuffling away. *I'll take that as an agreement*, Sabeline's thoughts grumbled as she crawled along after him. She had only travelled a few feet when Nivres stopped. Poking her head up, Sabeline cast her eyes around the new area. They had not travelled far from where the group was sitting, but from this new vantage, they wouldn't immediately be able to see them sneaking into the settlement. The patrol was nowhere to be seen either. "All clear." She uttered, dropping back into a crouch.

Nivres said nothing, but she watched as he reached out and gripped one of the stakes with both hands, the clawed fingers digging deep into the wood. With a great heave, the wood immediately shifted in the dirt. *I guess Nivres was right, this fence isn't architecturally sound*. The dragon remained silent, despite the obvious strain lining his body. She couldn't help but wonder whether he wished he was in his dragon form, despite his pledge to himself. Nivres's feet shifted a little as he dug them in, before hauling the stake upwards.

Leaping into action, Sabeline darted through the small gap, her armour just scraping the edge of the wood. As she turned, Nivres held the stake up with one hand, hurriedly stepping through and letting the stake fall. Sabeline's body immediately braced at the sound and her eyes darted from side to side, anticipating a Chaos Convocation member to round the corner and discover them at any second. While she scanned the surroundings, Nivres stepped towards the hanging lantern, staying within the darker shadows of the night.

No one is coming. Either they hadn't heard the sound of their fence being ravaged, or the sound had seemed much louder to her than it really was. Clambering to her feet, she made her way to the lantern and Nivres. It was affixed to a metal hook, higher than either of them could possibly reach. "Climb onto my shoulders. Hurry." Nivres muttered.

Nodding in affirmative, Sabeline manoeuvred herself so that she was almost in a piggy back position on the dragon's back. He tucked his arms back to support as she hoisted herself further up with her hands, eventually managing to stand on the dragon's shoulders. His hands wrapped around each of her ankles to aid in her balance. Her cheeks felt warm and she was pretty certain it had nothing to do with the heat of the lantern light. *By the goddess, focus! He touched me, so what? We're in the middle of a battle here!*

Brushing the thoughts aside, she stretched out her hands, the tips of her fingers just grazing the hook. "Can you move a step forward?" She muttered down. The dragon obliged, keeping her balanced. She reached again, gripping the metal loop of the lantern and pulling it free of its holder. It was heavier than she expected, especially for a makeshift operation. Holding it up, her gaze roamed over the metal work in a steady inspection. The craftsmanship was exquisite. Whoever had made this was no simple blacksmith or crafter. The Chaos Convocation either had connections, had a craftsman who was a master (unlikely but not impossible) or had stolen it. All of those possibilities did not sit well within her. *Just how many secrets does The Chaos Convocation hold?*

She would dwell on that later, when this job was done. Perhaps Nivres knew more or maybe this would be new information. She couldn't help but feel as though there was more to this lantern's story. But she passed it down to Nivres all the same and deftly leapt off of his back. The dragon expertly curled his claws around a pane of glass, pulling it free and leaving an open space. *So the fire and oil can spread faster,* Sabeline realised. He tossed the glass panel to the ground, letting it shatter. Then before Sabeline could blink, he threw the lantern with perfect aim at the fence.

The orange flames licked against the wood, almost as if to sample the taste as the lantern fell. It broke into a mangled mess of pieces in the dry dirt and Sabeline felt a pang that such a finely made thing had to be destroyed. It wasn't long before the flames progressed from tasting to consuming the fence in a glorious display.

She stood there transfixed for a moment until Nivres grabbed her arm and gently pulled her along with him deeper into the settlement.

She hurried along until the dragon dragged her down behind some boxes as a flurry of people ran by. From the commotion she could hear in the distance, it seemed their distraction was well and truly working.

"So, strike the settlement leader's building, take out as many as we can, reduce the place to ash and be back at the cave by sunrise. Was that not the next part of the plan?" She grinned, as another bunch of people came hurrying by their hiding place.

"That sounds about right." Nivres returned with a smile of his own.

"Well then, we best get a move on." She continued good naturedly. The thrill of battle pounded through her blood as her limbs itched to execute moves learned only by the Knights of Idrelas. She could never imagine giving this feeling up. It was something that called to her, that felt right. It was as if she was born to be a Knight, to do the things others would not dare attempt. *Such as taking on the Chaos Convocation with a dragon in the form of a man.*

"The settlement leader's building will be in the centre." Nivres interrupted her musings.

"Where it is most protected." Of course. She knew that strategy well enough. "Will the leader be there or will they have gone to help with the fire?" She did not know how the Chaos Convocation worked in terms of hierarchy, but she had a feeling the leader of mercenaries, thieves and murderers would probably let the smallest amount of power go to their head.

"They will most likely remain in the building, trying to save their precious spoils. Gold, artefacts, that kind of thing. For the Chaos Convocation, individual lives do not mean much, well except to the individual, but riches above all else, must be protected." The disgust was evident in Nivres's voice. The philosophy was so far removed from anything she had known. Gold over Mariel's life? Over Echoris's? Bersaba's? It was inconceivable. She felt a snarl pulling at her lips.

"Well at least we know what to expect from the filthy coward." Sabeline growled. *I will take great pleasure in bringing him down.* As a single set of hurried footsteps echoed closer, she ducked down again, tracking the person with malice in her gaze.

"Indeed." Nivres agreed. "We've seen a good amount of

people come down this route towards the fire and…" He craned his head up towards the sky, Sabeline followed his motion, taking note of the wisps of smoke dancing delicately in the air. "If that smoke is reaching us, they're not controlling the flames well." The dragon continued and Sabeline swore she could hear the bemusement in his words.

"It's too risky to exit either side." She agreed, glancing both ways and appraising each direction. They would most likely end up in the middle of Chaos Convocation members and ultimately, their presence would be discovered. Turning behind her, a rickety wall was closer to them than she thought. Her and Nivres were between boxes and an unkempt shack. *Even the poorest of Idrelas do not live in such squalor.* The building was small, much smaller than the others around it and though the Chaos Convocation clearly had much to learn about construction and architecture, the shack appeared sturdy enough. "What about going up?" She murmured, drawing Nivres's attention. She saw him out of the corner of her eye following her line of sight.

A grin stretched across his mouth, the most inhuman one she'd ever seen on a mortal face. "That would work."

She wasted no more time. Giving another glance either side and seeing the area was clear, Sabeline hauled herself up onto the large crate in front of her. With care, she crawled and clambered over the rest that had been stacked. Gripping the edge of the highest one, she pulled herself once more, staying low to the surface. It would do no good for someone to glance up at the smoke and see her standing there. A decent gap lay between her and the mismatched roof.

The vision of Nivres matching her movements with determination as he followed the route she'd carved out greeted her sight, as she quickly checked down on her left. A memory slammed into her so fast and painful that a gasp left her lips and was lost in the night. She had been with Mariel and Echoris, traversing a colossal hill in the Great Green Plateau. The three of them had been investigating reports of a shadow hound in the area (which had later turned out to be a missing farm dog). But it was not the thrill of the hunt, or the climbing that had her trying to contain the unexpected emotional onslaught. It was the companionship. Moving together as one, trusting her sisters in arms with her life. A laugh of elation or relief. The victory singing in their veins after bringing down a vicious foe and raising their weapons high, clanking them together in quick celebration before continuing with the mission. *By the goddess, it has been so long. I had almost forgotten what it was like to fight side by side.*

She was drawn back to the here and now as Nivres reached her, his movements stilling.

"Is everything alright?" He questioned.

Goddess damn it! Some remnant of emotion must still have been plastered on her face for him to ask. Making sure her expression smoothed to one of indifference, she snapped out "I am fine, thank you." *Get yourself under control, you'll get yourself or Nivres killed otherwise!*

The dragon did not appear convinced but thankfully said nothing else.

"The only way is to jump for it." She said, nodding towards the roof.

"Can you make it?" Nivres asked. His tone wasn't filled with doubt, nor concern, which oddly, made her heart swell. It was as though he was trying to learn just how skilled she was.

"Of course I can. The question should be; can you keep up dragon?" She countered and before Nivres could utter another sound, she stepped two paces back, sprinted forward and launched herself across the gap. She hit the roof, landing with perfection and tossed him a triumphant grin from over her shoulder.

With a shrug, the dragon followed suit, jumping over the gap. But Sabeline watched with growing horror as he stumbled upon landing, his form falling backwards over the roof edge.

22

Fear Amid Flame

She rushed forward, sabatons clacking against the patchwork wooden roof as her heartbeat echoed in her ears. Her surroundings disappeared as all focus was directed at the spot where the dragon had disappeared. Nivres could not have perished. Not now. She would not allow it.

Half frantic, Sabeline dropped down at the edge and peered over, eyes roaming in desperation. *There.* The breath whooshed out of her lungs as her sight landed on Nivres's form, clinging to a small metal pole sticking haphazardly out of the wall. Goddess damn him! Reining in her emotions, Sabeline leaned forward, reaching out her hand. Thankfully, he hadn't fallen too far. "Guess you can't keep up after all dragon." She taunted with a light heart, grasping Nivres's forearm.

The dragon smiled at her words as he hauled himself up with her assistance. "I guess not." He replied, as she secured him on the roof. They sat there for a second or two, before Sabeline rose. Now that Nivres was safe, her senses slammed back into awareness. The smoke billowed above her and across the night sky as she gazed across the roofs of the settlement. Ash lay heavy in the air and the scent of burning extended further with every moment that passed. Cries and shouts met her ears along with the occasional sloosh of water as the Chaos Convocation tried in vain to manage the fire. They had to get to the Settlement Leader's residence fast, if they escaped in the confusion, there would be no chance left of tracking them. She turned, fixing the dragon with her gaze as he stood. "Do not do that again."

Nivres seemed to understand how serious she was. Good. She didn't want to think about the fear that flooded her being as he fell off the precipice beyond her reach. He gave her a solemn nod in return. "Let's go then. I think I see the Leader's... Hut from here." She had no idea what to call the large building in the centre, dilapidated and as ramshackle as the rest of the buildings. Hut was being generous.

The dragon stepped forward and stood beside her. "Yes, that would be the place." He affirmed, following her stare. "The biggest building would have more locations to store the spoils of battle. They are most likely ensuring nothing is left behind."

Her lip curled into a sneer. What good would gold be if they all perished? They couldn't take it with them. Disgust filled her as the logic and priorities of the Chaos Convocation were put before her. If riches were so important to them, she would ensure this Leader suffered before meeting their end at her blade. The ghost of a smirk glanced across her mouth as a beautiful plan formed in her mind. *Oh yes, death by itself is too good for these people.*

"Then let us make sure they don't leave with it." Sabeline

uttered, darting forward with Nivres at her side.

With care, Sabeline continued a path across the rooftops, keeping a wary eye on the dragon. He seemed determined to match pace with her after his earlier mishap and she noticed he planned his movements with more caution. Good. After several more minutes traversing the shack tops, Nivres dropped to his haunches and his hand reached out to prevent Sabeline from travelling any further. Curious, she glanced down at the dragon.

"What is it?" *Why would he stop us now? The leader's residence is just ahead!*

The dragon inclined his head towards the ground. "Apart from our distraction, there are more people here. We'll have to take care."

She followed his golden gaze. Various ruffians in all manner of attire were hurriedly carrying boxes of different sizes and large sacks, while a woman in a dark blue robe shouted orders and directions at them. As Sabeline watched the scene, one of the sack seams ripped open, pouring gold coins onto the ground. The woman leapt for them, screaming obscenities at the hefty mercenary. *What a pitiful display.*

"I take it she is the leader then." Sabeline mused, keeping her eyes locked on the robed woman who was now digging at the ground and shoving the spilled gold into her pockets.

Nivres shook his head. "Unfortunately not. Blue robes mean she's the second in command. She has to be pretty skilled scum to have authority over the rest of these villains." He finished with a growl.

"So who would be best to take out first, her little army, her or the leader?" Sabeline wondered. Would it be easier to get rid of the goons, who would be called in to defend their leader and potentially be used as a distraction letting the leader get away, or go after the head of the settlement, as without leadership they'd probably be at a loss as to what to do. *For saying they're called the Chaos Convocation, they sure rely a lot on hierarchy.* Though no matter which way they went about the deed, she'd still be able to pull off her special torture. A dark grin stole across her lips at the thought.

"We'll work our way up. The lesser ones first, then the second in command and last the leader. If we do it right, they'll still be trying to protect their valuables when we burst in."

"Understood." She was no stranger to stealth. At least for this part of the plan. "Shall we go then?"

Nivres smirked. "I believe the adage is ladies first is it not?"

Her lips quirked. "Spoken like a true gentleman."

As soon as the words finished leaving her mouth, Sabeline flipped over the side of the building, clinging to the edge of the roof. No one had spotted her movement. Perfect. She continued steadily scaling down the side, finally dropping to the ground and hiding behind one of the wagons being piled up with goodies.

Within seconds, a thin, spindly woman decked out in leather armour approached the wagon. A scarf covered the lower half of her face, whilst the skin on the left half was decorated in an inked oath. Sabeline sucked in a breath.

Just my luck. An assassin.

The assassin crept closer while Sabeline shuffled further back, crouching low. She glanced down at the wagon, but it was built too close to the ground for a person to be able to crawl beneath. *Goddess damn it!* Sucking in a breath, Sabeline remained frozen, scarcely daring to move even a finger. If the assassin peered the wrong way, she'd catch sight of her. She may be hidden from the bodies ambling around with their precious spoils, but there was nothing to conceal Sabeline with someone this close.

Keeping a wary eye on the assassin, Sabeline watched as she tossed a hefty sack onto the wagon. *Stronger than she appears.* That did not bode well. The assassin threw another item. *How much stuff is she moving?* That put a damper on her plans to wait quietly until the assassin left. If the assassin had a fair amount to move, Sabeline couldn't afford to wait. Time was of the essence.

When the assassin shifted to collect another of the Convocation's spoils, she carefully shuffled further back, all the while keeping her gaze fixed on the assassin's form. There wasn't a horse attached to the wagon, whether that was because they'd bolted in a panic at the scent of fire or if one of the bigger built men was going to pull it, Sabeline couldn't be sure. But it did mean she would be out in the open. *Great choices, one assassin or a whole mob?* She squeezed her eyes shut, weighing the decision. It was going to have to be the assassin wasn't it? The advantage of surprise was on her side, after all, Sabeline was certain the assassin hadn't noticed her. *If she had, I'd be dead.* She had a better chance of taking care of the assassin quickly and quietly, without the surrounding minions noticing, then taking them all on and potentially losing their chance at the Leader.

Decision made, Sabeline's eyes flashed open and she crawled forward softly, glancing at the assassin every few seconds. She was still undetected. *Good.* The assassin turned away from the wagon again and Sabeline padded over the last bit of ground before raising herself back into a crouch. She was at the very edge of the cart. Heart pounding in her chest, she endured the agonising wait for the assassin to manoeuvre.

A slam indicated the assassin had placed yet more material objects on the wagon. While she still had the fabric of a sack clenched in her hands, the assassin paused and Sabeline's heart almost stopped as the assassin's narrow eyes glanced to the side meeting her own.

The assassin's gaze widened and with moments before she sounded an alarm, Sabeline reached out with the speed of a snake, ensnaring the assassin's leg in her grip. Immediately, she yanked back with all the force she could muster, causing the surprised assassin to fall on her back as Sabeline continued dragging her out of sight behind the wagon.

The assassin recovered quicker than Sabeline had anticipated, thrashing and blocking Sabeline's attempt to knock her out. Instead, a wayward kick landed on her jaw. *Goddess damn assassins!* She'd worry about the pain later. Thinking fast, she threw herself on top of the assassin, (who'd managed to twist onto her front) and slammed her head into the dirt.

While stunned, Sabeline divested her of the arrows secured in a quiver affixed to her back. For extra security, she also patted down the assassin's side, claiming the several daggers and tossing them to the side along with arrows. "If someone needs that many weapons, then they're compensating for a lack of skill." Sabeline whispered to the groaning assassin.

Successfully knocking the assassin out with a quick elbow jab, she planned her next move. Admittedly, she had expected more of a fight from the assassin. She'd heard stories from the other knights who had encountered them that they were notoriously difficult to battle, usually for their array of weapons. While not highly skilled in all the weapons they possessed, it was hard for an opponent to determine which until it was too late. She'd been lucky at subduing this one so fast, but if the Leader had anymore stashed away to call on, she feared whether her and Nivres would be able to defeat them.

Shuffling past the unconscious assassin, she peered around the wagon. Only to be met with the sight of several groaning or prone bodies on the ground. Nivres stood there in the middle of it all, a little scuffed, but otherwise fine. He sent a sharp toothed grin her way and shrugged. "Couldn't let you have all the fun."

"How did you...I didn't hear anything..." Sabeline marvelled, emerging from behind the cart and taking in all the defeated mercenaries, thieves and was that... "You took down the second in command too?" She asked surprised, rethinking her earlier fear about being able to take down more than one assassin. *By the goddess, what skills does he possess to be able to do this?*

"Well, she did prove to be difficult. I told you, to be second in command, she had to be proficient in what she does."

"And what did that turn out to be?" She asked, curious. Maybe it would give her an idea of how well trained the Leader was.

"Knives. Both throwing and using them in combat." Nivres growled and Sabeline caught sight of a bleeding slash across his right cheek she hadn't been able to see from her secured position. It seemed she wasn't as subtle in her observations as she thought, considering Nivres had caught sight of her gaze. "Don't worry, I got her back for it. Come Sabeline, the Leader awaits." The dragon uttered, stepping away and closer to the large hut.

Just before following him, Sabeline glanced back at the Second in Command, lying unconscious on her back. This time, she noticed the line of burnt flesh on the Second in Command's right cheek.

A perfect mirror of the wound given to Nivres.

23

Purpose

"Please tell me we are not going through the front door." Sabeline hissed as she stood on one side of the rickety, thrown together bits of wood half hanging off the opening. It wasn't much of a door, she would admit, but surely Nivres had to know how bad a plan it was to enter that way. There could be a bunch of assassins or thugs in there for all they knew, lying in wait just behind that sorry excuse for an entrance.

"It would be what they least expect." The dragon smirked at her from where he stood on the opposite side.

"It's what everyone expects." She retorted. Maybe they just didn't expect a human to walk in and start blowing flames everywhere and that's why Nivres was so sure of their entrance, but there were probably still a dozen archers or knife throwers on the other side all poised to strike the main door.

"Then it is a good thing this isn't the main entrance isn't it?" Nivres continued smirking at her and Sabeline got the distinct impression the dragon was trying to either tease or jest with her.

"If this isn't the main entrance then what is it?" Surely it would make sense for all the Chaos Convocation members to transport the goods out of the biggest door of the Leader's shack, which up until now, she'd assumed was this one.

"Transport door. It's probably tucked out of the way near the back of the room or sometimes they're down a dismal, tiny hallway that's been specially built." Nivres huffed, distain coating his tone.

"But why? Surely speed would be of the essence if you're trying to transport ill-gotten spoils." Sabeline puzzled. This set up made little sense to her. Why go through the effort of disguising a door so effectively, when that would hinder the transportation of gold, gems or whatever else the Chaos Convocation had managed to lay their thieving hands on?

"Oh trust me, they want to get it out as fast as possible, but they also want to do it with few members aware it's happening. The Leaders don't want the rest of the settlement to know how much they have or see them shifting it, so then members can't grab and dash off with anything in the evacuation or retreat." Nivres growled.

"That's…" Sabeline trailed off. She couldn't even think of a word for how appalled she was. She didn't think anything further could have surprised her regarding the Chaos Convocation's greed, but going to all the effort of disguising a door, just so members couldn't run off with a few coins? It wasn't like they'd be able to grab much if they were running for their lives after all. If indeed they even gave their lives any kind of priority over materialistic riches. *These people would probably get on well with King Falon.* Her lip curled at the thought of the man who had once held her loyalty.

"So," she began, dismissing the image of Falon's sneering face, "we go through this transport door and then go for the Leader? Exercising stealth and caution of course."

"Of course." Nivres repeated, though there was a slight lilt in his voice making her think they had different definitions of the term caution. Well, it was too late to turn back now. She'd agreed to do this, right the wrongs of her past, see the world with a more open mind. And if that meant she'd have to keep Nivres safe and watch his back while they were in there, then so be it. *May the Goddess protect us both.*

"Ready then?" She asked after sucking in a deep breath.

"Idrelas Knights first." Nivres grinned, pushing open the door. Sabeline was surprised the thing still clung resolutely to the wood. She'd half expected it to clatter to the ground.

"Arrogant dragons second." The muttered words left her lips as she stepped carefully inside.

It seemed this was one of those purpose-built hallways Nivres had alluded to earlier. Wide enough that heavy or large loads could be brought through, but small enough to walk in single file or in pairs. *Clever, utilising as much as possible while trying to be as discreet as possible.*

She stepped at a slower pace, hoping that no floorboard would suddenly creak and alert anyone to come down here. The shadows seemed to soak into the very walls, illuminated by only a single torch affixed to the wall.

"They will be expecting the couriers to come back through this way." Nivres whispered, so close that she could feel his breath on the back of her neck. "Any noise will be disregarded as them returning for more goods."

Understood. In other words, it was alright to move faster. With that encouraging sentiment, Sabeline picked up the pace.

It wasn't long before she was facing another door, only this one appeared a little more well kept and sturdy. Nivres was right about these hallways being small. Her hand reached out and with gentle force, pushed the door.

A steady creak echoed around her as the door swung freely to the side. She felt the warmth of Nivres by her shoulder as he stood closer than she'd ever expected. Her cheeks began to grow hot at the realisation. *No, knights do not blush for goddess's sake! I do not have time to entertain these thoughts, I need to focus.*

With a quick shake of her head, Sabeline stepped through, with Nivres mirroring her movements.

As she emerged, Sabeline cast her gaze around, taking note of the shattered pieces of wood, no doubt from boxes or crates concealing the door, scattered around them. The room seemed oddly empty. "I do not like this." She murmured as Nivres stepped beside her. The air felt strange, as if there were eyes on her, but she could see no one. Her gaze slid over to the dragon, who wore an expression of both confusion and alertness.

"Nor do I." He muttered back, before his golden eyes widened.

"What...?" Was all that escaped her mouth before Nivres tackled her to the ground as a ball of purple energy blasted into the wall above them.

A menacing growl rumbled next to her ear. The sound was full of threat, warning and general malice that it sent a shiver down her spine. She'd heard many creatures during her missions, howls of rage, snarls of displeasure, cries of defeat, but this...Nothing she recalled had ever made a similar noise to the one emanating above her. It promised suffering.

Sabeline shifted a little, her armour clanking as she did. It seemed her movements had broken through to Nivres, who was still pinning her in place with his body. At her movements, he rose off her and it didn't escape her notice that as the dragon stood, that terrible growl followed him.

She scrambled to her feet, drawing her blade and adopting a defensive position. *Come on then, do your worst.* She flicked her gaze around the room again, but still saw nothing. But someone was here. They had to be. In her experience, pulsating purple energy balls did not appear from nowhere and judging by the increased volume of rumbling from Nivres, she was best to be on her guard.

She risked a glance at the dragon. He appeared to be tracking an entity across the room, his eyes following…something, never straying from their target. Curious, Sabeline tried to match the direction of his narrowed glare. There were only a few more crates piled on top of each other, a scrap of fabric that presumably, used to be a fine rug and a medium sized table with a single lit candle in the middle and plenty of small pouches spilling out gold. She couldn't see…Wait…there!

By the table corner, a portion of the air seemed off. It shimmered and flowed as if made of water. "Is that…?" She already had a pretty good theory, but if Nivres could confirm it…

"Camouflage Cast." He snarled in answer to her unfinished question.

Dammit, that's what she thought. And there was only one thing she knew able to do that. *By the Goddess, why us?*

"We can see you, sorcerer. So you can drop the fancy illusion." She spat towards the shimmer.

She hadn't exactly expected the sorcerer to listen to her, so when the flowing air became more corporeal, vague surprise etched its way onto her features before she quickly discarded it. Nivres still continued to growl ominously beside her and Sabeline was impressed he'd been able to keep up the intimidation for so long.

"Chaos's Bane." A male voice spoke with simple authority. This was a man used to having people carry out orders. Gripping her sword tighter, Sabeline raised it slightly higher. *He will not live to see morning.* The promise to herself steadied her pounding heart. She was a knight. She'd taken down worse things than a coward sorcerer shooting energy balls in a ramshackle hut.

Nivres growled louder at the words and she found herself wondering how that was even possible, considering the dragon hadn't let up on the deafening, threatening noise since the magic was thrown their way. While the dragon was intimidating the sorcerer, Sabeline took the opportunity to swiftly flick her gaze around. There didn't appear to be anyone else in the hut. Certainly not the rows of assassins, archers or swordsmen she'd been envisioning and preparing for. There weren't any more strange shimmers in the air that she could see either, meaning no guards or security were concealed by yet more illusions. It was just the sorcerer. The Chaos Convocation leader alone. *He must be confident in his skill to face us by himself.*

"I have heard rumours of you, Chaos's Bane. The man who controls fire, burns down our settlements and strongholds. To what end? We will always be in Idrelas. It is our right to own its riches, whatever form they take."

Her hold on the blade increased as she gritted her teeth.

Who did this…. this… ingrate think he was! "The riches of the land do not belong to one person, nor to one group alone. The Chaos Convocation's greed and lust for trouble will be your undoing." Sabeline spat at the sorcerer, who appeared entirely unaffected by her words. *Someone like them is too far gone to be reasoned with.*

The sorcerer opened his mouth to say something, (no doubt about to inform her why she was wrong), but before a word even slipped passed his thin lips, Sabeline felt heat rush by the side of her face. A fireball careened through the air, heading straight for the Leader. She risked a glance at Nivres, who had wisps of smoke dancing out from the corners of his lips.

Moving her eyes back to the Leader, Sabeline watched as he waved his hand, creating some kind of defensive barrier. The fireball ricocheted off the invisible wall, slamming with speed into the far-left corner and immediately engulfing the wood in flames. *That is not good.*

"It seems the time for talking is over." The sorcerer hissed.

"Typical Chaos Convocation, always wanting the last say." Nivres rumbled beside her.

Another fireball came hurtling out of the dragon's mouth and this time, she wasn't going to stand idly by. Especially as time was now of the essence, due to the growing flames spreading across the hut. Racing after the fireball, she kept her gaze trained on the sorcerer. The moment he moved his hands to protect himself, she dropped, sliding the last few paces across the ground and letting her sabatons hit him with full force in the shin.

He crumpled in front of her, the fireball flying overhead and consuming the wall in flickering orange and yellow. Rising to her feet, she pointed the blade at the sorcerer's neck, resting it on the skin so that if he so much as moved, it would cause the sword to pierce his flesh.

She didn't expect the Leader to throw a smirk her way as she glared down at him. *Why does he wear that expression? Surely he knows I won't be releasing him. Or does he think I will show him mercy? After all, they know of Nivres, but not of me.*

"You left my hands free." The sorcerer let out in a strained whisper and before she could blink, one of his hands moved in front of her. Magic gathered in a swirling mass beneath her torso, shooting her into the air and she heard her blade clatter to the ground as it was ripped from her fingers.

The blazing wall of fire greeted her vision, growing closer as she plummeted towards it. *Brace yourself,* was all Sabeline could think as she slammed into the fire. The roar of flame and collapsing wood weren't enough to drown out Nivres's anguished, panicked cries screaming into her ears.

24

Everything

Everything hurt. Her limbs ached under the weight of the armour and there was a crushing feeling emanating along her chest and back, though that could be due to the fact she was under a fair amount of flaming debris. *By the goddess, this has all gone straight to damnation.*

A scratching cough clawed its way out of her throat as the roar of fire echoed all around. She had to move. If she didn't, she was as good as dead. *I haven't come this far just to die at the hands of a greed driven nobody magician.* The angry, determined thought fuelled Sabeline's body. With great effort, she moved her sluggish arms and wrapped her fingers around some of the wood decorating her chest.

Sucking in a deep breath, she pushed upwards, extending her arms until they shook with the effort, screaming at her to just give up and drop the wood back down. But that would be easy. She wasn't known for taking the easy way. Especially when death himself was facing her down far too soon for the second time. She had survived Falon. She would survive this. She had to. After all, who would torment Nivres if she was gone?

That thought almost caused her to drop the wood. The dragon was becoming her friend. It was perfectly normal to have those thoughts about friends. Wasn't it? Of course it was. *Focus!* Tucking the internal argument away for another time and gritting her teeth, Sabeline hauled the plank off her, shoving it to the side. More pieces scattered around her at the motion, but at least these were small and easy enough to claw her way through. Well, maybe in normal circumstances.

Her face stung; her arms barely felt like they existed after moving the main problem out of the way. She hadn't even tried her legs yet…Ah yes. There they were. At least she hadn't broken anything. *Thank the goddess for small mercies.* There was no choice. She was going to have to keep going and break free of this debris, before the fire consumed her whole. She'd have to deal with the consequences when they finally left this settlement behind. *Never have I wanted to return to a cave so much.*

With renewed determination flowing through her, Sabeline clamped her lips shut. The last thing she wanted to do was make a sound and draw the sorcerer's attention back to her. Bending her knees brought her legs up and she ignored the agony shooting down her shins as she did. Using them as leverage, she managed to haul herself up into a crouch. More wood scattered and slid, clanking to the floor with a hollow thud. Clambering up, her hands wrapped around the last few parts and shoved them to the side as much as she was able.

Finally, her head broke free and with haste, she stumbled out of the pile. There was no time to check the extent of her injuries. *Probably for the best, I can tell it's not going to be good.* Fire remained swirling around her, licking and flickering over each crevice and surface. From the sight greeting her, it wouldn't be long before the whole place collapsed.

Frantic, she pivoted, eyes searching through the havoc in an effort to locate Nivres. He had to be here somewhere. He wouldn't have left her, Sabeline knew that much. So where….?

An anguished scream erupted to her left, it's high pitch carrying with ease over the constant crackling of dancing flame. *Nivres.* Oh goddess, she needed to get over there. Her armour clanked and groaned as she forced herself to move across the floor, each step feeling heavier than it should. There was no time to dwell on such things. Nivres needed her help. She could not let him down. Not now when they were so close to finishing this quest. Sabeline had started this with him and they'd have to kill her if they thought she would finish this without the dragon. Perhaps ever since she had begun hunting Nivres, the goddess had irrevocably bound their destinies.

Evading flame and crackling debris, she finally arrived to where she needed to be. Her face still tingled and felt as though it was covered in some kind of grit. While her limbs didn't quite scream in protest with each movement anymore, the ache still throbbed painfully down every sinew, pulsating against her muscles. But it was nothing compared to the vision that greeted her.

The dragon in human form stood tall and proud, despite the darkening patch of crimson Sabeline could make out spreading across his basic armour. The sorcerer must have struck him good for the wound to be bleeding that much. His golden gaze was narrowed as his arm stretched out before him. Following it, Sabeline's eyes set upon the sorcerer.

Nivres's hand was wrapped around the Leader's neck, in a very unforgiving fashion. An assessment tickled the back of her mind that perhaps the scream hadn't come from Nivres's mouth after all. But the urge to get over there still strummed strong in her soul. There was no way she was going to let the dragon have all the fun and claim the victory single handed.

Edging closer, it seemed Nivres and the sorcerer were completely unaware of her presence. That could serve her well. A stealth attack would be advantageous if the two men remained in their current positions. Creeping nearer, Sabeline was drawn to a sudden halt as a seething voice hissed above the flame. "If any harm has come to her, not even death will save you from the reach of my vengeance."

A spluttering cough escaped the sorcerer's lips before strangled words followed. "You are the bane of Chaos. I knew you would come for me one day. But that woman is nothing."

Sabeline watched as Nivres pulled the sorcerer forward by his throat and slammed him back into the crumbling wall with such force that the remaining structure trembled. A choked gasp dragged from the Leader's mouth before Nivres's growling fury-soaked response caused her lips to part in shock.

"She is everything."

25

Escape

Those three words rampaged through her like a pack of shadow hounds, causing her heart to sing and heat to flood her cheeks. *Goddess damn it, I do not blush!* Taking a swift breath, Sabeline attempted to tamper down her body's responses to that very interesting statement. She could ask him about it later, when they were both alive and safe. Right now, that wasn't a guarantee. Especially when a wheezed-out bark of laughter caused her eyes to narrow back on the magician.

"The great Bane of Chaos tamed by a mere woman. Does she know how much of the Convocation you've slaughtered? Do you fear the way she would look at you if she did?"

Who in all of Idrelas did this fool think he was? He had female assassins, mercenaries and thieves at his beck and call. Did he think just because she'd come with Nivres (who she was gathering had gained some kind of reputation within the organisation) that she was the weak one? Oh no. That insult wasn't going to stand. Seething anger slithered through Sabeline as she kept the sorcerer and Nivres in her sights, creeping further around some charred debris.

She watched as Nivres growled, his lip curling to reveal canines too pointed and sharp to belong to a mortal man. His fingers clenched tighter around the Leader's throat.

"Must have hit a nerve Chaos's Bane. Am I right?" On the one hand, Sabeline admired the sorcerer's defiance. She'd go down fighting too if she was in his position. On the other, it did mean she'd have to put up with his barbed words until she could kill him. Goddess knew after such an insult, Sabeline wasn't about to let him continue breathing. Almost there…

With care, she reached down her greave, curling her fingertips around the concealed dagger she'd secured there. Her sword may be gone, lost in this crumbling hellscape, but she would never be defenceless. A Knight of Idrelas would have a short life indeed if they didn't have any contingency plans.

Sabeline stepped forward, the dagger now secure in her grasp. She was aiming to come from a direction that would let Nivres see her, but keep her concealed from the Leader's view until the last possible second. A few more steps and she caught the dragon's golden gaze as it slid over to her. His eyes widened and she managed a small twitch of her lips and a nod in his direction. His eyes travelled down to the dagger in her grasp and he seemed to understand her line of thought. Nivres gave an almost imperceptible nod back, before turning his attention back to the smug, but struggling sorcerer.

"Not even close." He snarled out in answer to the Leader's question. She only had a brief second to take in the confused expression now adorning the magician's face before darting from her position. Giving over to her instincts, Sabeline thrust forward, plunging the dagger upwards into the sorcerer's right side. A shocked gasp escaped his mouth as Sabeline twisted the weapon deeper. "I am not nothing. It is a shame you learned that too late." She whispered into his ear before yanking the blade back out. Nivres took the opportunity to release his grip on the Leader's throat, letting him drop in a heap to the ground.

Thick blood coated the dagger and was rapidly spreading across the magician's robes. *If he is not already dead, he soon will be.* She secured the blade back within her armour before turning to the dragon. He almost looked as if he wanted to say something to her, but a piece of falling flaming debris landing to the side of them put a stop to any words.

"We need to get out of here. Now." She implored, dragging Nivres's attention back to the current situation.

"Right. Yes. Of course. The quickest way would be for me to change into my true form, but I cannot do that here with wayward bits of building falling on our heads."

"Fine, so we get out of here, find a reasonably safe spot in this inferno of a settlement for you to change, then we fly." Sounded simple enough. "Over there." Sabeline pointed to a large but alit hole in the wall after glancing around. "We'll have to go through there. Any other way is blocked off and if we don't go soon, we will die." She emphasised, cutting off whatever protest was about to spill from the dragon's lips. She already had burns; she could feel them itching across her skin. A few more wouldn't make a difference.

Without any further thought, she reached over and grabbed Nivres's hand, sprinting with him and leaping through the hole. Flames brushed against her armour, reaching out to dance across the flesh of her neck as she and the dragon broke through, landing on the other side.

It is not much better out here. The thought trickled through her mind as she took in the other buildings consumed by orange and yellow fire, glowing embers drifting along in the wind like fireflies as they travelled upwards to meet black plumes of rolling smoke so thick that it blocked out the stars. Suddenly she felt herself be pulled along, running again though this time with Nivres's hand wrapped around hers in a tight grip.

The lack of people and sound as they hurried along made her think either the members were dead or had cut their losses and cleared out. *At least we don't have to worry about being caught on the way out, that's something.* The dragon finally released her as they stepped into the circular centre of the settlement, each building far enough away that the flames couldn't reach them. *Yet.*

"Hurry Nivres." She called, as a groan reached her ears. Out of respect, she kept her focus trained on the ever-encroaching inferno, leaving the dragon to alter forms without fear.

It was only when claws scooped her up and the ground became further and further away did Sabeline allow herself to rest, the pain of her injuries returning with vengeance as she did.

***

"You do not have to watch me as though I am some kind of fragile flower." She huffed, peeling away another piece of her armour and discarding it beside her on the cave floor. Never had she been so relieved to be back underground, though the dragon had barely let her out of his sight. "We were in a battle, injuries happen. You should know that more than most." *Goddess knows I expected to come out with a scrape or two, no warrior wouldn't.*

Heaving off her sabatons with more effort than they were worth, she placed them with the rest of the pieces she'd been able to remove. Movement caught her attention and she turned to see Nivres coming closer to her, aware of his large tail flicking in agitation similar to a cat's. *Why me? Why do I have to deal with a sudden over-protective beast?* Sabeline swallowed the heavy sigh threatening to leave her mouth.

Nivres's jaws came closer to her body, before the dragon opened them wider and turned his head just a bit. Copious amounts of green fell onto her lap and with care, Sabeline plucked one clump between her fingers. Tilweed. She would have to ask Nivres where he was getting all this from. *No doubt a secret stash hidden somewhere within this labyrinth of tunnels, but still, producing this much tilweed cannot be normal.*

"Thank you," She uttered, with a slight nod. Nivres tipped his great head in return before moving to the side, it was as if he wanted to put distance between them, but at the same time, resented the idea. *Quick, before he is too far...* Sucking in a deep breath, Sabeline braced herself for the consequences of her next words. The matter needed to be addressed and address it she would, even if the dragon had been acting out of sorts since they'd returned.

"When I searched for you, after being thrown into the wall, I saw you holding the sorcerer by the neck. I was trying to come up with a plan when I heard him speak and say I was nothing. Can you guess what else I heard?" Sabeline was surprised to find how soft her voice was, despite her heart deciding to take flight with all the pounding of a griffin's wings within it's cage. Glancing up at the dragon, he was still, as though her words had turned him to a statue.

A second passed. Then another as she kept her gaze fixed

on Nivres. The time was brief, but it felt as though an eternity had passed as she waited for the dragon to speak.

"I did not know you were present for that." The sentence was just as careful and gentle as her words had been, but Sabeline detected something else too. Something she couldn't name.

"That was the point. I was trying not to alert you both to my presence." She jested in an attempt to free them both from the sudden atmosphere weighing down on them. Nivres remained still, mouth clamped shut.

This time she could not stop the sigh that spilled out of her. "I'm not asking for the kingdom Nivres. All I want to know is what you meant by that. It's a statement that leaves a lot more questions than answers."

Another flick of the tail. At least that was something. She'd begun to worry he would turn to stone in order to avoid speaking with her. *I do not want to push him, but if he doesn't say something soon, goddess help me I'll...*

A sigh blew from Nivres's jaws, reflecting her own earlier action, although Sabeline noted hers hadn't been accompanied by a cloud of smoke. Her gaze followed the billowing tendrils as they rolled across the cave above her. Anything to distract herself from the tension soaking the air.

"It was, I mean, you had just been thrown by an energy blast into a flaming wall Sabeline. Then you fell, in a cacophony of wood, ash and flame. It was, I...I can't watch that again." She waited as Nivres swallowed hard before continuing. "In that instant, I had to destroy the sorcerer and I'd have done anything to ensure his body lay beneath my feet. Then, when I had him cornered, he spewed that *filth*. I didn't know if there was still breath in your body and he thought fit to insult you."

The pounding of her heart had progressed as she listened to Nivres, the emotion clear in each word that left his lips. Did she want to hear anymore? Was she truly prepared for another change in so short a time, no matter what that might be? Ascilia used to have a phrase she'd utter at an opportune moment and Sabeline heard it echo in her ears as if the knight herself stood there whispering it. *You reap what you sow.* Without her permission, Sabeline's hand curled into a fist, the tips of her fingers pressing deep into her palms as the skin of her knuckles turned white like a phantom. She had started this, now she had to accept the consequences. It was better to air this now, rather than let it haunt her waking thoughts and cause it to fester. At least, that's what she tried to tell herself.

"It caused such a fury within me, as if I had become the embodiment of rage itself. How dare an honourless fool say such a thing? You have courage, respect and honour. Everything he and his convocation lack. And..." The dragon cut himself off but she could see the conflict raging within his golden gaze.

"And?" Sabeline prompted with care. *What am I doing? I could have left him to finish there and be done with it. Dammit, too late now.*

"And I am fond of you Sabeline, Bringer of Truth, Knight of Idrelas."

"Well, that is a good thing is it not? Friends are supposed to be fond of each..." Sabeline let her voice die as Nivres fixed her in place with his stare.

"I am fond of you Sabeline, Bringer of Truth, Knight of Idrelas." The dragon repeated. "Perhaps more than I should be."

26

Hollow Hearts

The impact of the words thundered through her like a storm. She had been right. She hadn't been prepared for that answer. But now it was out there, crackling between her and the dragon as Sabeline remained silent, gazing wide-eyed at Nivres as he shuffled his claws. "I.."

Her lips started to form something, but she trailed off as hectic thoughts assaulted her mind. Yes she had been coming around to the idea of Nivres as a friend. The agony she'd felt when he'd slipped from that settlement rooftop and the panic that had run through her in Dunsaw couldn't be denied. She'd be a fool to do so and if there was one thing Sabeline prided herself on, it was practicality. Without warning, she'd come to care for the great beast. But to feel something akin to love….

Love was not practical nor logical. Sabeline was aware of this. That and there was still much about dragons she was unaware of. Perhaps they felt emotions on a grander scale or were more confident in identifying how they felt more than mere mortals. Nivres also had the benefit of not being burdened with a lifetime of hatred against her. On the other hand, Sabeline had just freed herself from that burden only a few days ago.

Her fingers clenched across the dirt of the cave floor as she gritted her teeth. Yes, Nivres made her blush and her heart did strange things around him from time to time. But it was not love. *Not yet.*

"I," She tried again, lifting her gaze from the floor and trailing it back to the dragon. "I care for you Nivres. But right now, I do not think I can return the sentiment the same way. Please understand."

This was why she preferred being on the battlefield. There was no awkwardness, no tension thrumming through the air. Everyone on each side knew what they were getting into and at the end, you either rejoiced or were on your way to the goddess. Simple. Easy. Familiar.

The silence continued to stretch to the point of pain before Nivres caressed the air with his voice. "I think I understand, Bringer of Truth. But your words give me hope. Though I will make one request of you."

"Name it and I shall fulfil it." By the goddess, right now he could ask her to capture a star and she'd do it. Anything to ease the hurt she knew she'd caused, even if he claimed to understand her reasoning.

"If there comes a point where you are certain you would not be able to return my feelings in full, I request you tell me the moment you know. It would be better that way."

Sabeline swallowed hard. It was fair, what he was asking. But the thought of ever saying those words to the dragon caused her heart to plummet into her stomach and stay there. *You owe Nivres this at least.*

"Very well. If I ever feel that I cannot return the same, I agree to inform you as soon as I am able." Why did agreeing to the dragon's terms hurt more than Falon's betrayal?

Nivres nodded, crimson scales glinting in the smaller firelight. They still needed to keep warm, but after the night's events, Sabeline was grateful the dragon had made the usual colossal fire a bit more demure.

"Thank you. Now I'm sure you need your rest in light of your injuries. I'll leave you to sort yourself out." A dismissal if she'd ever heard one.

"Right. Yes." Those two quiet words were all she could manage as Nivres shifted to full height and began padding towards one of the tunnels. Almost as if compelled, Sabeline couldn't help but utter "Goodnight Nivres," to his retreating back.

The soft echoing "Goodnight Sabeline," that funnelled back to her was enough to raise her heart back up from the pit of her stomach.

***

Flying up from the ground, Sabeline cast her eyes around as her blood rushed through her ears. Her breath came in harsh pants as she glared into the darkness, illuminated only by the dying flames of the signature fire pit. *The cave. Dreams, that's all it was.*

She tried to catch the wisps of images as they drifted towards the recesses of her mind. There had been fire, much of it. Thick smoke too, but for once she had no fear as she wandered through it, no memory of that day from her childhood stalking each step like the flame. Nivres had been there too. But why and what he was doing was already becoming a fog as she tried to recall. Something had caused her to panic, it had caused her eyes to open with the speed of a clawton cat.

A sigh huffed out of her chest as she calmed her breathing. Just a dream. A nightmare. *This is what I get for pushing memories and feelings aside and vowing to deal with them later.* Though the nightmare had vanished, Sabeline had a feeling sleep had finished with her. Giving herself a quick once over, she was satisfied to see her makeshift bandages and tilweed paste were all still in place. She couldn't have tossed around that much at least.

With nothing else to do, Sabeline found her gaze drifting towards the tunnel Nivres had disappeared through. *Maybe I should check on him?* She shook her head, banishing the question from her mind. He didn't want to see her, he wanted to get away from her to gather his thoughts. That much had been obvious from his dismissal. Her eyes flicked over to the tunnel again. Still…

Heaving herself up and taking one cautious step after the other, she drifted over towards the entrance. In her bandages and white linen, she really hoped he wouldn't think a ghoul or other creature had breached the cave. The fire provided just enough light to make it a little way through the tunnel. *He can't be that far. Just a quick check and then I'll come back.*

Another step. Before she knew it, Sabeline was striding down the cavern in search of Nivres.

As her feet wandered, she noticed that the firelight had receded much quicker than she'd anticipated. Letting her hand glide across the cavern wall, bumps and ridges brushed against her bandaged flesh as Sabeline tried to feel for some sort of archway or opening. Maybe she'd made a mistake coming down here. *What was I thinking, coming to check on*

Nivres when he currently wants nothing to do with me? Well, she'd come this far. A sigh breathed past her lips against the silence. Maybe it was her own selfish desires, her need to know the dragon was alright, that drove her, but all she knew was that she was committed.

Stepping over and knocking into rocky crevices, she padded with care a little further. *If he's not in the next cavern, I'll turn back.* The resolute thought both assured and disappointed her. True to his word, she had not encountered any traps like that first night as she'd searched. The notion filled her with new determination. With her eyes now able to pick out shapes amidst the gloom, Sabeline withdrew her arm from the wall as an opening made itself known. *Just a quick peek and if he's not there, I'll turn back.*

Edging around the wall and taking care not to kick any rocks by accident, Sabeline manoeuvred with grace into the new area. The darkness was not so thick here, though she supposed that might be to do with a cluster of flames dancing delicately on melted candles set into a shelf carved out of the rock. Taking a few steps further, she cast her gaze around. *I am surprised by how big this room is.* The size was a promising sign, perhaps the dragon was here after all.

The glow of the candle lights illuminated various trinkets, though above all else, Sabeline found her eyes sliding over to a portrait set in a gilded gold frame, the light flickering over the subject's face. Walking over, Sabeline crouched to get a better look, holding back a hiss as the motion caused her injuries to sting.

It was a woman, captured in eternal radiant beauty by the artist. She'd never had her portrait taken, no one wanted to capture blood stained, filth drenched knights, even if they had just returned from a battle to protect the people. *Or thought it was a battle to protect the people.* Sabeline buried the thought before it could form further. She was making it up for it now wasn't she? The Chaos Convocation would be wiped from the face of Idrelas, she'd sworn it to Nivres. Turning her attention back to the portrait, Sabeline drew her gaze across soulful wide eyes that matched the colour of her beautiful blond tresses. Wait…matched? She'd only ever seen one creature with eyes of gold. Wrapping her hands around the frame, Sabeline rose, turning the picture in the light until…ah yes. There.

The bottom of the frame had been inlaid with a plaque; a single word etched in perfect calligraphy across the smooth surface. *Myvanna*. With care, Sabeline placed the portrait where it had been. It almost felt like the portrait's eyes were watching her, judging her. Somehow, it felt right that she should say something to it. "You don't know me," Sabeline whispered, hardly daring to be louder than a breath, "but your brother saved me when he could have simply eaten or killed me, like the King wanted." *That no good, backstabbing, traitorous, royal...* "I have agreed to help Nivres in his justice against the people who tortured and murdered you. However, he has confessed his affections for me along the way and I do not know yet if I can return the same fully." Sabeline let her eyes fall from the portrait. It was probably better not to mention that she'd been trying to murder Nivres for quite some time before their sudden acquaintance. "If one day I am able to care for him as he cares for me, I hope the union would have your blessing. Be well in the care of the Goddess, Myvanna dragon born."

Nothing more crept past her lips as Sabeline stepped away

from the painting and deeper into the room. She had not expected to pay respects to Myvanna on her search, but honouring the dragon's memory felt right. However the simple fact Myvanna's picture was here gave credence to the importance of this room. Nivres would not want to be far from his sister's memory.

An odd sliver of jealousy ran through her as she walked. Nivres had acquired a portrait of his sister in her human form to keep close, though all she had of her family were fading memories, overtaken by ash and flame. Even her second family in the knights, there were no paintings to mourn the loss of or carry with her. Coldness washed over her as a terrifying thought overtook all else. *What if one day, I forget Mariel's face? Or what Echoris's armour looks like? Ascilia's overbearing attitude or Bersaba's kindness?*

Swallowing hard, Sabeline sucked in a deep breath. She would not forget. She couldn't forget. They had been her family in all but blood. She would not disrespect them that way. Marching further across the ground, thoughts swimming through her head, she did not see the warm bulk until she collided with it.

By the goddess, now I've done it... Sabeline heard her heartbeat echoing in her skull as she waited for the dragon to stir. There was a brief snort and a wisp of smoke, though Nivres did not move any further. *I have fulfilled what I set out to do, Nivres is fine, I should head back and pretend this never happened.* She blamed her irrational nightmare for the all-consuming need to check on the dragon. The nightmare she could barely recall, except for the fear. He was here and he was well. That was all she needed to know.

Turning, Sabeline hoped to wander away as swiftly as

possible. Placing one foot forward, she was just about to take another step, when a confused sleep-ridden utterance of her name caused her to stop as though she'd been hit with a stunning spell. Peering over her shoulder, she found herself staring into the second set of golden eyes she'd encountered this night, although these pair were becoming more aware by the minute.

By the goddess, why is it always me?

"Sabeline?" The utterance of her name came stronger now as the dragon blinked away the last of sleep. Great. There was no way she could sneak out now or pretend she was just a dream (like Kilyn had attempted to do to her once.) A burning sensation racked her heart. She was still the Bringer of Truth and it would be foolish to turn away now.

Sabeline tried not to shift under Nivre's penetrating gaze. She would not show weakness, despite being in nothing but bandages and her under shirt. *This mess is of my own doing and I must now make truth of it.* "Sorry, I did not mean to disturb your sleep." She spoke at a normal level, after all what was the use in whispering now?

"What are you doing here? Is the cave under attack?" Those reptilian eyes widened at the dragon's own realisation, before his gaze flicked away from her, becoming more intent on the cavernous archway. Sabeline felt a slight sting in her chest at his assumption. *He believes I would only come because of danger?*

"No, we are safe. I-" She wrapped her left fingers around her partially bandaged right arm, glancing away from Nivres. "It was for a stupid reason that I came here. I shouldn't have intruded. I'm sorry, Nivres." The thoughts and images of the dream swirled across her mind, reinforcing her words.

Was it ridiculous to check on a friend after such a nightmare? Sabeline didn't know anymore. The Knights of Idrelas were sent to dispatch creatures, beings and forces that often looked like the imaginings of the darkest dreams. Facing such threats on a regular basis had caused her and her fellow knights to become mostly immune to nightmares. She doubted any of them knew how to act after such a night vision now.

Letting go of her arm (the tilweed was starting to itch under the linen), she padded across the uneven ground, hoping to slip past the dragon.

"Wait," the gentle rumble rolled through the air, putting an end to the quiet hanging between her and the dragon. "It is not a ridiculous reason if it caused you to seek me out." Nivres shifted before her, settling down again now that she'd informed him of no immediate danger.

Sabeline halted in her movements. Should she tell him? Would he still think it was not a silly reason after she revealed the truth? *What does it matter anymore? There is nothing left to lose now.* "I had a dream." By the goddess, that wasn't her most eloquent of openings, but with those four words, Sabeline already felt some of the heaviness lift from her chest. Flicking her eyes back up to the dragon's face, she tried to gauge Nivres's reaction. There were no outward signs of disapproval. A sliver of confidence swelled within her and she grabbed it before it could slip through, ploughing on with her story. "Some of it remains like a fog in my mind, but other parts, I remember clearly. There were flames and fire, I was running for something. I cannot remember what, that part is lost to me. But I remember finding you, amidst smoke and ruin. You were in your other form, human. Everything else has been forgotten, but there was a narrowed flash of gold in the gloom."

It sounded so foolish to her own ears. She couldn't even recall half of the night vision for goddess's sake! *Nivres will change his mind, he will not thank me for disturbing his rest...*

Instead, the calm question of "Was it the fire that caused you to come here?" interrupted her raging thoughts.

"What?"

"You have not had the best life experiences with fire Sabeline, first with your childhood and now today." Nivres uttered in a gentle tone, as if trying not to scare her further, but his eyes...his eyes seemed pained. "Perhaps that manifested itself into a nightmare?"

"No, no that's not it." She answered with vehemence. In her dream, the memory of that day hadn't even crossed her mind. The fear hadn't spread throughout her until later. Until... "You." The realisation struck her like one of those energy blasts as she gazed at Nivres with wide eyes.

"Me?" The dragon now seemed concerned.

"Yes. The fear only manifested after I saw you. I thought, I thought you were in harm's way. I thought something had happened to you and I wasn't able to reach you." An echo of the dream flashed brightly through her memory. Sabeline had been scared for him. Scared that even with all her skills and training, she was still unable to help her...her friend.

Nivres now seemed less concerned, which puzzled her. What had he been thinking? "You feared being unable to help me in a time of peril?"

"Yes." Sabeline nodded, without any trace of uncertainty.

"And that is why you came here? To ensure I was safe?"

Her hand reached out and tugged a loose scrap of bandage, twisting it back and forth with her fingers. It was fine. She could admit to that. Friends checked up on each other, she had done it with her sisters in arms thousands of times. "I had to see you were alright, despite our last conversation of the evening. I didn't intend to wake you, I thought just a quick glance to ensure you were here and breathing would be enough to satisfy my worry."

The dragon let out a little humming noise, which sounded content in nature to Sabeline's ears. "If you have such dark visions at night again, you are always welcome to satisfy your worry. I would rather be awake to dispel your terror, then let you wander with it alone in the darkness."

I do not deserve him. Not after everything I have done. Despite her self-deprecating thoughts, warmth buried into her heart and her lips flickered into a small smile. "I hold you to the same oath."

Nivres continued with that strange noise. "Agreed." He rumbled, before continuing "if you wish, you could remain in this part of the cavern till morning. It may continue to reassure you."

Gratefulness filled her at the offer, but she shook her head. "Thank you, but I don't want to disturb your rest any further. Go back to sleep Nivres and I'll do the same. I feel better now, I promise."

"Very well, if you are certain. Goodnight Bringer of Truth."

"Goodnight Nivres."

With care she padded a little further away, waiting until Nivres had curled back up and closed his eyes. After a moment's hesitation, Sabeline crept back towards the dragon before sitting by the cave wall and letting herself drift back into a more peaceful oblivion.

27

Forest Trouble

She had crept from the cave and out into the strange woodland as the slivers of dawn grew across the sky. It would not do for Nivres to wake and see her slumped against the wall, especially after she'd reassured him that she was fine. *It doesn't look good, the Bringer of Truth going back on her word.* Hoping that breakfast would be a peace offering (after all, it had seemed to go down well last time) she had decided to hunt. And this time she was armed with a sword.

Though Sabeline could already imagine being scolded for gallivanting around this strange forest while still healing. There was no doubt the tilweed was helping, but still, the odd limb ached and twinged or itched from the repairing burns. But she did not want Nivres to worry any more than necessary and catching breakfast would be the perfect way to prove she was on the mend. *Now, what to get?*

She curled her fingers tighter around the blade in her hand, moving it up and down slightly to test the weight. Oh yes, she'd be able to bring back more than a weasel or some other rodent this time. *Just as long as I don't run into any goddess damned bracken trolls again.* Edging further into the forest, Sabeline took care to avoid crunching branches and bracken underfoot. Anything could be alerted to her presence and if so, she'd lose her tactical advantage. Best to stay quiet as much as possible.

A sudden blur of colour caused her eyes to slide to the left. Remaining still, she drew in a breath before slowly releasing it. With care, Sabeline inclined her head in the same direction, providing a better vantage. Nothing met her gaze which was a good sign, it meant whatever had darted past was unconcerned with making her breakfast instead. Taking one step forward and then another, Sabeline reached out and gently pushed some thin overhanging branches aside, resting them on top of a thicker tree limb.

A glade, previously hidden to her sight lay before her and best of all, an unconcerned deer grazed in the middle. *It seems the goddess is smiling upon me today.* Bending down, so the deer would not be alerted to her presence, Sabeline observed the creature and its surroundings for a few seconds. It was the only other being in the clearing, which thankfully meant she would not have to fight scavengers or predators to claim the kill. Her lips pulled into a smirk. *I shall make this quick.*

***

Dragging her fresh kill towards the cave by hand was not as easy as she'd hoped. Cursing her still healing limbs, she plunged her fingers harder into the carcass and yanked it across the forest floor. Huffing pants escaped her chest as she summoned her strength and dragged it a few more steps. Goddess she hated feeling like this. *This is why I despise recovering from injuries. Of course, in the line of duty I expect to be wounded but the healing time is as torturous as Falon.* Frustration began to bubble in her blood. She could do this dammit. She'd hauled bigger and uglier creatures along than one simple deer.

With a pained grunt, she dragged her kill a few steps more. Glancing up, the mouth of the cave loomed in the distance like some ominous foe. *Almost there.* Gritting her teeth, she prepared to pull the deer again. Before she could, a low growl reached her ears, rumbling through the foliage and causing her heart to pick up its pace. Great. It seemed she was going to have to fight after all.

Whatever it was, it knew she was aware of it. She could tell from one hunter to another. That and the fact previously quiet, undetectable footsteps were now uncaring of the noise they made. Planting her feet, Sabeline half turned behind her, confident that was where the growl was emanating from.

Her gaze narrowed. There. Something dark, with hints of green slunk through the trees. Dropping the deer, Sabeline moved one hand to rest on the handle of her sword where it lay secure in her scabbard. She caught a glimpse of eyes the colour of the forest leaves and a flash of long, bared fangs before the rest of the creature strode into view.

A sabre-toothed tree panther. She should have expected one to be roaming about this unnatural forest of all places. Still keeping her position, Sabeline wrapped her fingers around her sword handle and gradually began pulling it out. The panther still stalked towards her, though it had changed from emitting a low growl to a complete feline battle cry.

Its paws flew across the ground as it barrelled towards her. Just as she went to slash at its chest, the beast leapt into the air, catching her with its back paws and knocking her to the ground. There was no time to stab up at its underbelly and releasing a growl of her own, Sabeline jumped back to her feet. The panther stalked in a circle around her, occasionally reaching out a paw with all claws fully extended to take a swipe at her. With a swing of her sword, she felt the sword make contact with the panther's leg the next time it tried.

A pained hiss erupted from it and while the creature was off guard, Sabeline swung again but the feline shuffled back at the last moment. Heaving pants started to spill from her as her weakened limbs protested from this prolonged suffering. *It is life or death now and I refuse to be beaten by a forest cat.* Between pants, a sound that could have been a laugh wheezed out while the panther still watched her with caution in its gaze.

"Come on then, if you want my deer, you'll have to take it from my cold hands." She spat, raising her sword and aiming the tip towards her agitated foe. The panther growled in response and lifted one paw, ready to spring forward.

Until an all-consuming roar shook through the air. The very trees trembled around her under the weight of the sound. The panther that had been so ready to end her life moments ago now gazed at her with wide eyes, curling its tail around its legs and in her next breath, the feline darted back into the trees.

Shaking off the sudden shock, Sabeline snapped her head in each direction. If that noise could frighten off the panther, then she should be ready for the creature to spring out and… .Oh.

Her gaze landed on the mouth of the cave, where a crimson dragon stood tall casting his eyes around, almost as if he was searching for something. She watched as the dragon opened his jaws and released another terrible roar that caused several nesting birds to erupt from the trees and fly as far away as possible.

Why do I get the feeling that I'm in trouble?

28

Instinctual

"I thought getting us breakfast would be a good idea," Sabeline grumbled as Nivres nudged her back with his snout, herding her towards the cave entrance. "And you can stop that. I am fully capable of walking back without your aid."

By the goddess, since the dragon's searching gaze had landed on her, she'd been ushered towards the cave and shielded by Nivres's bulk and wings from anything else that might have wandered out of the trees.

"You decided to hunt breakfast while still in your undershirts and bandaged. Your wounds are not completely healed, I can smell it under the tilweed stench." Nivres growled in return.

The dragon may have had a point there, but she'd still been able to swing her sword around in a few offensive and defensive motions. He was making it sound as if she'd decided to wander around completely defenceless and take down the deer with her bare hands. Though she had been secretly pleased when he'd decided to lift up her kill in one of his clawed hands and carry it back on her behalf.

"I had my sword and I'm healed enough to strike some blows with it. I am a knight, if you recall. I have been in far worse condition in my lifetime than this." She deemed it best not to mention the forest panther and how close it had come to shredding her unguarded torso.

Nivres huffed over her shoulder as they traversed through the cave. "I have left you with scars, made by my own claw. I would rather burn than not aid in your recovery from the sorcerer's assault. And that starts with your rest, not wrestling with sabre-toothed forest panthers."

"How did you…?" The question would help distract her from the warmth spreading through her soul at Nivres admittance. He carried guilt with him from the consequential injuries she'd sustained when he'd first brought her here (though honestly, she had been more focused on the emotional pain, hatred and betrayal than the deep puncture marks) and this was his way of making amends.

"Believe it or not Bringer of Truth, but dragons do have a well-defined and sensitive sense of smell. And the lingering scent of panther is cloying my snout."

Damnation. She should have known. "The panther was… unexpected."

Nivres said nothing in return, but Sabeine could almost sense a self-satisfied smile to himself. *It is a good thing we are almost to the main chamber; he will no longer be able to hide his expressions.*

The shadows along the cavern walls began to elongate and dance as the almighty glow of the fire stretched beyond the arch of the main chamber. As they stepped in, Sabeline expected the dragon to sequester himself over towards the flames and prepare the deer. However, Nivres remained by her side.

Her gaze flickered over as she continued to wander towards her makeshift nook of space. Really, it just held some sheets on the floor, along with her armour and sword scattered around the fabric, but it was hers all the same. He did not seem to be acting any different than normal, his behaviour unchanged apart from the unusual decision to follow her to her area.

It was odd, but not enough to raise a fuss over. Bending her legs and crouching down, Sabeline shifted herself until she was sitting somewhat comfortably. The dragon imitated her, also sitting by her side. Once settled, she watched as Nivres began preparing her kill with his claws. *Why would he wish to do that so far from the fire?* It didn't make any logical sense. He would only have to move again to roast the meat, unless he was planning on breathing fire over it. But again, that didn't seem very practical in her eyes.

Well, no doubt Nivres had his own reasons for behaving in this manner. Deciding to question it no more, she turned her attention to where the bandages had come loose, thanks to her tussle with the panther. Running her fingers over the fabric, some of the green tilweed colouring had leached into the white. Beneath that, the paste had hardened, cracking and falling away in solid chunks. No wonder she felt like she wanted to scratch her skin off. A sigh breathed through her lips. There was no choice but to wash the paste off and soak the bandages before reapplying everything.

Come to think of it, I have not bathed since being brought here. The dragon would never let her go to a river to bathe and while it had been necessary to do so a few times in her past, she was unsure about river bathing in this particular forest. With her luck during her recent forays, she'd probably run into a frost eel or something equally dangerous lurking within the water.

Opening her mouth, she readied herself to ask Nivres but before any words could leave her throat, the dragon stepped forward towards the fire. At the same time, Sabeline felt a scaled tail wrap gently around her, lifting her up with great care and carrying her along.

Now she was confused. *What is he doing?* She sent a questioning look Nivres's way, but to her annoyance, he was keeping his gaze on the deer and fire in front of them. *This is pleasant though.* The thought came unbidden and Sabeline became acutely aware of the warmth surrounding her as she remained cradled safely within the thick muscle of the dragon's tail. Perhaps she could enjoy it, just this once.

It was only a few seconds more before they arrived at the fire and Nivres crouched down beside it, though his tail remained securely around her as he began placing the deer on the roasting spit. "Nivres, I do not wish to pry, but is there a particular reason I'm now being carried from place to place?" Sabeline asked with an air of caution.

The dragon snorted. "To keep you safe."

"Safe from what exactly? You and I are the only beings here."

She watched as his mouth twisted before he spoke again. "It is instinctual, and I will not battle my instincts on this matter. The need to protect is currently whirling like a storm within me."

Right. Well then. There wasn't really much she could say in response to that, apart from desperately trying to ignore the heat flooding her cheeks. *By the goddess, we've been over this, knights do not blush!* Clearing her throat, she tried for some reassurance. "But why? I am fine Nivres, I am able to walk and move. I may ache, but the injuries are no worse than before. I know when I can handle things and when I cannot. I am here, I am present. There is no need for your instincts to torment you so." *No matter how good this feels.*

"You misunderstand Sabeline. It is not a torment, nor despite the evidence before my eyes, is it logical. You already know that I care for you Bringer of Truth. I could have lost you to an overgrown cat mere hours ago. Let my instincts revel in the fact that you are still here, still present and that I will let nothing enter this cavern to harm you. It may mean being by your side for a little while until my instinctual responses settle once more, but please do not deny me this."

She swallowed hard as her heartbeat echoed like a roar in her ears. She knew he cared for her; he had said it outright the previous day leading to the awkward night. She had taken his confession; she had taken his comfort during the night. Perhaps it was time to give something back in return.

"If that is the case, then I would be honoured to have you remain by my side Nivres, for however long your instincts require."

The dragon let out a long sigh and from his position, his shoulders seemed to relax, as though a great weight had been lifted from him. He sent a smile her way, showing his fangs, before returning his attention to the roasting spit.

Sabeline crossed her arms on top of the crimson tail she was enveloped in, before resting her head atop them as she too watched the deer turn amidst joyous flames. She knew it wasn't love. Not yet. But she also had a feeling that her heart was balancing on a precipice.

And she didn't know how much longer it would be until it fell.

29

Protection Detail

"Where do we strike next?" She uttered around a mouthful of fresh roasted deer. Nivres had finally released her from his tail, but it remained coiled on the ground surrounding her. She needed a distraction from the swaying desires of her heart and destroying another part of the Chaos Convocation was just as good as any.

The dragon huffed, little plumes of smoke escaping his snout as he did. She thought she could detect some humour in the noise he created, which did not bode well.

"We are not striking anything until you are healed." Nivres replied, before closing his jaws around a large chunk of meat.

"Surely you jest? I'm almost back to full health."

Those reptilian eyes glanced sideways at her before he echoed one of the words she'd spoken. "Almost."

Sabeline narrowed her own in return. "Almost is just as good. A Knight has no time to fully rest and recover. As soon as we deem ourselves able, we go back into battle. And right now, I am deeming myself able Nivres." By the goddess, what had she come to? Having to beg to go back into the fight. She was grateful her sisters and arms were not here to witness such a thing.

"You are strong Bringer of Truth, of that there is no doubt. But I will not risk you further. I remind you the forest panther almost stole your life this morning. If you did not have such lingering weakness in your muscles, I have no doubt you would have defeated the beast. But do not ask me to watch as a Chaos Convocation member knocks a blade from your arms and impales you with their own weapon. *Please.*"

The distress in his voice and how it cracked on the word *please* caused her to swallow hard, hurting her throat. When put like that, there wasn't really much she could say in return, was there? Because he spoke the truth and they both knew it. As unlikely as it would be for one of those goddess damned scoundrels to catch her off guard, it was still a possibility. One that Nivres had clearly been running through his head for a while. Though maybe, just maybe, she could get the dragon to compromise.

"Alright. Alright Nivres. I would never ask you to do that. But why do we not plan today and then on the morrow or the day after, when I am fully healed, we strike together? Is that not fair?"

The dragon chewed slowly, hopefully considering her words as she waited with bated breath. *Please let him agree, by the goddess I'll go mad if he demands bed rest with nothing to do.*

"That is fair." He eventually agreed, dipping his head. "We can begin preparations after our meal."

"Excellent." She agreed, grinning as she turned her head to gaze up at him. The dragon mimicked her actions before she felt his tail come to rest against her body, the end curling around her knees.

After a few more mouthfuls of meat, Sabeline reached beside her, picking up discarded stone and rock, examining them between her fingers. Ah yes, this one would do. Just what she needed. The dragon was still chomping away above her, so she began etching away the basics into the ground with the sharp point of the stone.

Sabeline continued to carve white lines into the rock beneath them as the dragon's crimson head lowered to her level. A rumbled approval right next to her ear almost made her drop the stone she was using. *Almost.* "That is fine work. You have only been to one intact settlement and yet you draw out a map as though you have put an end to them all your life."

A pleased blush warmed her cheeks, though it disappeared as quickly as it had arrived. *Good. Knights do not blush, even a little bit for goddess's sake.* "Yes, well, it is a good skill to have, knowing and remembering one's surroundings. Especially in the realm of battle." She spoke, hoping for an indifferent tone. Though from the knowing glance Nivres directed at her, it was clear she had not succeeded.

"All settlements are similar in structure and layout, so while the fire was effective last time, it also affected us. This time I suggest a more subtle approach, here." She tapped her finger over one line, closest to what would be the Leader's hut.

"Ah, so you think it would be best to go straight for the Leader and the rest will fall apart?"

"Take out all the leadership and higher-ranking members and the rest will not know what to do. In the confusion, then would be best to light the fires. There would be no time to ferry away any spoils and those that may survive and search for other settlements would be disgraced as what self-respecting member of the Chaos Convocation would be seen without any of their precious gold or items?" She couldn't disguise the sneer that wrapped around the last part of her explanation.

"Yes, not only would this deplete their numbers through death, but also ensures any survivors would not be allowed back into the fold, thus decreasing them even more. Using their own obsession with riches against them. Truly magnificent."

The eager rumbling that emanated from Nivres sent a thrill of her own running through her. It was the anticipation of what was to come, the foreseeing of the battle ahead. This feeling would always be a part of her, she knew. Once a knight, always a knight. But for the first time, she realised that it was not only her or her sisters in arms that felt this way. It was part of Nivres too and thus, he understood. They may have been enemies once, but she was coming to understand that there was little difference between them.

***

They had continued to plan for the rest of the morning, ensuring no detail was left unchecked, nothing overlooked. It was solid and between them, Sabeline had no doubt it would be perfectly executed. Though once it was done and everything settled, she had asked Nivres something else that had begun to bother her. Where in all of Idrelas could she bathe?

The dragon had been surprised at first, it was probably not the most expected question to arise after an intense strategy session. But he had smiled and brought her through the tunnels to this place. An underground heated spring, with the clearest water she'd ever laid eyes on. Some stones had been placed around it to make it seem more of a pool, while streams of steam cascaded upwards through the air.

Nivres had left shortly after bringing her down here and now the blessed warm water was soaking into her tired, sore limbs, soothing the itch from the dried tilweed and making her feel cleaner than she'd been in weeks. Forget Falon with his over perfumed ointments and cloying bubbles sticking to her ready for slaughter. No, this, right here was perfect. She'd take this spring over the castle baths any day.

Sinking lower into the water, a contented sigh left her lips and mingled with the tendrils of steam. Her life had always been full of hardship, but at least now her experience was paying off. She was used to pain. Used to being sent into battle and ending the lives of both monsters and men. But there was also the aid the Knights gave, carrying food to villages in need, helping find those that were missing. It was a double-edged sword, she had had to be both fierce and protective, logical and emotional. And now she was turning it all on the Chaos Convocation, for the dragon that had been by her side since the fateful day Falon had decided her services were no longer required. *In the very public and humiliating manner that he did.* Gritting her teeth, Sabeline dropped lower so the water rested beneath her chin. She would never forgive, and she would never forget. Maybe one day, she could convince Nivres to light him on fire and see how he liked it.

It would do no good to dwell on those thoughts now. She needed to focus on the battle ahead. She would not let Nivres down. It was not an option. And if there were any sorcerers lurking within the depths of the next settlement, they would soon be acquainted with the edge of her blade. With the conviction settling deep within her, determination thrummed through her blood, pounding like the war drums of old. They would do this together. Both her and Nivres. They would win and they would be fine. With this spring working wonders on her body, maybe she could convince Nivres to strike tomorrow. If it took another soak in here before going out to persuade him she was healed, then she wasn't going to argue. For once.

All too soon, in her opinion, though it had most likely been hours, it was time to leave the water. Nivres had thoughtfully left a towel for her, though she did wonder how he'd come by it and where exactly it had been hiding until now. The fabric looked clean, so at least it hadn't been stored in the dirt and forgotten about.

Drying herself off, Sabeline pulled her underclothes back on, forgoing another round of tilweed and bandages. Her skin needed to breathe, goddess damn it. Padding along the tunnels and back to the main chamber, she prepared herself for bargaining with Nivres about tomorrow. By the time she stepped through the archway, a flawless argument was ready to fly from her lips.

Just as she opened her mouth, Sabeline snapped it shut again, glancing around the main chamber. The fire still bloomed; scattered piles of hoarded treasure still decorated the corners. Her little nook of sheets and armour was just how it had been left. But Nivres was not among them.

The dragon was gone.

30

Apart

That no good, sweet talking giant lizard! If he doesn't get himself killed, I'll do it! Gritting her teeth, Sabeline stomped around the various caverns, though with each one she checked and with no sign of Nivres, it was becoming more and more apparent the idiotic reptile had left her here.

Fury pounded through her blood in unison with each step. She was almost healed, goddess damn him! She'd explained this several times. She didn't care if those instincts he'd alluded to had convinced him that this was a good idea. The dragon should have known better. Should have known *her* better by now. She didn't need protecting. She could fight her own battles and Nivres's too while she was at it. Clenching her hands until they were balled up fists by her side, Sabeline stalked back to the main chamber.

The etched lines she'd made on the ground hours ago stared up at her, startling white against the dirt. Her eyes narrowed as other diagrams and lines emerged around the area she'd drawn. Those new ones…they were not her handiwork.

Bending down, Sabeline brushed some of the dirt away, revealing a more complete picture.

The bulk of the settlement she'd sketched with the rock was the same, but on one side, it had been extended to include another area. This part had been marked with the word "Storehouses". So, this settlement was larger than the last one. Something Nivres had chosen to omit when discussing strategy. Had it been his plan all along to leave her here? Letting her come up with a battle formation, knowing he was to leave her behind? Maybe he had thought he could make quick work of this one and would be back before she realised he was gone. Her lip curled. *Then he is a fool.*

There were arrows carved towards possible entry points and Sabeline committed each one to memory. Words were marked into the rock, the large letters spelling out *Sentinel Pass.* With care, Sabeline arranged herself into a sitting position, keeping her gaze fixed on the diagram. Sentinel Pass. It was not overly familiar to her; she'd found herself travelling through it once or twice but that was all. However at those times, there were no buildings, huts or structures. *This settlement has to be new.*

It would make practical sense, plenty of land made up Sentinel Pass. Enough to create a large, functioning settlement. A sudden thought caused dread to creep within her heart. What if this particular place was more than a settlement? What if this was the equivalent of a Chaos Convocation city? Would Nivres even realise? Cursing his name for the umpteenth time, Sabeline stood, before pacing across the ground. There was nothing for it. She was going to have to wait for the dragon to return. No, that wouldn't do. She refused to be idle with worry. She'd give him until dusk. Sabeline gave a sharp, satisfied nod to herself. Yes, she'd give him until dusk. And if he had not returned to the cave by then, she was going to drag him back by his tail.

***

She had sharpened her blade with a whetstone she'd found amongst some cultivated treasures. She had adorned her armour once more. She had ventured through the cave system and its various caverns. She had examined and *borrowed* another dagger to give her a dual set. She had sharpened both the new one and the one she had had since the beginning of her life here. And still the dragon was absent.

There was only so much she could do to distract herself from her thoughts and Sabeline was fairly sure she had committed every task she knew of in this place. Fury still sang in her blood at Nivres's disregard, but it was a softer quieter tone compared to the worry and fear that was now rising to overcome it. Though she had no doubt the minute she laid eyes on the damned fire breathing lizard, the anger would rear its head like a wave on the ocean. So she'd heard at least. She had never seen the sea.

Bersaba had spoken of the water and so had Mariel. Great expanses of open water that crashed onto shores of dry sand and craggy rocks covered in rich salty plants that only grew in the salt of the sea. Rubbing a hand across her protected heart at the memory, she buried it once more within her soul. She had lost her sisters in arms thanks to Falon's manipulative and maniacal actions. She refused to lose Nivres to people who were just like him.

Drawing in a deep, shuddering breath, Sabeline released it before rising to her feet and heading towards the carved stone archway that would take her towards the entrance tunnel.

Her blade was secured in its scabbard, the familiar weight an instant comfort. A dagger was secured and hidden within each greave. As she stepped towards the arch, Sabeline turned her head, gazing at the large fire still burning in glorious flickering motions before continuing on the route that would lead her towards the forest.

Emerging from the darkness of the underground, Sabeline found that the beginnings of dusk were settling over the land. On instinct, she cast her gaze upwards, searching the skies for any flash of crimson, any streak of scarlet. *Goddess damn him.* If the stubborn lizard had just had faith in her... Sabeline shook her head violently, tearing her eyes away from the now lilac sky. It would do no good to dwell on such notions. There would be plenty of time for that *after* she'd brought him home.

But how was she going to do that? The few times she'd ventured into this strange forest, she was under the impression the only way to leave was by flight. It had seemed as though whatever lived in the forest, stayed in the forest. Apart from Nivres. Her valiant war steed remained within Falon's stables. She hoped the other knights were looking after Hylix well.

Without her steed and without Nivres, how in goddess's name was she going to break free of the forest and travel to Sentinel Pass? She stood a little straighter as determination flooded through her. She'd do it one way or another. There was no choice, no alternative. She had to get to Sentinel Pass, no matter the cost. And there was only one way to start.

Her sabatons clanked as she placed one foot in front of the other and trekked through the foliage, deeper into the unknown. It was hard to believe that she had traversed the same path at daybreak. *If it was dangerous this morn, then the threat will only increase as the darkness descends.* Dying wasn't an option either.

She wandered further, casting her gaze around, wary of the slightest movement of branches, the rustle of a bush or what could be footsteps in the distance. It would be folly to let her guard down, even for a moment. Perhaps she could follow the birds? They could come and go as they pleased from this place. Out of everything potentially living here, following the birds seemed like her best hope. No doubt whatever creatures lived near the break of trees leading out, ventured no further.

But with night fast approaching, there would only be a short amount of time before the birds flew to their nests to roost. And travelling on foot would not be fast enough to keep up. Goddess damn it, she needed to find something that could traverse the forest fast and continue on to Sentinel Pass.

Adding urgency to her steps, Sabeline began tracking the few birds she could see. It was a start at least. A particular one with speckled white, brown and dark green plumage seemed aware of her, unlike the others. Sabeline had the odd feeling it knew what her purpose was as the bird stared back at her from a branch with glistening black eyes.

Suddenly, the bird pulled its head back and opened its beak wide, letting out three sharp, loud calls. The sound pierced through her and she was just about to cover her ears in case the creature started again, when a much deeper, vaguely familiar growl echoed through the trees.

Moving her hand to the handle of her blade, Sabeline wrapped her fingers around it, pulling her eyes away from the bird and directing them towards the trees instead. She knew that growl. She'd heard it only this morning.

The Sabre-Toothed Forest Panther had returned.

31

An Unexpected Battle

Sharp eyes glowing with intelligence appraised her form, while she carefully began pulling the blade from its sheath. Would it leap from the trees and go for a direct assault? Sabeline could only imagine those elongated fangs sinking into her neck or shoulder as the panther went in for the kill. She wouldn't let that happen. It was probably still furious after this morning's bout, so she wouldn't put it past the creature to take that option.

Continuing to drag the blade out, she kept her gaze fixed on the beast, just as it was doing to her. Sabeline knew this dance all too well, sizing up the opponent, taking their measure, trying to come up with a plan for every move they could make while they did the same in turn. But eventually, someone had to make the first move. *This time, it might as well be me.*

Yanking the last part of the blade free, her feet flew across the ground as the panther sprang into the air. She continued to run, ducking her head but the panther's natural foliage camouflage still brushed against her hair as it travelled above her. With haste, she turned. The panther had landed and its claws had sunk into the earth stabilising it's return to land. It whipped its head around and let out a mighty hiss. *Intimidation tactics do not work on me.*

Ignoring the hiss, she charged forward, hoping to throw the feline off balance with her unexpected move. It would need time to reassess now that it's hiss had failed, and she was counting on the delay. Sabeline did not stop as the panther continued to direct all manner of sounds towards her. As she got close, she thought she saw a flicker of fear enter the panther's eyes.

Swinging her blade, it seemed the beast in its desperation also tried to strike. Goddess damn it! Pain erupted across her arm. The damned thing had managed to get its cursed claws through her armour's weak point. Gritting her teeth, she ignored the stinging flesh and hoped in desperation the scent of her blood wouldn't attract anything else. She glanced over at the beast, who was also roaring at its shoulder. A fine strip of red glared brightly against the green and brown colouring. It seemed her strike had landed after all. She couldn't help it as one side of her lips pulled into a smirk.

They were equal near enough. That much she could tell from the blows they'd just given each other. If the battle continued for much longer, not only would it continue to waste valuable time in rescuing the Nivres, but Sabeline had a feeling it would end with either both her and the panther dead by each other's hand, or at least grievously injured to the point continuing to fight would be impossible. Neither options were acceptable. Her eyes flickered over the beast. It was a good size. And fast too. Maybe…just maybe….

There was no other choice. She was going to do it. *Goddess I hope this works.* While the beast was still distracted by its injury, Sabeline positioned herself out of its view. She only had one chance. And it wasn't going to be easy. It wasn't long before the beast turned away from its wound, no doubt trying to seek her out. Before it could search for too long, Sabeline took one step, then another, leaping into the air. *Stay still, stay still...*

With a hard thump, she crashed onto the panther's flank, sinking her fingers into its leaves and clumps of bark. The creature, no doubt feeling her weight, snapped its head round at her. Gripping tight, Sabeline hauled herself up the side while the panther repeatedly attempted to shake her off. Finally, she crawled across its back, positioning herself between the beast's shoulder blades. Perfect. It wouldn't be able to reach her with either claw or fang here.

Once again, her fingers curled around the creature's fur and foliage in a secure grip as the panther changed tactics and tried to buck her off. Sabeline hunkered down, lowering her torso so that it ran parallel against the panther's back. The feline sprinted towards the treeline, turning its body at the last moment and slamming its side into the trunk, hissing and spitting the entire time. Still she held on. It was now a battle of endurance and acceptance.

She had done this many years ago, when she had first travelled to become a knight. Part of the training had included taming wild horses. The kingdom had been in short supply after a heavy number of thoroughbreds had been stolen and this was the solution. Have the knight initiates train by taming. It would test endurance, skill, strength and determination. Well, so she and the others had been told. She had never had to use that training again in her knightly duties. Until now. *Maybe the mentors did know a thing or two....*

She noted deep pants coming from the panther as it tried slamming into a tree trunk again, only this time it was more of a half-hearted effort. Almost there. The creature flopped to the ground and she could feel the muscles beneath her relax from their tense state.

"You don't know me and I don't know you. But a dear friend of mine is in trouble and I need to get to him. You are my best bet and I'm sorry it had to be this way. But if you take me to Sentinel Pass, you can then come straight back to the forest. Do we have an accord?" It felt right to speak to the sabre-toothed forest panther. It had been a worthy opponent and even though she didn't know whether it could understand her, it deserved her respect.

The beast let out some grumbling huffs before rising to its paws, seemingly recovered enough. It turned its head back a little and Sabeline found herself meeting its gaze. Holding her breath, she waited one heartbeat, then two. The panther let out a noise akin to a meow before lowering its head again.

"I'll take that as an affirmative." She exhaled in relief. "Thank you."

The panther grumbled something back before padding through the trees. Now she was well and truly on her way.

Hold on Nivres, you idiotic lizard. I'm coming.

32

Entrapment

Nivres prided himself on one thing and one thing in particular against his opponents. He never, under any circumstances, underestimated them. Even when the Bringer of Truth had been trying to slay him, he had known if anyone were to succeed, it would have been her. He had grown to love her tenacity, even more so now it was no longer directed at seeing him bleed out under her blade.

The Chaos Convocation had murdered his sister, dear sweet Myvanna. He knew what they were capable of. The members were nothing but filth, driven by greed and a lust for violence and suffering. Over time, as he fulfilled his oath, the organisation had named him Chaos's Bane, with very few survivors of his assaults spreading the word of a man who could control fire. He preferred it that way. Let them underestimate *him*. No doubt they had come to their own conclusions about his motivations and what he was. But he had been prolific enough to garner a reputation amongst the scum.

That was probably the reason why he was currently locked

in chains within the Leader's dungeon.

Gritting his fangs together, he tried to pull his arms downward, but the heavy, iron shackles around his wrists tightened around his flesh. Glaring upwards, he caught the glow of ancient runes blazing across the cuffs before disappearing once more. A sneer etched it's way onto his lips while a growl rumbled within his chest. How could he have let this happen?

He was a dragon, goddess damn it! He was supposed to sense an ambush before it happened and leave them all in a blaze. But this time…this time his thoughts had been elsewhere.

His head hung, chains rattling at the movement (they'd taken the liberty of collaring him like a dog against the wall, for which they'd pay), as a sigh breathed past his fangs. The Bringer of Truth had haunted his thoughts. The deception he'd engaged in, it was all for her safety. A necessary endeavour to ensure she didn't fall before his eyes, while he was unable to do anything, unable to move, to *get* to her as she suffered. Not again. The fact she'd still not been at full strength only fueled the desire to keep that nightmarish image from becoming a reality. His eyes clenched shut before he opened them to greet the gloom again. How she must hate him for what he'd done.

And despite it all, he'd been missing her as he'd infiltrated the Sentinel Pass settlement. Missing her logic, her planning, her capability. Missing her company, missing knowing she'd have his back. He'd longed for her presence beside him, ready to begin the slaughter together. But he was wholly to blame for her absence. Nivres huffed once, without humour. And look where his great plan had gotten him. Captured and trussed up in some scum's dungeon.

He could only imagine what Sabeline would say or think if she saw him now. The image of her, in full armour and brandishing a blood soaked blade while she stood before him, no doubt with fury burning in her eyes, warmed his heart and a sense of comfort flooded through his blood. He'd never expected to fall in love with a warrior maiden, much less one that had dedicated herself to ending his existence, but it was undeniable. As certain as the moon rose and the sun set, he loved Sabeline, The Bringer of Truth.

He would take her ire, her anger, her fury. He deserved it after his deceit. She had been right, no matter the circumstances, they were better going into battle together, rather than alone. He would not leave her behind again. That is, if she would want to see him again after all this.

The ominous sound of a heavy set door opening drew him out of his melancholy. Raising his head, Nivres's mouth set into a hard line and he positioned himself as straight and tall as the infernal chains would allow. Whoever this was, he would not give them the satisfaction of seeing him so defeated. Defiance would rule.

The cacophony of footsteps reached his ears. More than one then, wasn't he a lucky dragon? At least they hadn't figured that part out yet. A clear testament to their stupidity if there ever was one. Within moments, a figure flanked by two others appeared before him. Both humans on the left and right were dressed in blue robes. Interesting. So there were two second in commands here. Which meant the one in the middle had to be…

"Chaos's Bane." A self-assured, distinctly feminine voice echoed. "How nice of you to pay us a visit."

His golden eyes narrowed as the middle figure grasped her hood, pulling it from her head. She was pale-skinned, with hair like spun gold. And a hard glint to her eyes that gave the impression she had seen too much too soon. It was that above all else that caused his skin to prickle. Whoever this Leader was, she controlled the Sentinel Pass settlement and that wasn't something to be taken lightly.

She kept her eyes on him. Did she think that would unnerve him? Please. He was a dragon, it would take more than an appraising look to make him break.

"It's polite to respond." She grinned.

He'd humour her. "You didn't ask a question and said nothing of worth that warranted a response."

The grin slipped enough for him to notice, before she slapped it back on her lips in full force. Idly he wondered what her speciality was. She was confident enough to stand before the man that controlled fire after all. Then again, her confidence might have been from the fact he was shackled and could hardly move.

"True enough. You'll have to forgive my impertinence, I just can't believe I have the great Bane himself at my mercy." She said with happiness, though there was an edge to her words. An edge that promised something unpleasant.

"How can you be so sure it is not the other way around? Perhaps this is all a part of my master plan." Nivres returned, hoping the lie would unsettle her.

Instead the damned woman laughed. "Not many plans end up with the saboteur himself caught and locked in rune enchanted chains. These were made by a friend of mine, a sorcerer. Though I heard you lit him and his settlement up a few nights ago. Fitting then, that his magical signature prevents your escape." The woman walked forward, leaning over slowly, she plucked one of the chains causing it to glow and dim. It was unfortunate she hadn't come closer. He'd have sunk his fangs into her flesh and bathed in her blood.

She carried on speaking, as if oblivious to all the ways he was concocting killing her. "Oh how I've waited for this day Chaos's Bane. I admit I thought it would have been much more difficult to have you at my feet. But perhaps we were lucky and you weren't at your best, hmm?"

Nivres couldn't help the roar that ripped through him, though the..the…vile pondscum of a woman before him was unaffected.

"That's what I thought." She smirked, "Well no matter, what's done is done. Gives me more of a chance to savour the moment, take my time. Works to my advantage really."

"What are you talking about?" Nivres spat. She was starting to test his patience.

"And they said you were intelligent. Let me make it clear to you, I'm going to do everything you've done. You've destroyed our settlements, our takings, our hauls and our numbers. I'm going to destroy *you*. And the best part? I can burn too."

With that, the woman reached out, wrapping her fingers around the bare part of his arm she could reach. Nivres fought the urge to shudder in disgust, until an all consuming coldness like ice spread across the flesh she was touching. It was unrelenting, never spreading, just entirely focused on the point beneath the pondscum's awful grip. It was so cold that it felt as if it was burning. But that was preposterous, he'd never been burned by anything in his life…

The pondscum released her grip and with it, the cold sensation disappeared. She had the audacity to step back and shoot him a winning smirk. "Not bad, don't you think?"

Still glaring, Nivres snapped his head to the side, gaze falling on the arm she'd done something to. Wait, that couldn't be right…the skin was red. Bright red and the air felt like it was tormenting him further each time it caressed the area. Had it…had it *blistered* in places?

"What have you done witch?" He whipped his head back to face her and her perfectly smug expression. The dragon decided then and there that as soon as he broke free, he'd rip that look right off her face with his talons.

"Oh, so close. Not a witch I'm afraid." The pondscum held her hand out, palm up. Where there was nothing, a hefty ball of ice began to form above it. Nivres figured out her intentions at the last moment, quickly moving his head. The ice ball shattered a hairsbreadth next to his cheek.

"Damn," The pondscum pouted, "Missed." Another ice ball started to form; this time bigger than its predecessor. "Oh well, we're just getting started."

33

Calm Before the Storm

The muscles and bracken moved in perfect rhythm under her hands as the forest panther raced across the land. The only sounds that had accompanied them were the panther's paws thudding over dirt paths and the occasional heavy pant. It was strange to traverse the land as she once did, without solely being dropped off into towns and settlements by Nivres.

Nivres. It had been far too long. Sabeline cast her gaze upwards again, as she'd done so many times on this journey that she no longer counted. Each time she'd hoped for a flash of crimson, a scarlet streak against the now darkened sky. But alas, no such luck. And with each failed sighting, the worry churned in her gut.

Something's not right. Both her and the panther were getting closer to Sentinel Pass and the lack of ash on the wind or crackling heat in the distance caused her eyes to narrow. Goddess damn him! Fury blazed brighter than any fire, burning away the worry momentarily as Sabeline gritted her teeth. She knew it. She knew the dragon shouldn't have gone without her. Now here she was, on a forest panther she'd corralled and travelling for hours to save him from whatever mess he'd ended up in. She was sure that this time Nivres had bitten off more than he could chew. The main question plaguing her was just how much.

"Almost there." She murmured with softness to the panther. It gave a huff in return, which she took to mean *thank the goddess*. The ground thundered as the beast increased its pace and Sabeline curled her fingers tighter around the branch like sinews near its shoulder blades.

It wasn't long before wooden structures appeared on the horizon, haphazard towers and buildings cobbled together from whatever had been to hand, much like the previous Chaos Convocation Settlement. Lights flickered in the odd openings resembling windows and Sabeline could just about see flickering lanterns spread across a wide area. *How am I supposed to find him in this place?* Even from this distance, the sheer size was unnerving.

Only a few minutes more and the panther slowed before coming to a stop at the ridge. Here they were close, but not close enough to be detected by the guards Sabeline noted scurrying around the gate. *By the goddess.* How had such a place gone undetected? She could understand the smaller settlements slipping past Falon's ever watchful gaze, but this? This was a city. A fully functioning city built by thieves, assassins and other unscrupulous scum. And somewhere within was her dragon.

Wait a minute, her dragon? Where had that notion come from? Despite his declaration, he wasn't hers. *Not yet at least...* Shaking her head and vehemently ignoring that last thought, she released her grip and carefully manoeuvred her legs, sliding off the beast in a hurried dismount. "Thank you for bringing me here." She uttered, placing one hand back on the panther's shoulder.

Sabeline drew in a deep breath before releasing it, while keeping her eyes on the gate. "You can head on home; you've done enough for me today. I will either come out of this place riding a dragon, or not come out at all."

The sabre-toothed forest panther let out a soft whine and she turned her head, meeting its soulful gaze. "It is alright, my fate will be defined here. I can feel it. Neither I, you, or the goddess herself can change that. We took each other on though, did we not? And we were both worthy opponents." Sabeline managed to quirk her lips at the panther, and it looked somewhat reassured. "If I survive, I will find you in the forest. You have my word."

With that, she let her hand fall from the beast. The panther placed one front paw to the side and then another before turning and padding quietly away from her. *At least if nothing else, my worthiest foe will be alive.* It would have done no good to drag the panther into her fight. It belonged to the forest, the foliage and all things green and earth. Whereas she belonged here. Staring down a Chaos Convocation city as her sword hummed for bloodshed.

The familiar anticipation of battle crept along her bones and ever so gently, she let her hand rest on the hilt of her blade. She had not lied to the panther when she had spoken about fate. It was an almost tangible thing before her, but still unseen to her eyes. *If only Echoris were here, she would be able to divine what fate awaits me.* Perhaps it was better not to know. There would be no risk of overconfidence or no shadow lingering at the back of her mind. She would take everything as it was meant to be. And for a knight, that would mean head on and without mercy.

Sabeline curled her fingers tighter around the hilt, just as a great roaring cry shook the air and split the stillness of the night. Her mouth dropped open in a gasp, as her fevered blood cooled to snow. Her stomach became a cavernous pit, in which a great weight suddenly sat. That cry, no mortal could conjure a sound so thunderous. *Nivres.* What were they doing to him?

Swallowing the bile that had risen in her mouth, Sabeline drew in a deep, shaking breath. Her instincts were screaming at her to run down the ridge and slaughter everyone and everything she came across, but she tampered them down. What good would she be to Nivres if she died at the gate? No, in order to save him, she would have to apply logic.

Watching. Waiting. Finding the patterns in the guards' movements and observing points of the Sentinel Pass city for a short while. That should give her enough of an advantage. And she would do it, so that they would both survive.

Even though the next agonised, otherworldly scream reached the heavens and caused a tear to fall down her cheek.

34

Silent Death

The stars were high by the time Sabeline felt confidence strum under her skin at the patterns she'd been able to ascertain from her vantage point. *This has taken too long.* The thought caused her to grit her teeth. The dragon's screams had long grown hoarse and each one had been like a dagger plunged into her heart.

But now the time was upon her. Rising from her crouch, she edged down the narrow ravine. A wince etched its way onto her face every time the slightest pebble dislodged and rolled from under her feet. It would be just her luck to get caught before she'd even stepped through the gate. Then who would save Nivres? No. She could not let such thoughts allow to despair to creep into her soul. She would save Nivres. And when she did, by the goddess, she'd throttle him for going off on this ridiculous plan without her. Because he had to be alright. She was no fool, no creature made a sound like that unless they were in great agony. But as long as he was alive, there was still a chance. And a chance was all she needed.

Using the night as cover and sticking to where the shadows

lay thickest, Sabeline continued to traverse the steep decline. A grudging respect welled within her. Whoever was the Leader here had an eye for strategy. Fortifying defences by embedding a city within this rough landscape was a clever move. *If the Sentinel Pass Leader is able to construct to their advantage, then I must ensure absolute caution. Anything could lie in wait beyond the gate.* She had the feeling that the sorcerer had been an easy win compared to this place.

Finally, she was close enough. Shuffling behind a large rock, Sabeline waited, keeping her gaze on the two guards stationed just ahead to the side of her. The glow of lanterns affixed to the wall bathed them in a yellow light, giving her the perfect view. They would change in a few moments, she was sure, but this would give her ample time to inspect their armour for any weak points. It was crude armour, mainly leather and chainmail. Her blade would do its work before they could even get through the metal plating that adorned her form. Her lips twitched as the familiar anticipation of battle began to sing in her veins. This would be quick. Then all she had to do was slip in, find Nivres and get them both out of this damned place. Or die trying.

The sound of footsteps caught her attention and Sabeline flicked her gaze to the sides. Ah, here they were. Right on time. Remaining hidden, the guards changed over without much fuss or preamble. Excellent. Now the previous guards would advise command the changeover was smooth and it would be a long time yet before the change would happen again. With care, she wrapped her fingertips around the hilt of her blade and gently withdrew it from the scabbard. Feeling its weight in her hand was a comfort. Taking in one deep breath, Sabeline slowly released it. *Now or never.*

Slipping out from behind the rock, she ignored the slight pang of fear at being out in the open, making sure to stay downwind. Keeping her footsteps light, Sabeline continued ever closer. She could use the shadows to her advantage but those lanterns, they would be a problem. As soon as she was within their glow, she would have to act fast. At least the guards had remained still in their vigilance. They had kept their faces forward, they would not see her coming from the side. *Thank the goddess.*

Sabeline took another step. Then another. She was a hair's breadth away, positioned just outside the lantern's light. Tightening her grip on the hilt, she twisted the blade in her hand. Her dragon lay beyond the gate and these two were in her way. Eyes narrowed, Sabeline darted behind the first guard and before he could even blink, she plunged her blade upwards into the back of his chest. It was quick, clean and probably a better death than any member of the Chaos Convocation deserved. She waited until his body was limp before pulling her sword free from the flesh and leather. *This is what you get when you do not invest in good armour.* Perhaps she would be in luck and all within the city would be clad in similar, easy to slice through garments.

The body fell with a thump once the last part of her blade was free and she grit her teeth. The sound would not be missed by the other guard. She had to move. Now. Losing no time, she sped forward, almost colliding with the guard who was making their way towards her location. The image of crimson scales and golden eyes danced across her mind. Fresh fury and determination pounded through her with every heartbeat. Her eyes focused on the exposed neck of the guard and with one clean swipe, she despatched his head from his shoulders. Blood began to pool across the ground where the two parts landed.

Sabeline remained still for a moment, breaths coming out in a quick pant. That was the easy part. Closing her eyes, she briefly let the vision of a scarlet dragon surrounded by flames dance under her eyelids. Opening them once more, she headed towards the gate, cutting through the weak chain that acted as a barrier and heaved the wooden structure aside, just enough so she could edge through.

Hold on Nivres. I am coming. And nothing and no one was going to get in her way.

Ramshackle but sturdy buildings opened up before her, reminiscent of jaws widening. *This place will swallow me whole if I let it.* Each flickering flame of the lanterns traversing the area seemed ominous against the silence she found herself in. It would not do to dwell here for too long. Stepping forward, she let the darkness cover her as she stood against one of the wooden walls.

It seemed even though she had entered through the main gate, this part of the cobbled together city was considered the outskirts. Letting her gaze wander over the buildings surrounding her like jagged fangs, Sabeline noted that these were simple. Most were made of whatever wood had apparently been available and the rooftops constructed of cheaper materials like grasses and hays. Good for keeping the rain out, but it offered little else in terms of luxury.

It would be foolish to dally here too long. The place had an eerie feeling to it, as if an ambush could take place and the surroundings would not be disturbed. Maybe that was the intention. After all, the silence almost seemed unnatural the longer she stood. Flicking her gaze to the rooftops and then the nooks and crannies nearby, no silhouettes or figures were poised ready to strike her. *By the Goddess, please let it remain like this until I reach the Leader's residence.* It was an unlikely wish, but she hoped the Goddess heard her plea. The quicker she reached Nivres, the better.

Determination fluttered through her once more. As much as she had detested hearing the dragon's cries, as much as each one had pained her, there was one thing she could cling to upon hearing that heart wrenching sound. Nivres was *alive*. And she was going to drag the damn dragon out of here by his tail if she had to. Darting forward, Sabeline weaved amongst the surrounding shadows, taking care to avoid any pathways that looked like they would be in regular use.

She had expected to encounter the odd wanderer on her travels, despite the late hour. Surely, they did not just guard the main gate and leave the rest unattended? From what she'd gathered so far, she did not think so. This leader, whoever they were, would not be so lax in their judgement. So where were these members? Even in the small settlement they had secured victory against, there had been many residents still up and about. A city such as this? She should have seen someone else by now.

Keeping a rein on the growing suspicions and rising fears within her, Sabeline continued on. She could not let such feelings consume her, not when Nivres still drew breath. Perhaps these parts had reduced patrols at this time. Maybe they kept the focus towards the centre, the more fortified and protected part. *Because that is where their treasures are kept*, the thought caused disgust to swell within her like the tide before it retreated as fast as it had begun. *Treasures like Nivres, Chaos's Bane.*

By the goddess, why had she not thought of it before? To have captured Chaos's Bane, would that not be a crowning achievement to brag about? To call all members to see that this settlement had captured the being that had plagued their organisation for so long? Nausea echoed in her stomach the more she saw the logic of such thoughts. The screaming of the dragon, she had assumed, had been at the hands of the Leader, and perhaps it had been. But what if…what if they had then given Nivres over to the city? Hundreds if not thousands of furious, skilled people without morals bearing down on the being with vengence in their hearts for lost members, settlements and of course, gold and valuables.

Swallowing down the bile rising in her throat, her feet flew across the ground of their own accord, little clouds of dust swirling into the air with each step before disappearing into the night. If anyone appeared in front of her now, she would cut them down without hesitation. Only one all-consuming objective pounded through her soul in perfect rhythm with her frantic heart. *Find Nivres. Find him now.*

She did not know how long it had been since fear had taken hold of her actions, but another quick glance at her surroundings revealed the buildings were slightly changing. These ones seemed sturdier, made of stone and wood while the rooftops were interwoven with tiles of pottery and metal. *I must be getting close.* Still no figures emerged from their hiding places, no one lay in wait to ambush her. Slowing her steps, Sabeline wandered forward with caution. Entering a new area of the city could mean that different rules were in force here. The first one that sprang forth in her mind was an increased patrol.

Ducking around a small corner, a clattering up ahead caused

her to still. Her fingers itched to raise her blade, but if her movement was spotted, everything would be undone. Refusing to let out a breath, her gaze detected two men at the other end of the path. One had fallen, various items spilled around him. Items that shone and sparkled under the dim lantern flames. Sabeline watched as the other pulled his companion to his feet, both of them hurriedly gathering their haul. Words floated on the air and she strained her ears to hear their murmurings.

"Of course you would fall. We didn't grab all this stuff for you to damage it on the way to the arena!"

"I'm sorry alright? I was in a rush. Chaos's Bane, can you believe it?"

"I'd believe it a lot faster if we could get there!"

"Right, right. That's all of it. Come on, let's go!"

The men dashed off but were still slowed by their overloaded arms. They would be extra careful now not to drop anything, Sabeline mused. And what of this arena they had spoken of? Was it an actual arena, or the name given to a particular area? Either way, they had mentioned Nivres. Whatever this arena was, she had to get to it and soon. Her dragon may not have been turned over to the masses as she had previously thought, but if it was becoming common knowledge he was here, it may not be long until her vision became reality.

Slipping out of her hiding place, she peered around the right of the building. As predicted, the men had not gotten too far despite their eagerness, but far enough that she would be reasonably safe. Emerging from the wall, Sabeline followed. These fools would unknowingly take her to Nivres.

And if luck remained on her side, a Leader who would not

know death was coming until it was too late.

35

The Arena

Around her, the buildings shifted once more as she kept the Chaos Convocation fools in sight. Now constructions made of brick and mortar, strong against attacks, caused wariness to creep within her. She did not miss the fact that some of the architecture resembled watchtowers.

She had to be entering the heart of Sentinel Pass City. And a heart would be the most fortified and heavily guarded place of all. Sabeline suppressed the urge to lay a hand over her own at the thought.

Staying amongst the shadows, she continued to weave deeper into this vile place. Thankfully, the fools ahead of her never noticed her presence. *They are either aware and leading me to a trap or they are truly incompetent amongst familiar surroundings.* A loud clang as one of the men lost their grip on a golden vessel and plate echoed through the pathway, causing her to duck down while they scrambled to pick it up again. If they were pretending to be imbeciles, then their skills were unparalleled.

Wisps of conversation drifted on the wind as Sabeline kept her gaze roaming for any guards, warriors or archers that had been left behind from whatever was happening at the arena. If she strained her ears, she could make out some of the sentences shared between the two men.

"Do you think she really has him?"

"Only one way to find out. But about this, I don't think she'd lie."

"Or pull everyone in to see."

"True. Knowing her, it's going to be quite the show."

"Finally, Chaos's Bane will suffer for what he's done."

"Did you not hear the screaming on the way in? He's already suffering. I hope she shows him to us beaten and bloody."

Sabeline gritted her teeth as her fingers curled into her palm, forming a tense fist while the other flexed around the hilt of her blade. The fury pounding through her like the drums of war begged her to run forward and dispatch the two idiots for dishonouring her dragon in that manner. The sounds that had tortured her for half the night had caused them glee. Glee! *Before I am done, this whole place will feel my wrath.* Because she had one advantage. Nivres's reputation preceded him, but they had little if any idea that he was no longer alone. They would not be expecting her to steal him away, but that was just what she was going to do. Or die trying.

If there was one good thing from the snatches of conversation she could pick up, it was that they had referred to a "she." That had been intoned with respect, so either this "she" was the Leader or at least their second in command. She would find out soon enough, as it seemed she was following them to the looming construction just up ahead. All at once, it appeared well crafted but also cobbled together. Its silhouette was strange to the eye and it appeared more curved than anything. Sabeline unclenched her fist but kept a tight hold on her blade.

It was not much longer before she arrived at the structure and the two men disappeared into a large archway decorated with glowing lamps. While before the place had been eerily quiet, chatter, shouting and cheers emanated from the same archway. This had to be the arena. Though from the height and smoothness of the walls and lack of any other entrance, it appeared she had no choice but to enter through the same archway. At least she could disappear in the apparent crowd and perhaps if she stayed near the back, little notice would be taken of her.

Taking a deep breath, Sabeline closed her eyes, feeling resolve settle into her bones. She was so close. She was sure of it. Now was the time to define her own fate because she had a feeling that whatever waited for her beyond the archway, would change everything. Slowly, she let out the same breath and snapped open her eyelids. The archway called to her and without any more hesitation, she stepped through.

More lamps lit the way from their hung positions on the wall. Apart from that, there was little else in here. It was essentially a tunnel and nothing more. No hidden secrets. No traps. Steadily, her steps ascended into a run. The cool air of the night caressed her face as she emerged from the tunnel.

She was in a circular space which was surrounded by flickering fire poles in order to cast light onto the gathering. Flicking her eyes upwards, there was no roof to speak of, though she could not think why the arena would be designed in such a way. However, the main thing that greeted her vision was hundreds, if not thousands of rowdy people, dressed in various attire from armour to robes. Sabeline could already detect many of them were carrying several weapons on their bodies. Instead of taking up space across the arena, everyone appeared to be jostling or attempting to get closer to some kind of wooden platform. Even though the platform was raised in the centre, the people around her wanted to be at the very front.

If that was the place of importance, then that was where she must head. Sticking to the edges of the crowd, she edged as close as she dared to the platform. All it would take was one person to gaze at her for a second too long for them to realise she didn't belong here. The wooden floor was currently empty, but from the crowd's growing impatience, she imagined that was going to change shortly.

Sabeline kept her gaze steady as a hooded figure seemed to materialise out of the air, flanked by two others stepping on to the platform. Around her, the congregation of chaos erupted into deafening cheers and she winced at the onslaught to her ears. These figures were important then. Perhaps even the Leader themselves or this mysterious "she". The main hooded figure raised their arms and a hush descended, almost akin to dousing a candle flame. Once there was utter silence, the figure yelled one, jubilant sentence.

"Chaos Convocation of Sentinel Pass, I give you, Chaos's Bane!"

A shape was then unceremoniously thrown onto the wooden platform, procured by the two other figures. The sound of cheering immediately resumed, loud enough that even the Goddess herself was no doubt covering her ears. But Sabeline's voice remained silent as her eyes widened at the form on the wooden floor, bound by the wrists behind and at the ankles with biting, awful shackles.

One half whispered half breathed word left her lips, lost in the sea of overwhelming elation surrounding her.

"Nivres."

By the Goddess, what had they done to him? He was no mortal man, Nivres could take much more than expected. She could attest to that. He had always evaded her in the past, always took whatever attack she could throw his way and carried on as if her efforts were nothing. But this? From what Sabeline could see before her, the Chaos Convocation had poured every ounce of malice, ill intent and bloodlust onto her dragon.

Her dragon. She did not know when her mind had begun to think of him as such, without effort or further analysis. But as she continued to gaze in horror at his form, her heart throbbed painfully in her chest. There was no denying anymore. He was hers. It had just taken her this long to realise.

Swallowing hard, her eyes remained fixed on Nivres. The shackles she had noticed a few moments ago now seemed strange under her scrutiny. Yes, they were normal in shape and size, although perhaps thicker and with heavier chains but that wasn't what set them apart. Were those rune marks etched into the metal? Whatever they were, they were not written in the common tongue and they seemed to emanate a soft glow. Subtle but not imperceptible. *Curious.* She had a feeling that to save the dragon, she would need to unravel the secrets of those chains. He was bound in them for a reason and no matter how much she feared the answer, she would uncover it. There was no other choice.

Sucking in a deep breath, Sabeline moved her gaze away from the shackles. Reluctance hummed within her but she had to see. She had to know what her time had cost him. Was she a stranger to grievous injuries? No. She had seen many a man and woman succumbing to wounds on the battlefield or clinging to life even when it seemed impossible. She had sustained and survived a fair share herself. But this? This was not inflicted as a matter of honour. It had been cruel, merciless and unrelenting.

Dark wells of crimson were caked to the shackles and parts of it were flaking where the skin met metal. More scarlet streaks decorated his flesh, some dry like a mockery of war paint and others still fresh and bright. His chest still rose and fell thank the goddess, but his breaths appeared laboured. She did not want to contemplate how many bruises were potentially decorating his ribs. His golden eyes narrowed at all before him, shimmering with rage and pain. *They have not broken his spirit, not yet.* It was something she could hold onto at least. Some small piece of hope that she could still get them out of this goddess forsaken place alive.

The jubilant roars of the crowd came flooding back into her awareness. Maybe if she could cause a distraction, she could sneak around and grab Nivres before anyone knew? Foolish perhaps, but she could see no other option. Yes, she could wait and see if the Leaders dragged him off somewhere, before sneaking in but that would cost more time. And from his current state, Sabeline did not think her dragon would survive being subjected to another torture session. She would have to be quick and cunning.

She took one step before Nivres's lips curled into a cruel smirk. Then those lips parted and flames erupted in a concentrated ball of twisting fire below. The shock of the assembled members and Nivres's expression of satisfaction caused the same feeling to spread within her. Her dragon was sending a clear message, one she knew well. Never underestimate your enemy.

Without knowing it, he had provided the perfect distraction, now all she had to do was… A hissing sound pierced through the air and a silence drew over the crowd at the noise. A white plume had descended and with it a chill that even Sabeline could feel on the fringes of the gathering. After a few more seconds, Nivres's glorious flames had been doused, smothered by the overbearing chill. She managed to catch a glimpse of the ground, only to be met with scorch marks covered in glistening frost. Ice. They had poured ice over the flames. But how…

Snapping her head back up to the platform, the mist cleared to reveal the main hooded figure, arm still outstretched with splayed fingers coated in hard shards of sparkling ice. They peered over the platform and seemingly satisfied, turned their attention to her dragon. Goddess damn it, she had thought the sorcerer was bad. But to take down a…

All thoughts flew out of her head as the Leader grabbed Nivres by his bloodied garments and yanked him up. Sabeline caught defiance in his gaze before a resounding smack echoed through the quiet and Nivres's head snapped to the side. *Rage.* It rolled through her like a storm, consuming everything in its wake. How dare such filth torture her beast? How dare this… this…*troll* show him the ultimate disrespect? There was truly no honour here. She would feel nothing by destroying every last acre of this city. Starting with the arena.

Keeping a grip on her blade, she stepped forward letting

calm words flow from her lips, but ensuring there was an edge to them, a promise and threat all rolled into one. And she was going to make sure this entire band of filth heard her roar.

"Do that again and I'll be sure to remove your hand from your arm."

36

Standing Ground

She stood her ground as the Leader dropped Nivres as if he was nothing, before turning their hooded attention her way. Were they so much of a coward they refused to show their face? Pressing her lips into a thin line, Sabeline kept her gaze narrowed. She did not dare flicker her focus towards Nivres, even for a moment. If the Leader picked up on her movements, they could possibly use the dragon to carve out her vulnerabilities. And from the state of him, Nivres had already been through enough. *I refuse to let him endure anymore.*

The Leader's steps were measured as they walked towards the edge. Methodical. Confident. Still Sabeline stood her ground. "And who are you, to command me?" The words were a sneer, she could sense the disgust rolling through them. So, this Leader wasn't used to their authority being challenged. Interesting. Maybe they had been up in their ramshackle residence too long, giving orders from on high. Sabeline resisted the urge to snort. She would cut them down to size.

"The Bane of your Bane. Now let him go." Her hands tilted

the sword upwards slightly, a clear signal she would follow through on her threat. She had no doubt this Leader was intelligent enough to pick up on her cues.

"So, Chaos's Bane has picked up an accomplice since our last known reports. And you really think you can get him from our clutches? Ready to swoop in and save him? What a foolish woman you are. You can abandon hope now."

"I don't think so. I came for Chaos's Bane and I'm leaving with him. If you hand him over now, I give you my oath I won't raze this place to the ground and slaughter everybody standing here. Your choice." She refused to let this Leader get under her skin. Anger and fury were good motivators, but too much and they hindered battle more than helped. And this was a fight she couldn't afford to lose.

Though the features were still obscured, Sabeline thought the Leader almost seemed affronted. As if they couldn't believe the impertinence of her to talk back, let alone voice a threat. The crowd were still as silent as the grave, but the air was split by a high pitched, distinctly feminine cackle.

"You really are a fool. I'll give you my word instead, considering yours is mere folly. How about you die first? It'll spare you the pain of watching me kill Chaos's Bane slowly and painfully. It also means I get to torture him a little more when he watches the life leave your eyes. What do you say?"

This Leader underestimates, and it will be her undoing. Swirling her sword a few times, Sabeline caused those that had encroached a bit closer at their Leader's proclamation to shuffle back once more. "Alright. But as you have refused to hand him over, I would like you to note that I'll keep my oath." She ensured this was said in a calm, matter of fact tone. At least she had offered them a chance. Her honour was still intact if they refused and didn't believe her.

A sliver of delight danced within her as Sabeline watched the Leader gather themselves. Her calm confidence was getting to them, sowing the seeds of doubt. The first strike had been made. *The advantage goes to me.*

"One of the greatest evils of this world is holding onto hope in the face of overwhelming defeat." The Leader moved just enough so that Sabeline could see a smirk adorning pale lips, before they raised their voice to address the crowd. "Ladies and Gentleman, this hero has chosen death. Make sure she begs for the goddess to take her well before her heart stops beating."

A deafening roar and the clanging of various weapons being pulled or strung filled her ears. Amidst the eager, blood baying chants, a different voice cut through the vile cacophony. A voice that had been quiet until now. A voice she would know anywhere.

"Sabeline! Sabeline, run! You cannot secure a victory against this many. Please. I do not wish you to die for my mistake."

She let her eyes flicker over to her dragon. Those words had taken effort to speak, the rise and fall of his chest was once again erratic as he sucked in lungfuls of air. But those golden eyes. They were large, desperate, imploring and held her own for several seconds. Her heart missed a beat. After this was done, she would tell him. Tell him that despite everything, she loved him. Goddess dammit, he had set fire to her heart and had made his home there, nestled in the warmth.

He knew as well as she that there was no running. Even if she did, they would still chase her, hunt her down. And for how long? Days? Months? Years? That was no way to live.

No, she needed to put a stop to this tonight. "Do not worry Chaos's Bane. I have no intention of dying here." With that, she forced her attention towards the bloodthirsty crowd and moved into a defensive stance, raising her blade in front of her.

"Whoever draws the first blood gets to keep the largest treasure from the next raid." The Leader announced with unbridled glee. Damn them. It was just as she'd thought, this one was skilled in strategy.

Out of the corner of her eye, Sabeline caught a glimpse of a flash from her right. Dropping down, the swoosh of an axe breezed over the top of her head, close enough that she'd felt the weapon just miss strands of hair. Instead of rising to her feet, she swiped her blade into the assailant's shin. A scream echoed above her as she yanked the blade out of the flesh, leaving a deep crimson wound. The assailant crumpled to the ground beside her as Sabeline rose to her full height.

"Who would like to go next?"

The eagerness of the assembled members appeared to ebb slightly; no doubt due to the ongoing screams of agony next to her. Perhaps she had gone deeper than intended with her strike, but she cared not. *No doubt that that is only a fraction of what Nivres has endured.* Though her actions had given the members pause. They were hesitating.

Hesitation could cost your life. You either did something or didn't on the field of battle. It was another lesson that had been constantly reiterated to training knights and one of the most important. Hesitation would be the Chaos Convocation's last mistake. Before they could gather themselves enough to land a strike, Sabeline adjusted her stance and ploughed forward.

Her sword cut into flesh and snagged on bone. Scarlet drops decorated her armour and adorned her face like war paint before too long. The metal of her blade was now gleaming red, a river of it running down over the hilt and her fingers before dripping to the ground, leaving a macabre trail everywhere she stepped. She was no fool, despite what the Leader wanted to believe. Their shock had given her the advantage and momentum, but it would not last. The rest of the arena would at this moment, no doubt be considering the best way to kill her and they would not be so shy. A smirk pulled at her lips as she ran her blade through an archer's chest as they tried to get to higher ground. At least she would have the satisfaction of taking a portion of their members down. Yanking the blade out and kicking the body to the floor, Sabeline turned.

Only for pain to explode across the left side of her face, radiating from a point on her cheekbone. Snapping her gaze back, she was met with the visage of a large, gruff man, head back in laughter as weathered, heavy iron gauntlets encased his hands and part of his arms. No wonder her face was pounding. Those things were ridged too, for maximum damage. Dammit, her face was going to be bruised for days.

A sound akin to a snarl left her mouth as a metallic tang touched her tongue. Goddess curse him, those things had drawn blood. She'd put a stop to that laughter if it was the last thing she did. Tilting her head back, Sabeline aimed and spat a dark spray straight at the man's face.

It was something to behold, a warrior who thought themselves formidable being affronted by her spittle. Sabeline let a cruel smile etch it's way onto her lips. "There are no rules in war. You should know this by now."

"Then you won't mind another beating!" The man roared,

letting a fist fly. Thanks to his warning this time, Sabeline moved back, eyes following the trajectory of the punch as it harmlessly swiped across the air inches away from her face.

"If that is what you call a beating, then no, not at all."

She watched as his lips twisted in displeasure and the grit of his teeth before he came flying at her again. This time, she followed her earlier tactic. As the gauntlet laced fist barrelled towards her, Sabeline dropped down, keeping her grip tight on her blade as she swung it towards his shins. Instead of sinking deep into flesh and sinew, the metal clanged and the impact reverberated down the blade and through her fingers. Above her, a satisfied laugh echoed.

"You think you can get the best of me? Don't you know who I am? They call me The Blacksmith because both my hands and legs are protected by gauntlets and sabatons the likes of which you've never seen!"

"Your reputation must be awful indeed, because I've never heard of you." She rolled to the side as a punch tried to incapacitate her from above. *Just his hands and shins he said. That means everywhere else is unprotected.* She wouldn't get near his chest, not with him flinging his fists to protect it. But the legs…

The Blacksmith dragged his fist from the ground, thus removing any obstacle in her way. Bending her knees and digging her feet into the ground, Sabeline leapt from her crouched position with all the force she could muster. She briefly caught a glimpse of another punch being aimed her way. *Good. That will work to my advantage.* The Blacksmith stepped forward to better target her, just as the deafening sound of colliding metal filled the air. Staying crouched, Sabeline raised her hands to cover her head. Something large, heavy and egotistical tumbled over the top of her and she could feel the weight drag and pull across her armour as it fell.

A monumental thud came from her right. With care, Sabeline rose to her feet, taking one step and the another before surveying the sight before her. The Blacksmith was groaning, face down in the dirt. She took another step onto his back, making sure she pressed down hard. A muffled, pained moan emanated from the ground. "I was right then. Your reputation is worth nothing." With those solemn words, Sabeline narrowed her eyes and in one perfectly executed move, sunk her blade into The Blacksmith's back.

With a sneer, she yanked her weapon free, watching until the body went still. How many was that now? How much blood stained her armour? But she would not stop. These people had kept her dragon in captivity, laughed and cheered at his torture. If she were to die here, at least she would take her last breath knowing she'd significantly decreased their numbers. And if they were to succeed in their attempts, at least there were worse reasons to die than for love.

Pain once again appeared at the forefront of her mind as it pounded a rhythm across her cheek. The blood had stopped running at least and she could feel the trails stuck and dried to her skin. It would look worse than it was. Hopefully. Something ricocheted off her right pauldron, drawing her from her thoughts. Glancing to the side, Sabeline was met with a sleek, well-crafted arrow.

Damnation. Turning her head, her eyes landed on the archers. They had managed to get to higher ground before she could prevent them from doing so. Several of them were positioned amongst what appeared to be an audience area.

While the outer wall was smooth stone, the inner benches, floors and steps were crafted from wood. The different levels and benches gave the archers good cover, better range and overall, made it harder to get or aim anything back at them.

Their first arrow had glanced off her pauldron. The next one might make it through her head. She did not want to risk that, which left only one option. She had to go after them. Archers were fantastic long-range fighters, but up close, they were at a disadvantage. Mariel had known such a thing, which was why even though a bow was her proficiency, she had taken up a close combatted weapon. And Mariel didn't miss. All those training sessions and quests fighting alongside The Noble Arrow were about to come to fruition. *Thank you, my friend.*

With Mariel in her thoughts, Sabeline ran forward, plucking a discarded shield from the bodies and debris surrounding her. Gripping the handle tight, she kept her arm close to her chest, ready to raise it at the slightest hint of movement. It wasn't long before she was thrusting the shield over her head and in front of her face, hearing several thunks as arrows embedded themselves in the wood and clunked off the few metal components. She had a feeling that perhaps the archers hoped their repeated assaults would slow her pace, but she refused to yield her speed. A hum of satisfaction sang in her soul as she imagined their probable panic. Panic was the pre-emptive of fear. And fear was the pre-emptive of desperation. And that caused mistakes. Mistakes that she would take full advantage of.

But first, how to get up there? She assumed the Chaos Convocation didn't just climb up over each other to get to their places on these stands. Plus, the archers had gotten there relatively quickly. Some stairs perhaps? But where could they be...Ah, *there.* Sabeline veered a little to the left, charging towards an archway. It was much smaller than the main tunnel she'd entered through, but it was perfect for a staircase. The bombardment of arrows increased, to the point it would be her death to lower the shield for any longer than a few seconds. A good sign. She had to be on the right path.

Without hesitation, Sabeline charged into the archway and as expected, a set of simple stairs led upwards. Wasting no time, she put her foot on the first step when something flickered out of the corner of her eye. Bracing herself, she turned. *Please don't be a magical energy ball.* Instead, a basin of flames sat protected within glass. Someone here had to be a sorcerer or have some semblance of magical knowledge to produce this. It was not natural as far as she could tell. There were an array of sticks and poles stacked next to the basin. Curious, Sabeline lay down the shield and picked one up. It was fairly light, with a circular arch on the end. For a candle perhaps? *I wonder...*

Bringing the pole closer to the fire, she hovered it over the glass. Nothing. With delicacy, Sabeline tried tapping. Nothing. She did not have time to guess. She'd break the glass if she had to. Bringing the pole down hard, Sabeline waited for the glass to crack and shatter. Instead, her eyes widened as the pole passed *through* the glass and a small ball of flame separated itself from the main fire to nestle within that circular structure. With care, she pulled the pole out the same way, watching the flame glow. It was almost as if someone had crafted the fire into a sphere and placed it on the pole as an ornament. *This must be how they light the lamps.*

She drew her eyes away from the magical flame and looked

back at the stairs. Crafted from wood. Just like the stands where the archers were no doubt beginning to wonder what she was doing. Oh the Goddess had to be smiling down on her tonight. Descending back to the floor, Sabeline raised the pole out in front of her and placed the flame against the first step. Immediately, a whisper of flame leapt from the ball and ignited the step, far faster than any ordinary fire. For good measure, Sabeline held the flame against the next step, then the next, Soon, the entire stairway was swallowed in orange, yellow and red tones. *That should do it.*

Dropping the pole to the ground, Sabeline walked back out of the archway, just as flames engulfed it behind her. Screams of fear echoed across the arena as she glanced up. The fire was spreading at a rapid rate, licking and devouring all the wood it came across and when it couldn't find anymore, parts of it leapt over to the next stand, beginning the cycle anew.

Turning back to the platform, she raised her sword, ready to slice the Leader's throat open.

But the structure was abandoned.

37

Tracking the Dragon

Goddess damn them! The snow scum and her two minions must have scarpered with Nivres when they knew she was shedding more blood than their own side. A pang of regret stabbed through her for missing the expression on the Leader's face at the moment they must have figured it out.

Think, Sabeline, think. They could not have gotten far. Sure, the Leader would not care if they had to drag Nivres a hundred miles, but with time being of the essence and Nivres practically unable to stand, he would slow them down. It would be best to either improvise with a nearby residence, or if the Leader's domain was close, to return there. The hiss and clatter of falling wood drew her from her thoughts. Any survivors had already left the arena. Only her and the dead remained.

Quickly, but with care, Sabeline sheathed her sword. From the state of things, she would not need it for a few minutes. Better to keep it secure then become a hindrance. With her weapon safe, Sabeline dashed forward. The main tunnel was the only way in or out of this place. A groan came from above and her eyes snapped onto various flaming debris colliding with the tunnel area. It either shattered or landed by the entrance, with angry flames reaching, seeking another threshold to burn. And she was going to have to step through it. *Just my luck.*

She'd had enough of fire and smoke to last a lifetime. The memory of *that* day so long ago started to rise in the back of her mind along with the recent sorcerer skirmish. No. She couldn't let the images flood her senses. Later. Later when Nivres was safe. When he was safe, she could let the thoughts swallow her whole and muddle through her emotions. But not now. Now there was a mission to complete.

Drawing in a deep breath, a cough racked her chest for a moment as pungent smoke coiled down her throat. There was not much time. Soon the smog would be too thick, blinding her to the escape. Raising a hand to her mouth, she hurried forward before plunging through the crackling furnace that was once the tunnel. Flames continued to lick around the stone wall, trying to gain purchase. The lights of the lamps that had been whimsical to her only a short time ago now buzzed around their cages, yearning to join the ever-growing fire. *It would be all together best if I keep moving.*

Her steps felt heavy as she continued forward, the beat of her heart pounding in perfect cadence with her battered face. Goddess, she hoped Nivres wouldn't blame himself for the blow she'd received. She'd definitely had worse, but it wasn't exactly pleasant. And those instincts of his would no doubt rear their head. Instincts that had gotten them both into this mess. *If we get out of here alive, I am going to put a bell on him until the next moon.*

Finally, the semblance of clean air filled her lungs as she took the last few steps out of the tunnel. The arena may be falling to ash behind her, but at least she'd survived. And given the Chaos Convocation enough damage to think about. Maybe her earlier threat did not seem so idle to them now. She had said she'd raze the place to the ground. The arena was just the beginning.

But there were more pressing matters to attend to. Surveying the area, Sabeline's eyes sought out anything that could indicate which way the Leader had gone. Footprints would be nice, or a trail of frost. Maybe the odd trinket dropped here or there, but she would probably not be so lucky. *That* on the other hand...

Sabeline moved with care toward her right, crouching down to inspect markings coating the ground. They were dark, but the high flames illuminated it enough. The mark glistened in the fire's glow, almost like water. Taking her first two fingers, she dipped them into the substance. Wet and thicker than water. Her lip curled as realisation hummed through her. Blood. Blood from something that had been dragged across the ground. And she doubted the Leader was pulling her subordinates over the dirt. *Oh Nivres, I will make them suffer for this.*

Though her heart ached, she knew that this trail would be the only way to find Nivres. They must have been in a hurry. It was incompetent work to leave a trail such as this behind. Perhaps she had given the Leader too much strategic ideal. Though something told her this was not the case. She had best be prepared for anything. Rising to her feet, Sabeline wandered forward, keeping her gaze on the pathways for any sign of dragon blood.

There was far too much of it for her liking. Rounding another corner, she continued following the path Nivres had inadvertently left. She was certain she was being led deeper into the city, even though it did not seem that she had travelled too far from the arena. Taking her eyes from the ground, Sabeline gave a cursory glance at her surroundings. Big and bold buildings, though still cobbled together from whatever materials had been gathered, there had been significant effort put in to not make the buildings appear that way. *The equivalent of Chaos Convocation High Society no doubt.*

Though one building stood taller than the rest. It had been crafted from white stone and resembled a tower more than the typical house or hut construction she'd seen so far. The roof was again crafted from finer shale, there was no mixing of materials here. She could just make out windows embedded with thick glass, though it was a kind she had never laid eyes on before. Some parts appeared clear, but other sections were almost opaque and appeared rough rather than smooth. It was almost as if the glass had been created from the surface of a frozen lake….

Frozen lake. That was no glass. It was ice. Deceiving and impenetrable. So, this was it. *This is where the Chaos Convocation Leader of Sentinel Pass hides like a coward.* Flicking her gaze back to the ground, Nivres's trail stopped at the tower door up ahead. Should she charge it? Knock it down and hope for the best? Or would they be expecting that, waiting on the other side for her entrance?

Though as she approached, it seemed the decision had already been made for her. Two robed figures appeared from either side of the tower, dressed in the colours of the second in command. The pair came to a stop in front of the door.

They did not move again, but Sabeline's spine prickled as the hooded pair faced straight ahead, exactly towards her position. They were watching her. And they were waiting.

Slowly and deliberately, Sabeline reached for the hilt of her sword and drew it from its scabbard. With care, she twisted her wrist just enough so that light caught metal, illuminating all the dried and dark rivulets that she had yet to clean. That would send a sufficient message back to them.

If they want to fight, it will be their death.

38

At The Threshold

All was silent as Sabeline and the pair continued to regard each other. The two had made no further move towards her. Were they waiting to see if she would strike first? Or were they attempting to figure out her patterns, her moves before she had even made them? Her eyes narrowed. Regardless of their strategy, she did not have time to waste and she was not so easily intimidated by silence and stillness. Flicking her sword in a practised manner, Sabeline addressed the pair.

"I'm afraid I'm in rather a hurry. I need to get Chaos's Bane and burn this place into ash, ideally before dawn. The pair of you stand in the way of that. If you leave, I won't kill you. If you don't, then you have chosen death and I cannot promise it will be quick and painless." She had no qualms about taking her blade and slicing their throats open immediately, but it was the honourable thing to do, to give them a chance to run. Their fate was now in their hands.

She watched as the pair inclined their heads towards each other and whispered words on the wind that she could not make out floated between them. If they chose to leave, it would mean reaching Nivres much faster. But she had a feeling these two would remain. After all, they were second in command of this convocation city and she had a sense you did not get that position by remaining idle in the face of a threat.

"We have chosen to send you to the Goddess." Two voices spoke in unison before their forms raced across the ground. The momentum caused the hoods to fall back as Sabeline raised her sword in a defensive position. A clang cut through the quiet as metal clashed with metal. Her arms resonated with the sudden impact as Sabeline kept the hilt in a tight grip, using all her strength to keep the enemy sword from gaining an advantage.

It's wielder was a woman, staring up at her with a maniacal grin and confidence shimmering in her blue eyes. "I was trained by the finest swordmaster in the land, Mistress Fornight. You may have defeated others, but you have no chance against me."

Moving her blade upwards, she forced the woman's sword to rise, thus giving her an opening. Digging one foot into the ground, Sabeline raised her other and kicked the woman in the stomach hard. The woman stumbled, losing balance and as a result, her sword was no longer inches from Sabeline's face. The woman sneered. Clearly she had not anticipated Sabeline breaking free of her move. She noticed that was a great flaw of the Chaos Convocation, or maybe it was just this city that underestimated their opponents. *I think it is time to ruin her notion of an easy victory.*

"What an odd coincidence. So was I." She let a satisfied smile grace her lips as the second in command's expression turned to rage. Raising her sword, Sabeline stepped forward only for a force from behind to knock her to the ground. Damn her shoulders were going to ache in the morning. Twisting around onto her back and hissing at the pain, she was met with the visage of a man, with the same features as the woman. *Twins*. The thought was no more than a word, as her priority shifted to what the man had clutched in his hands. A mace. Perfect. Her armour probably had a bunch of concave dents from the blow of the spikes.

He held it above his head and her eyes widened as he began to bring the thing down towards her with speed. Rolling to the side, she narrowly missed the blow, the mace now stuck in the earth where her chest had been moments before. A flash of movement caught the corner of her eye and Sabeline rolled again, this time missing the woman impaling the sword into the ground, just where her head had been. On the ground, she was easy prey. She had to get up before they could recover.

Clutching the earth, she hauled herself up into a crouch and then with a final push, to her feet. It seemed the twin commands had also managed to reclaim their weapons from the dirt, as when she turned, both were flying towards her. Ducking her head, the mace and blade clashed above her as Sabeline spun, gathering her sword and aiming a precise slash at the nearest target.

A howl echoed through the air and her sword was pushed away with force. The man was gazing at her with fury blazing in his eyes as he held the mace by his sister's back. The robes she wore were blooming red like a rose across her side. Sabeline drew in some quick breaths. All this exertion was taking its toll. Yes she had fought many a hard and long battle. But she had had support, her sisters in arms by her side for each one. Here, she was taking on the entire settlement alone. Maybe it was true what they said about people no longer thinking rationally when they were in love. If Ascilia had proposed as a mission brief that she come here alone and take out the settlement, she would have laughed in her face.

"Mistress Fornight would be disappointed at your lack of defence." She couldn't help throw the barb their way.

At her words, the woman turned with gritted teeth and a snarl, though Sabeline noticed she was clutching her side with some ferocity. "I will cut you to pieces and let my brother pummel your remains into dust!" The woman hissed, while the man remained in a protective position in front of her.

Drawing in a deep breath, certain her small respite was over, she swirled her sword in an arch before gripping the hilt with both hands, bringing it parallel to her cheek and pointing it at a slight angle in their direction. "I did warn you that this course of action would be your deaths." Sabeline spoke with calmness. She'd already niggled at the pair, causing the woman at least to replace logic with anger. It had been easier and faster than she had expected, especially for a Second in Command but she would accept it without complaint. *The quicker they fall, the quicker I can reach Nivres.*

A cry of rage was the answer to her words and Sabeline remained still as the twins raced towards her. She kept her eyes trained on them, straining her ears for the slightest movement that would allow her to predict their next action. It was not often that a Knight would encounter a fighting duo, with practised moves and feeding off each other. Perhaps these pair thought they had the advantage. *Someone should tell them about Ivetta and Jaketta, The Twin Suns.*

There. The sound that broke the rhythm. The man was

breaking off just before the woman, coming around to Sabeline's right. She could guess the strategy, he was going to try and incapacitate her so that his now disadvantaged sister could land a blow. It might be fatal. It might not. She wasn't going to take the chance.

Darting to her left, she kept her grip steady on the blade. Drawing her arms back, Sabeline pushed the blade forward in a quick motion. The woman raised her own too late, no doubt hindered by her injury. The feeling of the blade sinking into soft flesh echoed through her hands, but she did not stop. Not until the blade pierced it's bloody end through the other side. She kept the blade there for a few moments, gazing into the dying eyes of one of the Sentinel Pass's Second in Command.

"May the Goddess show you the mercy you did not show me."

The woman's gaze widened at her words and in the next second, Sabeline yanked the blade free, standing over the body as it crumpled to the floor. A sound, a hollow cry filled with despair, reached her ears along with a muted thump. With a slight turn of her face, the figure of the man met her sight. He had fallen to his knees, head in his hands. The mace had been discarded by his side.

"If you still want to fight, I will oblige. But be warned, the only mercy I will show you, is reuniting you with your sister." She turned fully, as was only right.

The sobs subsided as the man raised his head and met her gaze. "I am honour bound to fight, but I cannot continue in this world without my twin." He raised himself to his feet, wrapping his fingers around the mace. "I hope you will still provide the mercy you promised."

"I am a warrior of my word." Sabeline assured, raising her

blade back up.

She would make this quick.

Hold on a little longer Nivres, I am almost there.

39

Lost and Found

A tendril of pity coiled around her heart as she gazed down into empty eyes that now stared into realms unknown. The unnamed man had fought with courage and skill, a feat to make his deceased sister proud. And now she had reunited them, as per her word. Sabeline wondered whether the Leader would already know what she'd done. If not, she was sure they would find out soon enough.

Wrenching her eyes away from the body, she turned her head towards the strange structure. Would stalking through the main entrance be too obvious? Perhaps she should search for alternative means of entry now that she had gained slightly more sufficient time. Caution laced her steps as Sabeline paced closer. She would not be so foolish as to assume the Leader could not appear before her at any moment. She flickered a wary glance at the ice masquerading as glass. With what she'd already encountered, no doubt the Leader would be able to melt and reconstruct it in mere seconds. Thus aiming attacks at her, and forming a shield against her retaliation. That would be a problem.

Approaching the tower, Sabeline stayed close to the stone. If any projectiles were to come her way, she refused to be an easy target. Edging around the curved wall, her sabatons pressed into the ground with silence. Moving in such a way, it was not long before she came upon the tower's rear. *Odd, there is nothing here.* Perhaps a little further to confuse foes maybe? But no. There was no other door hidden in the shadows or covered with foliage to keep its existence a secret. Nothing but stone. *Unless of course, it has been masked with magic.* Her trained gaze travelled every inch of the wall, searching for the slightest shimmer in the air, the smallest unnatural glisten that would reveal all. Nothing.

Narrowing her eyes, Sabeline continued on, following the curvature of the wall. If there was no rear entrance or exit, it could only mean one thing. Everybody here, either of low status or high, was required to go through the main door. Not that she was opposed to this idea, the damn nobles pandering to Falon were always uptight about lowborns and traders using the correct stupid door so they weren't seen. Ridiculous. But here in this place, the message and meaning was far more sinister. There was no hiding from the Leader. This was her residence and she knew all that entered and left. *If that is the way she wishes, then so be it.*

Keeping her sword firm, Sabeline approached the main door and wasting no time, raised her leg, thrusting it out in one deft kick. The door shuddered and rattled, before gently swinging aside mere inches. *Interesting, one kick alone would not be enough to bring down a door such as this.* Placing her hand flat against the surface, Sabeline pushed, opening the door wider before slipping inside. It fell shut behind her with a bang that reverberated and echoed through the tower. *If they did not know I was here, they will now.*

Turning her head, she performed a brief examination of the door. Ah. Just as she'd suspected. It hadn't been bolted or locked. An open invitation for her to enter, if she wasn't dead. She felt her heart quicken as an ominous tingle crept down her spine. Someone was confident and confidence meant they knew something she did not. And what that was, she would have no choice to discover. Her dragon was somewhere in this foul place, perhaps being tortured once more. Maybe the fight had gone out of him…No. She wouldn't, couldn't think like that. She'd play this Leader's little game and then drive her blade through their head.

With determination flooding through her anew, she flicked her sword up and marched onward with both swiftness and care.

***

So far, her travels had been mundane. She had stumbled upon a fortuitously well stocked kitchen and had grabbed some dried meat and bread. No doubt they had been starving Nivres as part of their disgusting fun. He would need to regain his strength when she found him and fast. She'd also found conference rooms, a banquet hall and one that judging from all the glittering icicles adorning the walls, was a personal training ground for the Leader.

Sabeline had suspected they would be keeping her dragon in the dungeon and if experience had taught her anything, all cultures and lands kept their dungeons below and out of sight. But despite her searching, she had yet to find a passageway leading further down into the depths of this place. Closing yet another door, she tried not to let disappointment take her as a sigh escaped her lips. He had to be here. She just needed to keep looking.

Suddenly, a clanging noise emanated from the door she had just closed. Had she missed something? She was sure it had been an ordinary bed chamber, most likely for guests. Perhaps she should check again, for prosperity's sake. Stretching out her fingers, Sabeline reached for the door knob. A splintering sound crackled from above and Sabeline snatched her fingers away just as tendrils of frost and ice spread over the door like a strange waterfall. The trails, at first thin, expanded and grew thicker, stretching over the door until it was completely sealed.

As she took a step back, the ice finally stopped moving, ending with a creaking, crystallising noise. The door was now impenetrable. *These rooms, they are a prison. Or a trap. And only the Leader can decide if you will be released, or if you will die.* But surely, they would not want these rooms to be common knowledge. Which would mean she had to be close to the bowels of this place. Secluded, out of the way, unnoticed. Leaving the preserved door, she carried on towards the end of the corridor.

It was only a few steps later when an inexplicable feeling drew her to the left. The air felt colder than before, causing her skin to prickle. An archway with no door was positioned in a way that one could easily miss at first glance, partially obscured by an embedded pillar. A clever thing, to construct a building in such a fashion. Wariness filled her as she approached, the image of the ice appearing, spreading and trapping her within the archway sprang forth in her mind. *Best be swift.*

With haste, she darted through the opening. No eerie sounds rang in her ears. No ice commenced its assault.

Satisfied, Sabeline wandered further. Lamps glowed on the walls as she continued on a downward slope, but the air felt dank and cloying with rot. The stone either side seemed damp and if it were not for the lamps, she was sure the place would be consumed in a cold darkness, with nothing but rats and wispy cobwebs to share it with.

Did it ever end? Already it felt as if she had traversed for miles, but perhaps the shadowed corners were tricking her mind. *By the Goddess, I hope I have not wandered into some kind of trap.* A bright glow up ahead caused her to squint, her eyes already growing accustomed to the dark in this cursed place. Blinking a few times, the hazy shapes became a thick array of lanterns clustered together, more than she had seen throughout this entire passageway.

They had to be there for a reason. She'd come too far to turn back in the face of such a thing. Holding her sword up, Sabeline wrapped her other hand around the hilt, keeping the blade poised upright in front of her face. With a quick shuffle of her feet, she repositioned her legs so they could quickly snap into a defensive or offensive stance before edging forward and passing under the light.

Eyes darting in each direction, she continued at a steady pace. This was not the place to be taken by surprise. A rattling came from her right, as if metal were being shifted. Before a whisper of thought could contemplate the sound further, a low groan intertwined with heavy pants followed. Could it be…?

Heart pounding like the drums of war, Sabeline quickened her pace but did not relax her stance. Not yet. It could still be a trick though she prayed the goddess would not be so cruel. Her gaze roamed, searching, seeking… *there*.

A silhouette partially illuminated by dim lantern glow. Chains stretched across the ground, circling around the figure slumped against the wall in a seated position. Long red hair that was once in a loose braid was now bedraggled and caked with dirt and blood. Marred skin could not hide the piercing gold of their eyes as they snapped to her own.

Beneath her armour, Sabeline swore her heart missed a beat as she sucked in a shaking breath. Without her consent, her grip on her blade became slack, but not enough that it fell to the ground, as one word echoed with a roar in her mind.

Nivres.

40

Reunion

She took one step forward, casting the lantern light upon her form. "Nivres." Sabeline uttered, as her heart beat rapidly between the prison of her bones. The dragon said nothing for a moment, but an expression of pure despair etched its way across his features.

"Have you not tortured me enough?" The question was filled with exhaustion, but she could still detect an edge to them.

What? Should she not be asking that? He had left her, due to some damned dragon instincts and had ended up in this completely avoidable state, leaving her to come drag him back by the tail. Then after all the worry, fear and fighting she'd endured, he had the audacity to ask her that?

Stomping forward, she let out whispered words that carried a harshness to them. "How dare you say that to me? I have been through a gauntlet worthy of the goddess herself to get here and free you from their clutches and this is the first thing you say to me?"

The dragon's chest heaved as he dragged weary eyes back

to her face with a smile. But it was a cold and knowing smile, sending a chill down her spine.

"Very good, Crysantha. You even have her voice perfect. But you will not dishonour her memory by torturing me further with this visage."

Confusion reigned across her thoughts. What in all of Idrelas was he talking about? And who was Crysantha? Whoever she was, Sabeline could deduce she wasn't exactly a merciful person if she had taken part in Nivres's torture. Perhaps it was the Leader? But she was born of ice, was she not? Why would Nivres think she was this Leader?

Had they done something to his eyes since bringing him back? Oh by the goddess she hoped not. They had seemed in perfect condition when she'd glimpsed them moments ago, but now she could not be so sure. Perhaps walking more into the light would break whatever was wrong with him? She stepped closer, only for Nivres to crawl back at her motion. A sting, worse than any other injury she'd sustained thus far, punctured her heart. He feared her? Why?

Stopping, she raised her hand and slipped her blade back into its scabbard. "I do not know who this Crysantha is, but it is clear she has done terrible things to you. I am not her Nivres. You know exactly who I am."

"Lies!" The dragon growled. "Sabeline is dead, your people killed her and now one of your sorcerers taunts me with her image, just like before."

Her eyes widened as his words crawled into her being. He thought her a trick, an illusion. He also thought her to be dead. *Oh Nivres, what horrors they have put you through.*

"I am glad you have such faith in my abilities, to think I would die before reaching you. I do not know what lies they fed you, but I am very much here. Battle weary, injured, with blood on my hands and the arena razed to the ground, but my heart still beats. I have not yet breathed my last you damned dragon."

Something flickered across his face, it was as if he wanted to believe what she was saying, but was scared to. Strange, all she had done was to try and advocate her living status. She had not fully expected the words to get through to him, but whatever she had said that he had clung to, it seemed to be unravelling his doubt.

This time, when he gazed at her, there was hesitant hope in his eyes. "You called me a dragon."

"Yes, well I have always called you that." She shrugged.

"Crysantha does not know what I truly am. Nor does the rest of the Chaos Convocation. They believe I am simply a powerful pyromancer."

"I have grown fond of flying on a particular crimson dragon's back. However, I came to drag him back by the tail for leaving me without a word and trying to take down a Convocation settlement of this size and stature by himself." Sabeline crossed her arms over her chest as she continued to gaze at him, letting a knowing expression appear on her face.

The dragon edged away from the wall, chains clanking as he shuffled forward. Eliminating the distance, she stepped closer and crouched down so they were both at the same height. She watched as wonder and relief flooded his face. Raising one hand, he brought it to her left cheek. As his hand cupped her skin, she could feel the grit of the dirt and the dried cuts gracing his fingers and palm.

"It is you. Sabeline, the Bringer of Truth." Her dragon uttered in awe.

"I should damn well hope so." She muttered back with a smile.

"What did they do to your face?"

She had hoped he wouldn't notice her newly acquired bruising, especially in this light. The last thing she needed was for those dragon instincts to rear their protective head again and hinder the escape. "Do not worry about it. My opponent suffered much worse I can assure you."

He nodded and his hand slipped from her cheek. She managed to catch it and lowered it gently back down. Nivres was weaker than she'd first thought. Glancing down, thick shackles still clung tightly to his wrists, attached to those heavy chains. "We need to get you out of here. What manner of manacles are these?" She had never seen ones with such runework and from the occasional glow they emitted, surely something special was required to break them. She had a feeling her blade would do nothing against such instruments.

Her dragon huffed. "They are designed to be unbreakable. The runes are a spell. Blood and death will not undo it, that much I have been informed of."

"But they have not told you what will?"

Nivres shook his head.

A sigh breathed through her lips. They were so close. So close to leaving this place behind. Except this Crysantha had planned for any event. *I will run my blade through her heart of ice and delight as it shatters.* The thought was comforting. "There must be something here that will tell us. May I?" She asked, reaching for his wrist.

Nivres nodded and with care, she held his hand, her eyes traversing the glowing runes. Runework had been more of Echoris's speciality. She was the one who knew ancient languages and still worshipped old gods mostly forgotten by the rest of Idrelas. Echoris had always been an enigma, but a powerful one who had always believed that just because something had been lost to time, it did not mean it was not worth learning about. She had taught Sabeline some basic runes once.

She tried to pull the memories of Echoris's lessons to the forefront of her mind, no matter how much the sadness welled within her at the knowledge she would likely never see Echoris again. One glittering symbol she was fairly certain meant *heart.*

Another etched nearby was either *bleed from* or *blood from*. But hadn't Nivres said blood would not break these bonds? Tearing her eyes away, she searched for the others, shimmering in the dark. *Wound* or *torture. Freedom. Gain.* Her gaze flitted between the runes lighting up in what seemed like an avid frenzy, as if they were encouraging her to find the answer within them.

Bleed from the heart to gain freedom and end this torture.

What did that mean? Had the Leader been wrong and blood was required after all? No, Sabeline did not think so. Someone with such an eye for strategy would not overlook such a detail. Then what?

Bleed from the heart...

That part was the key. If she could figure out what it was trying to tell her, then Nivres would be free. Now then, she'd already established it wasn't a direct reference to blood. So what else was a heart? A place of emotion, moral and honour. It was also vulnerable. She had seen enough people heartsick, broken by love. Is that what the riddle meant? Break a heart to earn freedom? No, it could not be. The final part implied an end to torture, becoming heartsick would only begin a new kind.

If that was not the case, then what else came from the heart? *Confession.* The word flew into her mind like an arrow. Confessions of any kind were raw, full of emotion and mostly guided by the heart. Her eyes widened and she felt her lips part at the realisation.

Nivres must have noticed, because his voice echoed in the silence. "What is it Sabeline? Have you found the answer?"

Pressing her lips back into a thin line, she swallowed, trying to dispel the sudden dryness of her mouth. She had sworn to herself had she not? That she would confess everything once she had her dragon back. And here he was, trapped, injured and if her interpretation of the runes was right, only her words to set him free.

She still gripped his hand in her own and in response, she curled her fingers gently around his own. "I believe so. But know that I had sworn an oath to say this once I discovered you. Though it appears these manacles require me to speak the words now in order for you to be free once more." She glanced at their joined hands, feeling Nivres grip her own as much as he was able. Her lips quirked at the motion before she turned her gaze to the dragon's face.

"I hated you once. You stood for everything I had lost and I believed with all my soul that you were a monster, only focused on destruction and causing more death and pain to innocents. Then the incident happened with Falon and I ended up in the last place I expected with the very nemesis I'd been hunting. Over time, we grew a kinship. When you confessed you cared for me more than that, I was not ready. There were still so many things in my mind I needed to sort through. Then you left for here and didn't return. And I knew I would do anything, *anything* to find you and bring you back to that damn cave that was starting to feel like a home. I've fought. I've killed. I've destroyed. And I still will if it means I get to keep you in one piece. Because by the goddess, I love you too, you insufferable lizard."

Nivres opened his mouth, but before any sound was uttered, the runes on the manacles glowed with brightness before dimming. Different ones now appeared in a red hue, blazing bright against the shackles. *Compassion and love are the opposite of pain and suffering.* Sabeline just managed to catch the phrase as the runes disappeared and the shackles fell with a soft clatter from her dragon's wrists and ankles.

Squeezing his hand, Sabeline released her grip as Nivres rubbed his wrists. The skin was pink and sore, crimson where they had dug into the flesh far too tightly. She would make them pay for this. But first… "Come on Nivres. Let us get out of here. There is no time to lose."

A brilliant smile flashed across his face, revealing his fangs. "I will follow you anywhere Bringer of Truth. After all, you hold my heart, just as it seems, I hold yours."

"Yes, well, we can discuss it further back at the cave." She muttered, attempting to fight the heat rising in her cheeks. *For the last time, knights do not blush dammit!* "Can you stand?"

In answer, the dragon gripped the wall and steadily dragged himself to his feet. She could already see his legs shaking at the effort. "You will not make it far. It will be easier if I carry you."

"Absolutely not, I do not need to be carried." He huffed with indignance.

"I am not asking, dragon." Sabeline reached an arm out,

ready to secure Nivres on to her back. Her hand had just curled around his waist when a soft feminine giggle caused her to still. Beneath her fingers, Nivres's muscles tensed.

"What a delightful little confession, Bane of Chaos's Bane. Now I know why you were so determined to reach him. Didn't anyone tell you? A heart makes you weak."

A beautiful clear icicle the size and thickness of a spear careened through the gloom from the voice's direction. Instinct spurred Sabeline to move and as she twisted, a gasp was drawn from her lips as the crafted ice plunged through her flesh.

A fierce, wrathful cry that promised suffering trembled through her ears as agony pulsed across each sinew. It took her a moment to realise the sound was coming from next to her. Sabeline had thought it might have been emanating from her own throat. She caught a glimpse of hands flashing near her shoulder and the sudden panic at the intentions sharpened her focus, turning the pain to a dull throb. With haste, she raised her arms, wrapping her fingers with care around Nivres's wrist as he prepared to pull out the spear. His gaze flickered to her own in confusion.

"I have been in enough fights to know pulling out a weapon is not a good idea, no matter how much instinct says otherwise." She huffed out, attempting to avoid gritting her teeth as the pain increased once more.

"Trust me." Nivres said simply in reply.

Of course she trusted him. Apart from the noble sentiment that had gotten them both into this mess in the first place, whereby he had up and left without a word. But that incident aside, she knew she trusted him, especially with her life. Sabeline nodded once, letting her fingers fall from his wrist.

Her lips pressed into a thin line and her eyes scrunched shut as fresh torment came in a wave through her flesh. Every inch of the ice stung and dragged as it was being pulled out. She had half a mind to scream at the dragon to just pull it faster, even if logic dictated that this way, he could ensure nothing ruptured further, causing more damage. She knew the moment it had been completely removed. It was an odd sensation, to feel air moving between open holes in the front and back of her shoulder. *It is also highly unpleasant.*

Unclenching her eyelids, Sabeline felt the blood begin to well and flow from the wounds. Nivres sent a reassuring look her way, before opening his mouth and spewing flame onto the injury. Oh by the Goddess that *hurt.* She couldn't think which had been worse, the spear sliding through her flesh, it being pulled out, or *this.* All she had known was white hot pain for the last several minutes and goddess damn it, she was sick of it.

It was another few seconds when Nivres murmured "I have to do the back too." Of course he did. She knew he had to, or else she'd bleed to death. It didn't mean she had to like it. Drawing in a few deep breaths as Nivres with great care, stepped around and examined the back of her shoulder, she slammed her teeth together at the new onslaught.

She was accustomed to pain. A knight was not a profession without injury after all. She had fought against tooth and claw. She had fought against weapons, magic and madness. One did not come away from such fights unscarred. But this? This was something she would not wish on anyone. Well, except maybe Crysantha. And Falon.

"It is done." The dragon uttered as the agony came to a jarring halt, replaced by a constant ache and throbbing pain.

"You are lucky that as you moved, the spear went through your shoulder, rather than your chest. If you had not done that, then I would have lost you." Nivres continued and she could hear the emotion in his voice at what could have been.

"Have you not heard?" She panted out, pulling her lips into a smile, "I am hard to kill. The snow scum had better guard her life, because I'm coming for it."

She glanced over at where Crysantha had been. The coward had gone. Had she thought the element of surprise would have been enough to kill them? Sabeline did not think so. If there was anything Crysantha had shown, it was that she was a good strategist. Perhaps the plan had been to incapacitate her all along, with her and Nivres not at full strength, the ice maiden would have the advantage. And if the spear had killed her? Well then, that would have been an unexpected treat for the wretch.

Sweat beaded across her forehead, despite the cool, dank air of the dungeon as she wandered forward, Nivres weak but fairly steady at her side. Nausea curled in her belly, but she brushed it aside. They had to get out of here. That was the priority. Something glimmered on the ground, catching her attention. A circular layer of frost decorated the area where Crysantha had been standing, but on the surface sat a piece of parchment, frost clinging to its edges.

Nivres was in no condition to bend down and retrieve the note, so with her good arm, Sabeline reached out, quickly snatching it from it's place. Holding it between them, her eyes roamed over the delicate but furious inked words.

If you live, come finish this.

"When someone receives an invitation, I believe it would be discourteous not to attend, do you not think Nivres?" She scrunched the parchment into a ball, watching as flakes of frost fluttered to the ground.

"Indeed Sabeline. And we are anything but ill-mannered." The dragon growled.

"I agree. So then, in a show of good manners, let's remove the bitch's head from her shoulders."

A triumphant war-cry echoed from Nivres's throat and she couldn't help the smirk that spread across her face.

As you wish, Crysantha.

41

Declarations

It was easy enough to deduce where the Leader would be. After all, Crysantha had been kind enough to leave glittering footsteps in an ominous trail. She wanted to be found and Sabeline was more than happy to oblige. Perhaps the Leader had gained a grudging respect for them both, from her note, there was almost an expectation there that they would survive. Sabeline held back a snort at the thought. No, Crysantha definitely wanted them dead and no doubt would want it as drawn out and painful as possible. Especially considering she had managed to decimate the Leader's organisation. *I have a feeling she will not forgive that so easily.*

Nivres's steps fell in a steady rhythm next to her. Flicking her gaze over his visage, she took a moment to study him. Colour had returned to his flesh and while pale, he was not as bone white and gaunt as she had first seen in this place. The wounds that had been inflicted however, still blazed bright across his skin. His breathing seemed to be gaining strength and she hoped to the Goddess that it continued that way. Maybe dragons had some kind of robust natural healing. Or maybe he was gathering whatever little strength he had left, determined to make Crysantha suffer as he had. No matter what possibility it may be, she could not help the worry marring her heart.

"You are staring."

The voice sent a jolt through her and her gaze shifted to meet Nivres's golden eyes looking at her with something akin to softness, while a smirk adorned his lips. In haste, she turned her head. It would be unbecoming to blush again so soon after the last time.

"Yes, well, you have been brutally tortured, dragon. To see what they have done to you, it shatters my heart and sets my blood aflame with rage." Sabeline ground the words out as if they were a poison. Oh she'd have Crysantha's head on a spike soon enough. But even then, she did not think that would quell her fury at the acts they had committed against her dragon.

"I will live Sabeline, that I can promise you. These injuries, they will heal. These wounds were nothing, *nothing* compared to believing you had breathed your last." She felt a wisp of touch on her chin as Nivres's fingers caressed the skin before gently turning her head back to face him. "You have my heart."

The words he spoke were simple, but they settled deep within her radiating warmth and comfort throughout her bones. What did one say in response to something like that? She could plunge a blade into a man twice her size without effort, but responding to such heartfelt declarations? It was certainly a new experience. Swallowing hard, she managed to utter "And you have mine."

It must have been good enough, because a brilliant smile

stretched across the dragon's face in response, though he still held her chin with a light touch. The air seemed to shift between them and anticipation curled in her belly. Something was about to happen; she just wasn't sure what exactly. Nivres was meeting her gaze as he came closer to her face, and when she felt his fingers lift her chin up, Sabeline allowed herself to follow the motion. He was only a hair's breadth away now.

Her blood thrummed under her skin as her heart echoed and throbbed, as if it was a caged creature desperate to break free. She did not know what to do, thoughts becoming quiet and loud all at once. Nivres gave her one last look, as though she had a power she knew not, then seemingly satisfied at whatever expression was gracing her face, she felt his lips descend upon her own.

It was not her first kiss. Plenty of men and even some women wanted the prestige of being with a Knight of Idrelas. There had been a man once who she thought she had loved during training, and then she had become a knight and he had grown jealous that she was far superior in battle than he. There was also the unwanted advances by visiting spoiled sons of the nobility, who didn't seem to grasp that despite the appropriate gowns and jewellery, they were still warriors who could have their heads within seconds. So no, this was not her first kiss.

But it was the first to cause the stars themselves to erupt behind her eyelids and scatter their light across every inch of her body as her lips responded enthusiastically to the dragon's own. With each caress, each brush of a dragon fang against her skin, each delicate movement that deliciously curled around her soul, it was as though an unspoken message resonated through her being and back to the dragon. *I love you. I care for you. I will always fight for you.*

After what felt like an age, she pulled away with reluctance, raising her fingertips to her slightly swollen lips as she drew in the deep breath she'd been denied during the embrace. *It is good to see he is just as affected.* The satisfied, slightly smug thought crossed her mind as she watched Nivres also take some panting breaths. There was a glimmer in his eyes that had not been there before and his cheeks seem flushed, but in a healthy way.

An unrestrained smile broke out across her face without her permission, though Nivres's responding one was all she needed. She loved this damned overgrown lizard. And she was going to make Crysantha suffer for the cruelty she'd inflicted upon them both. Loathe as she was to interrupt the moment, it could not be helped. "We still have an ice maiden to take down. But once that's done, perhaps we could do this again?"

"We had best make the fight quick then." The dragon smirked. "As there is no *perhaps* about it."

"Well then, what are we waiting for?" She responded, before turning and marching off at a slightly faster than usual pace through the rest of the dungeon, as her body still hummed from the kiss. It wasn't long before a rather elated dragon fell into step next to her.

***

Compared to her journey into the dungeons, it seemed they were free and back into Crysantha's residence only a short time later. There was a stillness in the air, an ominous quiet that did not sit well. Those glistening footprints had still been left in a gleaming trail. Sabeline tapped the dragon and pointed to the tracks, which seemed to be leading towards the direction of the entrance. Nivres gave her a sharp nod and with care, they began to traverse the route.

Much like before, nothing leapt out, no trap doors sprung open, only this time, no ice ricocheted over places they'd been or doors they'd passed through. They made it to the entrance with relative ease and an unsettling feeling grew within her at the realisation. Crysantha was obviously planning something. But she did not want to fight them in this stronghold. Why? It would have given her the advantage, a building she had made and knew all of the secrets to, compared to her and Nivres who knew little about its traps and tricks. Sabeline could think of only two reasons. Either Crysantha was leading them to what she knew to be a more dangerous or significant place, or she was just tired of cleaning their blood from her compound.

But to end this, truly end this, she and her dragon would have little choice other than to continue following the tracks. Pushing open the door, Sabeline slipped through, Nivres close behind. Smoke was thick now, rolling across the already dark sky like ocean waves, stars replaced by glowing embers caught in the cloying tide. Sabeline gave a swift cursory glance to the side. The bodies of the twins had disappeared.

"You did this?" Nivres uttered in awe, as she turned her head back, the glow of the Arena and apparently quite a few other buildings glaring orange against the dark in the distance.

"I needed to get to you. Nothing else mattered." She answered honestly. "And I had been courteous enough to warn them of my intentions if you recall. An opportunity arose to enact the plan much sooner than I expected."

The dragon let out an approving hum at her words. "I think whatever is left of the Chaos Convocation after this will be assigning you your own name, or would you prefer to keep Bane of Chaos's Bane?"

She could hear the amusement in his tone. "Perhaps they'll let me keep that one." She jested back, as a glistening array caught her attention, pulling her gaze to the ground. *So the footprints continue.* "But we still have that invitation to heed. Let's go."

Her feet dutifully followed the trail before them as her dragon again stepped beside her. She had noticed that since their reunion. Never in front. Never behind (well, for long anyway). Always side by side. It was the kind of gesture she was growing to like. *Though what I do not like is where this trail is leading.* Sabeline was sure she had roamed this area only mere hours ago. Her suspicions only deepened as the consuming glow of the flames grew closer with each step they took.

"We are heading back to that goddess forsaken place." Nivres voiced from her left.

"It would appear so." She murmured back, the glistening frost prints growing weaker until they stopped all together. They were not quite at the Arena, but the suffocating heat stroked her cheeks and filled her chest with each breath she took. Nivres of course, appeared mostly unaffected, as expected for a creature raised in flame and smoke.

Through the gloom ahead, a figure bathed in the dancing lights of the destroying fire also did not seem unperturbed by the consuming heat.

Though Sabeline reasoned that was probably due to the crafted armour of ice adorning their body.

Here we are, snow scum. Here we are.

42

Steel and Ice

"I see you have managed to crawl out of the dirt unscathed, like the pests you are." Crysantha's voice called above the crackling flames. If the Goddess was on her side, Sabeline was going to make damn sure she cut out the Leader's tongue before anything else.

"And yet it was us *pests* that have left you with a settlement in ruins, your men dead and are so feared by the Chaos Convocation itself, you gave one of us a title." Confidence laced her tone as she relayed the facts to Crysantha, satisfaction growing as the Leader's expression grew more infuriated with each one. Wrapping her fingers around the hilt of her blade, she withdrew it slowly and deliberately from its scabbard, keeping her gaze on Crysantha as she did. Once the sword was free, Sabeline swung her beloved weapon in a swift arch before continuing. "And I am more than happy to show you why your organisation is wise to do so."

"I will freeze you both and hang you as statues in my new quarters." The Leader growled back, stepping forward and growing more illuminated in the light of the scorching fire.

The armour she had crafted continued to glisten and gleam, though Sabeline noticed the ice was continually reforming, to replace parts that were melting or growing thin. *She must be exhausting a fair amount of power to ensure she is protected. That could work to our advantage.*

Her dragon took this moment to utter a few words of his own. "Not if I turn you to ash first." He did not raise his voice, or growl or roar, but the promised threat curling around each syllable sent a tingle of awareness down her spine. If Crysantha still did not fear them after that, then she was a fool.

"I did not heed your invitation to stand around discussing ice and flame. I would much rather just kill you and return home. After all, I am growing rather sick of this place." Sabeline let a malicious grin grace her lips, charging forward before either Crysantha or Nivres could react. The element of surprise would serve her well.

A few steps more and she would be in range. Raising her sword, Sabeline swung. The impact reverberated through her arms as the blade crunched through thin ice. Glancing down, the sight of the sword stuck in ice met her gaze. Crysantha had raised her forearm to block the blow. The initial surprise in the Leader's eyes had faded to a smug glint. *Damn her.* Wrenching the blade free, Sabeline was slightly satisfied to see a gaping chasm in the ice vambrace.

Each muscle and sinew in her shoulder screamed in protest as she raised her sword again, though Sabeline gritted her teeth, shoving the protests of the still healing flesh aside. If she was distracted by such a thing, it could mean the difference between victory and defeat. The blade arched through the air once more, but this time met nothing. The Leader had turned at the last moment. Before she could strike again, a dull throb rippled across her stomach. Flicking her eyes down, the visage of Crysantha punching her in the stomach, fist decorated in a thick gauntlet of ice greeted her. A painful ebb, but nothing more thanks to her armour. *Maybe that is her plan, to ensure I am distracted by pain, she would have known she would not break through my armour with such a move.*

Before Crysantha could move, Sabeline raised her right leg, letting her foot strike the Leader's shoulder hard. A crunching sound echoed and joined the crackling flames in symphony at the kick. Crysantha fell back, with new jagged cracks decorating the adorned ice.

Her foot ached a little, but she refused to let this new irritation take root in her mind. Aches, pains and injuries could be healed later. It was more imperative that she survived first. Striding forward, both sets of fingers curled around the hilt as she raised her blade, plunging it towards the ground where Crysantha's head lay.

She had just enough time to see the Leader's eyes grow wide, before Crysantha unfortunately regained her senses, throwing her head to the side and just missing the killing blow. The blade sunk into the dry ground. *Damn her again.*

"I see you are the only one fighting, Bane of a Bane. The Pyromancer hasn't even joined this battle yet." The Leader huffed out, rising back to her feet as Sabeline tried yanking her blade out of the earth. "Is that because despite everything, you are not worth the effort?" She goaded.

Her words had been intended to cut like a dagger, but they bounced off her armour as harmlessly as a rainfall. If Crysantha thought her barbs would cause her to become unfocused, she was sorely mistaken. "Have you thought that it's because he's still regaining strength from your torture and thus he's confident enough in my skills to let me handle you in the interim?" She retorted, feeling the blade finally loosen enough to be pulled free. "Perhaps," she continued, releasing the sword and swishing it a few times before pointing it at Crysantha, "it is you that is not worth the effort?"

She watched as an ugly, twisted expression formed on the Leader's face. "I am Crysantha of the Chaos Convocation! The most feared Mistress of Ice to walk Idrelas since the time of the Goddess! I am the lonely, cold death that waits for all those who get in my way! How dare you say I am not worth the effort!"

Sabeline blinked. She had not expected an impassioned, rage-filled, screeching speech. Rather, she had held her sword up near her chest in anticipation of another assault.

"I will show you why it is wise to fear me." Cryantha uttered in a much calmer, sombre tone. It did not escape Sabeline's notice that they were almost the same words she had uttered to the Leader earlier. She watched as the Leader raised her hands and Sabeline positioned her sword at a slight angle, still ensuring her chest was protected. A blast of ice ricocheted across the small distance between them, the chill felt as though it was seeping into her bones as crystalline shards as sharp as glass nicked her unsuspecting, exposed skin. Her feet felt heavy. Sabeline tried to lift them but panic started to bubble at the realisation she couldn't move. Bending her knees, she tried to walk forward but it was as though her feet were stuck to the floor.

The freezing blast subsided and immediately she glanced down, the flecks of ice dusting her eyelashes melting now the blast had stopped. Horror crawled within her at the sight. *Ice.*

Her feet were encased in ice. And like a living thing, it kept growing, tendrils of thick, frozen ice gradually forming over her shins. If it continued to form at this rate, it would be over her knees and up to her calves within the next few moments.

The panic no longer bubbled, but swelled like the sea, crashing through her in a wave. Swallowing hard, her eyes traversed the ice, searching for any way to break free. "What have you done?" Sabeline spat, refusing to give Crysantha the satisfaction of seeing her unnerved.

The Leader laughed. "I told you I'd turn you both into statues. You'll feel the ice crawl over your flesh until the very end, knowing there is nothing you can do about it."

"I would not say nothing." The words were not her own, but the speaker became apparent when a fireball careened past Crysantha's gloating face, hitting the ground just in front of the Leader. A warning shot. If Nivres had wanted to cause harm, Sabeline had no doubt he would not have missed.

The Leader turned away from her, uttering "Chaos's Bane" with such malice and disdain that she was tempted to throw her blade and see if it struck Crysantha in the chest. Crysantha continued to turn, strutting off without so much as a glance behind her. Indignation smoothed over the terror consuming her for a moment. How dare Crysantha dismiss her! When she got out of this, Sabeline was going to make damn sure the Leader knew she was still a threat.

A gasp escaped her lips as the ice tendrils coiled tight around her calves, the metal of the armour shifting uncomfortably as it was pressed against the flesh beneath. By the goddess, she needed to stop this cursed element and do it fast. Taking her blade and sucking in a deep breath, Sabeline brought it down across her legs. Parts of the ice cracked off in small chunks.

It was not the best result, but at least her actions had done something. Perhaps if she continued to hack at it?

Just as she raised her sword to try again, voices fluttered over the makeshift battlefield. Her heart gave a little leap at the familiar tones of Nivres, sounding strong and proud. *Not the time.* Striking the sword down again, she could not help listening.

"I am not known for mercy Crysantha, even less so when it comes to your organisation. By the time I'm done, you will join the ruins of your operation."

There was a humourless laugh. "Good. Mercy gets you nowhere. I had you in chains Chaos's Bane and I can put you right back in them. No one will come for you, especially as your lover is becoming a pretty little sculpture as we speak."

The surety of that utterance immediately caused Sabeline to bring the blade down in faster, repetitive motions. *I am the Bringer of Truth and by the goddess, I will not end my legacy this way.*

"I won't let you do either." Was all she heard before a great hissing noise ricocheted through the heavy air. It almost sounded like when the blacksmith poured water over molten metal. Glancing up from her encased legs, the image of Nivres throwing out a huge flaming trail, while Crysantha retaliated with one of ice greeted her vision. The opposing elements crashed into each other in the centre, causing the awful sound as they each tried to gain advantage over the other. Her gaze flickered over to her dragon. He appeared calm, steady. Using such fire did not seem to be draining his energy further as she'd feared. His golden eyes were narrowed slits as he kept the Leader in his sights. Each muscle was tensed, ready to move at the slightest threat. Her dragon looked every inch the human warrior.

It was the heat in the air that caused her cheeks to become flushed. She was most certainly not blushing at a time like this. She caught a quick glimpse of Crysantha's furious face before turning back to the ice that was now reaching her hips. They were both at an impasse, their elements equal opposites. Someone was going to have to try a new strategy in order to gain any advantage. Hoping it would be her dragon, she resumed chopping at the ice in earnest.

The tendrils starting to form on her hips were thin and with care, she slid her blade between them and the armour, ignoring the slight screeching of metal gliding across metal. With a flick of her wrist, she pried the ice from her body, satisfaction growing as they came away in large fractures. She had at least managed to reduce it's hold back down to her calves. Not much, true, but slowing the ice down was better than nothing.

It would be best to continue while the ice was disadvantaged. Forcing her sword between both the thick ice and armour in the same way as before, Sabeline pushed, letting her gaze fall back to the fight as she did.

Both Nivres and Crysantha were still at their impasse, she had assumed as much from the hissing sound still grating across her ears. She thought she saw those reptilian eyes glance in her direction for a moment before Nivres's flames disappeared. Before she could blink, her dragon had ducked, narrowly missing the force of ice that was no longer being held back. His lips parted in haste and a small shot of fire sprang from his mouth.

The flames landed directly on Crysantha's crafted greaves, melting them within seconds. Her pained cry cut through the night as the blast of ice came to an abrupt halt. Instead of attacking, the Leader now had to redirect her abilities to the flames licking across the fabric and flesh of her shins. Sabeline allowed a slither of pride to wrap around her heart.

The sound of footsteps to her side drew her attention away from the cursing Leader and Sabeline's lips stretched into a smile.

"You took your time, dragon."

"It was longer than I anticipated."

"I am familiar with the feeling tonight."

His eyes met her own and she could see the depth of emotion hiding behind them, all the things he longed to say but now was not the time. She hoped her own reflected the same. The pinch of cold against her hips caused a slight hiss to escape her mouth and Nivres turned his gaze away from her face to the insulting ice.

"I do not suppose you could offer some assistance with this?" She gestured unnecessarily to the encroaching tendrils.

"I thought you would never ask." Her dragon answered, though despite the playfulness of his words, he wore an expression carved from thunder itself.

With care, flames burst from his fingers, curling around the encasing ice like the embrace of a lover, destroying the crystalline form as Sabeline felt it dripping away until it was no more than a dark puddle soaking into the ground. Raising her left leg, she shook it, revelling in the movement. *Finally.*

Suddenly, an expression of agony crossed Nivres's face. *I swear on all that I am, I will never allow such an expression to adorn his face again.* Strands of cold began to consume the air around them. From her position, Sabeline could see Crysantha, apparently recovered, standing just beyond

Nivres's shoulder, with her hands raised. *Snow scum.* It wasn't hard to deduce she'd seen an opportunity and took it from the frost Sabeline could now detect decorating Nivres's neck, hair and dusting his shoulders.

But Crysantha can not see that she is too late from the position of my dragon. And oh, she was close. So tantalisingly close in her arrogance. Decision snapped into focus with her and refusing to hesitate, her feet darted just past Nivres.

With everything she had, Sabeline slammed her sword into Crysantha's body.

43

United Front

But it was not enough. Her blade had broken through the weakened ice, but not far enough to plunge into that cold heart. Even though she had not succeeded, Sabeline relished the expression of shock and surprise that had crossed Crysantha's face. Before the Leader could recover, Sabeline flexed her fingers, pulling the blade out in haste and swinging it through the air in another strike.

The Leader darted back, narrowly missing her blow but as Sabeline went to follow, Nivres stepped into view behind Crysantha, immediately shooting a fireball at her back. A grimace crossed Crysantha's face and Sabeline had no doubt the fire had melted away the thick ice coating the Leader's back. The scent of charred flesh reached her nose, confirming her suspicions. *Hopefully that will slow her down.*

Turning away from her, the Leader aimed an ice blast at Nivres. Facets of ice were starting to form and spread over Crysantha's exposed back. But it was a slow process, probably due to the ice blasts that she could see Nivres deflecting easily with flame. She had expected better. After all, she was just as much of a threat as her dragon. It was time to fulfil the promise she'd made to herself mere moments ago.

Racing forward, she kept her sword raised. Seconds later, it slashed through ice, fabric and skin in a perfect clean cut. A dark satisfaction welled within her as Crysantha cried out. She had the Leader's attention once more, as Crysantha's eyes blazed in fury while meeting her own narrowed and determined gaze. The crackle of ice split the air.

"Perhaps you should have covered your exposed weakness earlier. Just because I cannot blast elements around does not mean I can't send you to the Goddess."

"I will destroy you before you get the chance." Crysantha snarled out.

"Yes, because you are doing such a good job of that." Nivres drawled, though glancing to his face, Sabeline could see vengeance in his eyes as he kept the Leader in his sights.

"I will enjoy turning you both to ice and shattering your corpses!" The Leader spat out before sending a stream of ice in both directions. Nivres wasted no time in countering with his fire. Dropping to a crouch, the blast flew harmlessly over Sabeline's head. A jolt of annoyance flooded through her as once again, Crysantha remained more focused on Nivres, only throwing her a sparing glance. *That just won't do.*

Moving her blade so that both hands wrapped around the hilt, she remained crouching. Bringing her sword up so it was level with her cheek, she waited a second. Then another. Crysantha's leg shifted ever so slightly, revealing the thinner ice of the greaves. Without hesitation, she thrust the blade forward. Ice splintered and cracked as the weapon sank through flesh and bone. She was vaguely aware of a scream as she yanked the sword back out.

She rose to her feet as Crysantha crumpled to the ground. Her gaze flickered to the side as Nivres stepped beside her. The Leader's screams still echoed as they looked down at her, trying to fill her wound with ice. From the crystallised blood fragments Sabeline could see dropping to the ground like tiny rubies, it seemed the Leader was doing more harm than good with her healing attempt.

The moment Crysantha noticed them watching, an ice blast came careening from her hand. Sabeline felt herself being shifted just a bit as her dragon came to partially stand in front of her, diffusing the blast with more flame. Her heart swelled at the knowledge Nivres would act as her shield, though the now familiar sound of ice forming pulled her attention before she could ponder those thoughts further.

"She has formed a shield of her own." Sabeline muttered as Nivres fell into step beside her again, no longer blocking her with his body.

"Indeed." The dragon agreed, as they gazed upon a small circle of thick ice, reaching to the sky in jagged points.

"Whatever she is trying to do to the injury I gave her, it is not going as she hopes. She's trying to delay us."

"I have an idea; it may end this once and for all. Raise up your blade my dear heart, but keep hold of it." The dragon uttered, low enough so that Crysantha would not hear them in her makeshift fortress. Curious, Sabeline did as he instructed.

With care, Nivres's fingers covered her own around the hilt. Nothing happened for a moment. Nothing except for her heartbeat increasing significantly the longer her fingers remained touching her dragon's. Then in a mesmerising burst, tendrils of flame licked around the edges of her sword, growing until they'd encompassed all of the blade. She couldn't help the slight parting of her lips as she gazed at her beloved weapon. It looked like a sword of legend, one from an ancient tale where warriors wielded fantastical blades imbued with power.

A pleased rumble that was distinctly dragon in nature echoed next to her. "It will remain aflame while I grip the hilt with you."

Sabeline closed her mouth and tried to rein in her awe. "This better not melt my sword, dragon."

"I can promise you; your blade will remain unharmed." Nivres answered with a slight chuckle.

"If it can only remain aflame while you hold it, why do you not take it then and finish this?" The question left her lips as she attempted to release her fingers, but Nivres kept them covered and still with his own.

"I have no skill with a sword, only flame. It will take both of us to end this." She turned to meet his gaze. Sincerity swirled within those golden depths, along with love, trust and a plethora of other emotions she couldn't identify, but those were enough.

"Alright. Then do as I do. We have one chance at this." The dragon nodded at her words.

Keeping the blade in its current position, Sabeline darted forward, pleased to note Nivres mirroring her actions with precision. As they approached the ice, she adjusted the blade so that the tip was at a horizontal angle, Nivres's hand moving with her own. Both arms pulled back in perfect synchronisation. With one almighty thrust, the blade plunged through the ice as though it was no more solid than water. There was a crunch, then Sabeline felt the familiar impact of slicing through flesh.

The ice fortress fell away in melting chunks and breaking fragments to reveal Crysantha on her knees, a trail of blood falling from the corner of her lips. Her armour began to drip before becoming water and falling to the ground like a waterfall. The flaming sword was buried deep in her chest.

Nivres released his hold and the flames coating her sword disappeared. With narrowed eyes, she pulled her blade from Crysantha's body, ensuring it was done as slowly as possible. She had expected that to be it, but the Leader gurgled out a question, bubbles of blood forming on her lips as she did.

"Who are you? I must know who bested me."

Sabeline contemplated answering. It would be just what Crysantha deserved if she remained silent and did not answer. But she was a knight, first and foremost. And there was sombre honour in fulfilling a dying request.

"I was once known as the Bringer of Truth." She answered, sheathing her blade. After all, Crysantha was no threat now and everyone else here was either dead or had long fled.

A choked laugh came from the Leader. " You lie. News from High Point reaches us even here. The Bringer of Truth died by a…"

"Dragon?" Sabeline interrupted, "Interesting then, that I should be here side by side with my murderer."

A great scarlet reptilian head appeared next to her shoulder and Sabeline took deep satisfaction and pleasure in seeing the dying Leader's eyes widen at Nivres's shift in forms. But she could also tell the light was leaving them.

"Goodbye Crysantha." She muttered, as the Leader fell back, eyes still open in shock, but void of any life. Dismissing the body, Sabeline turned, running her hand over her dragon's snout.

"Let's go home Nivres."

44

Unresolved Matters

For the second time, Sabeline found herself in Nivres's water cavern. Only this time, she was insistent that the dragon either get in the water as well or remain on the edge with his head turned the other way. After what had happened previously, she was not going to take a chance.

Perhaps sensing her ire, Nivres had chosen to remain on the side and she had dutifully plastered tilweed paste over his various injuries, before applying some to her face. She'd caught sight of her reflection on her way into the pool. The hit had definitely left quite the bruise.

The water seeped into her bones, the warmth lapping over her skin and turning the cold sting of Crysantha's ice into mere memory. But despite the water's soothing nature, Sabeline's heart beat like a trapped thing trying to escape and she could feel the tension still unwilling to unwind from her muscles. She glanced over to the dragon, still keeping his promise and protecting her modesty. She may love him, but unresolved matters needed to be addressed. And remaining in dragon form was not going to delay her from asking.

Drawing in a deep breath, Sabeline braced herself for what she was about to do. By the goddess, going into battle was easier than starting such a conversation. But it had to be done, otherwise matters would fester within her soul, tainting this new found love of theirs. "Why did you do it?" Her voice was soft, much to her aggravation. Dammit, the words were supposed to come out strong and fierce, not leave her sounding so...vulnerable. Her lip curled at the very notion.

Thankfully, Nivres did not ask her to elaborate. She watched as he inclined his reptilian head towards her, just enough so that he could probably see her out of the corner of his eye. "I wanted to protect you, my instincts were tearing me apart at the need to keep you safe and bringing you headlong into another fight so soon after your great injuries...the very idea nearly ruined me. But I knew time was of the essence to get to Sentinel Pass before news reached them of the sorcerer's settlement. With you safe in the cave, my plan was to go, dispose of them quickly and return within a few hours."

"And do you not think you could have told me? Goddess Nivres, I am a knight. If we are injured, we're patched up just enough so that we can get back into the fight. My body is trained to go from one battle to another despite sustained injuries. You did not ask me and instead let your instincts rule your head." She let the previously restrained fury seep into her voice as she continued, "Do you have any idea what it was like to find you missing and to realise where you'd gone? Finding out that you'd taken on a Chaos Convocation city by yourself? Do you have any idea what I had to do to get there? You may have thought you were protecting me, but that didn't happen did it? Instead if I hadn't come after you, you'd probably be dead by now and I'd still be waiting for an idiot lizard to return!" Her breath came out in ragged pants as her words grew louder. He needed to know, goddess damn him. Know that despite everything, he hadn't protected her at all.

A distinctly dragon rumble echoed around the walls of the cavern as Sabeline noted his tail whipping back and forth. Had she made him angry? Or was he frustrated at himself? No matter, she did not regret her words. They were the truth after all. "I am sorry my heart, I thought I could take care of it. I had failed to protect you from the sorcerer, but I would not fail again. I swore it to myself as my instincts clouded my mind."

So that was it. The memory of her careening through the air and being buried beneath wood and flame still haunted her dragon. Enough for him to give over to his instincts. She swallowed hard before returning in a less furious tone. "Imagine if it had been the other way around Nivres, what if you were to find me missing after a promise made, then realised I had decided to take on that settlement by myself? I do not think you would be best pleased either."

The dragon huffed, little puffs of smoke spilling from his nostrils as he did. "You are right. I understand your fury. I realised it once they had captured me that I would face your anger if we were to meet again and that I could have ruined everything by breaking your trust. That was just as much a torture as the wounds they inflicted."

"That is another thing dragon, if we were to be logical, I received what amounts to one major attack from the sorcerer, the results of which caused a few injuries. You were brutally harmed for an inordinate amount of time, repeatedly." She glanced away, crossing her arms over her submerged chest.

"I heard your screams, you know. Listening to such raw, deafening pain, knowing you can do *nothing* about it, knowing that no matter how much you want to rush in, you *can't* because that could jeopardise the entire operation even more…It is not something I would like to relive any time soon Nivres."

"It seems I am the fool, Sabeline. By trying to protect you, I inflicted more harm then I would ever have imagined. On both of us. To imagine seeing you the same way you must have seen me, it is a torment. No being should have to go through such a thing."

A heavy sigh escaped her chest as some tension began to uncoil from her form. "The consequences of this night, the memories, these are things that we both must learn to live with. There is no cure for them. Next time, despite what your instincts command, talk to me first before flying off and being all noble. If you do not, then you will have well and truly broken any trust I would have for you. This time, I will forgive you. Your instincts clouded your judgement and I am guessing you have not had to deal with such…intense insistence from them in terms of a lover for…some time."

By the goddess, that last part had been difficult to word. Truly, she did not know too much of her dragon's past, other than of Myvanna but it was perhaps safe to assume he may have had previous experiences with matters of the heart, just as she had. *It is just the heat from the pool, I am not blushing. Knights do not blush while having such serious discussions!* Shaking her head, Sabeline turned back to her dragon, who shifted slightly.

"I thank you for your forgiveness, my heart. You have my oath that I will not do such a thing again. A vow I will uphold with honour." Sincerity coated his voice, intertwining with solemnity. The pledge nestled into her soul, as serious as the fire in which he breathed. She did not doubt him.

"I thank you for making such a vow. I believe you, Nivres." The dragon appeared to relax at her acceptance. "Now if you don't mind, I think I have spent long enough in these healing waters of yours."

Once Nivres had flicked his head back fully to face the cave wall, her fingers gripped the stone and Sabeline hauled herself out, the loud echo of sloshing water filling the comfortable silence. Swiftly but with care, she rubbed the cloths Nivres had carried down over her skin, mindful of the various cuts and tender parts, in particular her cauterised shoulder and tilweed pasted cheek. Hurriedly, she reached for the white shirt and brown trousers that Nivres had obtained from somewhere in his hoard. The lack of armour felt odd, but she would endure the feeling. After all, her armour required a rather deep clean and her sword would need sharpening again. But this would be enough for now.

"You can turn now." She uttered and the dragon wasted no time in swivelling to meet her gaze. He padded around the pool to her and before she could move, his great crimson tail curled around her, gently bringing her closer to his hide as his head came down to rest next to her good cheek, warm breath ruffling the top of her head.

Reaching up her own hands, Sabeline let her fingers rest against his jaw as she pulled him down a little further and pressed her head against his scaled snout, closing her eyes. She understood. They were here. They were together. They were alive. And for now, they were safe.

An angry, rage-filled shout echoed around the entirety of

the cave, breaking the moment. "We know you're in here, beast! Come out and face us!"

Sabeline sighed again, releasing Nivres's face. *Just my luck.*

The words were powerful, surrounding her and Nivres with their torment and grief. Her eyes narrowed as she detected that last emotion disguised within the rage. Was it a wayward Chaos Convocation member, who in their emotional wisdom thought it wise to take on a dragon? But no… that could not be right. The Chaos Convocation were not aware of Nivres's true nature. Her dragon rumbled beside her.

"How dare such fiends interrupt us, how dare they approach our territory?" Despite the offence in his tone, Sabeline couldn't help the leap of her heart at his use of *us* and *our*.

"They must have tracked our flight back here. I cannot imagine these intruders would have discovered this place by any other means." She attempted to sooth his ire, but her efforts were soon destroyed as further shouts flooded the cavern.

"What is the matter, beast? Too afraid to pay for your crime? No matter, we shall ensure justice is served!"

Her dragon roared in response and scales slipped through her grasp as Sabeline tried to place her hand on his side. Her eyes followed his movements as he stalked towards the arch, no doubt fire raging in his throat ready to incinerate whoever was here for the insult. But something about that voice…it tugged at the wisps of her memory. And the words themselves…Sabeline narrowed her gaze. She was missing something. This was no Chaos Convocation member, and she was not familiar with anyone else for the voice to give her pause except…

Her mouth parted as her eyes widened. It was impossible.

Inconceivable. And yet it was the truth. *By the goddess, they have come to avenge my honour.* A further outraged roar shook the cavern, signalling Nivres had encountered them. Damnation, she had to get up there. Now. Without further thought, her feet flew across the cave floor.

Ignoring the pain and stabs of the rocky terrain across her bare flesh, Sabeline rushed through the tunnels towards the entrance. Her heart practically hammered against the skin of her chest as fear unlike any she'd felt before conquered her soul and sang a victorious anthem within her blood. They could not kill her dragon. And her dragon could not kill them. She would not allow it. And there was only one way to stop it.

Finally, the dappled sunlight dancing across the entrance greeted her vision. Sounds of weapons clanging, armour shifting and a dragon rumbling met her ears. Drawing on the last of her strength as her breath left in heavy pants, Sabeline leapt through the entrance and screamed with everything she had. "Stop!"

One reptilian gaze turned in her direction, along with three very human, very shocked ones. "Sabeline?" The one with short, braided ginger hair uttered, as though afraid she was not before them and merely a ghost. She could understand the sentiment, for the same was echoing in her mind.

"Kilyn." Sabeline uttered back, before turning to the others and nodding at each. "Echoris. Bersaba."

Nivres shifted behind them, causing Kilyn, Echoris and Bersaba to return their attention to him, weapons once again raised. "It's alright," Sabeline hastened to speak, "Nivres has proven himself an honourable dragon. He is no threat to us and ours."

She could see that her sisters in arms were dubious, but nonetheless they heeded her words and a warmth spread through her as they sheathed their respective weapons. "But you are supposed to be dead. This beast killed you." Bersaba reasoned, presumably trying to make sense of the unexpected situation they had all found themselves in.

Nivres huffed. "I am not a mindless creature, surviving solely on instinct Knight. I am able to make reasonable decisions, such as sparing the Bringer of Truth."

The notable surprise across their faces at Nivres's ability to speak would have caused her to laugh, if she had not experienced the same notions. "He speaks the truth. He could have easily chosen to kill me, but instead Nivres chose to spare my life. It is quite the tale, one that would take a place of honour in our halls, should it not be imperative Falon believe me still to be dead."

Her sisters in arms shared glances with each other before Echoris spoke. "The King has grown worse since your apparent death. We fear for ourselves and the Knighthood. Something is stirring within him. It may be death to leave, but death also to stay."

"Then what can be done?" She returned, trying to quell the horror of the vision Echoris painted. She had thought the King had targeted her in a moment of madness, but to have all his most skilled warriors filled with fear at his plans....This went beyond sacrificing her and keeping her sisters in arms locked in their tower.

"We do not know. We are watching and waiting, trying to plan our next move. We do not know for sure he seeks our deaths, but I have a feeling he wants to disband us. The reasons why remain unclear." Bersaba interjected.

"We know one thing with absolute certainty." Kilyn piped up. "There is something terribly wrong with the King. This is not the Falon we serve."

There was a moment of silence before Sabeline spoke again. "If he has become this bad, how have you been able to come here? I imagine in his current state, Falon would not sanction a revenge mission."

Kilyn let out a hearty laugh. "Of course not. Ascilia approved it. Despite her authoritarian attitude, she does care. And she definitely wished to uphold the tradition of seeking vengeance for a fallen Knight. So we volunteered and snuck out in secret. Ascilia just told Falon we were running some patrols, making sure reputations were intact after your… erhm…death. He seemed pretty satisfied with that."

"And we are certainly not going to inform him you're alive. Though the others will be pleased to know you were not killed after all." Bersaba grinned.

Nivres shifted again, this time padding closer to her side and ensuring his tail wrapped around the front of her. Glancing at their faces, Sabeline thought only Echoris seemed to understand the importance of the gesture. When she flicked her gaze towards Sabeline, Echoris gave a slight nod. *She knows.*

"Is it wise to tell the others of your creed?" Nivres rumbled.

"Of course it is. Knights are loyal to each other, dragon. I have absolute trust in all my sisters in arms. They would die before revealing this information to Falon." She ensured her words were laced with the confidence she felt as she met his gaze, though she noticed out of the corner of her eye Kilyn, Bersaba and Echoris nodding with a solemn air.

"The bonds of knighthood make us family. And family do

not betray each other." Echoris intoned with such seriousness that it would be folly not to believe her words.

Her dragon seemed satisfied and inclined his head towards Echoris. "I will hold you to that, spider born."

Turning to Echoris, Sabeline watched her eyes widen in surprise before she nodded. The Cursed One had always been a mystery, talking little of her past. Sabeline certainly wasn't going to press for her secrets now and it seemed Kilyn and Bersaba were of the same mind.

"Perhaps you should all come into the cavern so we can discuss matters further. It would be far safer than continuing out here." She offered, in an attempt to ease the awkward feeling her dragon had unintentionally created.

"Good plan. Some of the things we've seen in the forest wouldn't hesitate to have us for breakfast." Kilyn agreed with a stretch.

"Indeed, have you seen those sabre toothed forest panthers? If they were to get hold of you, you might as well pray to the goddess for a merciful death." Bersaba said, her tone lighter while Echoris nodded along with her words.

Her dragon also joined in, rumbling out an agreeable sound. Damnation, she hadn't exactly told him how she'd made it to Sentinel Pass, just that she'd had to go through a lot to get there and he hadn't pressed the matter.

As her sisters in arms stepped with some trepidation towards the cave, the realisation that she would have to tell her story, all of it, to both her friends and her beloved gripped her.

After Kilyn, Bersaba and Echoris entered, she felt Nivres uncoil his tail from her and with a glance up at him, he inclined his head towards the entrance. Walking side by side, a sense of peace and pride washed over her.

During the events of the last day, she had thought she would lose the dragon who had made a home in her heart. And she had accepted long ago that she would probably never see her fellow knights again. Now to have them both, at this moment, it was more than she'd dared to dream.

She would tell them all. She owed them both that much.

45

New Beginnings

And tell she did. Once Kilyn Bersaba and Echoris had been settled in the main chamber, Nivres nestled around the ridiculously sized fire, while she positioned herself close to them all.

She spoke of everything, from the sacrifice, to Nivres sparing her life, to the Chaos Convocation and finally the events of the previous night, including their love for each other. She noted her dragon become particularly restless when she mentioned riding the same forest panther that had tried to take her life and had gently placed a hand on his tail. That part of the story was never going to go well with him.

After the last words left Sabeline's lips, there was quiet for a moment before Echoris uttered, "A tale worthy of our halls indeed. I will make sure it is told and kept from the ears of the King."

In turn, her sisters in arms revealed everything that had happened since the sacrifice. How Falon was growing into someone they no longer recognised, but yet at times, he seemed like the old King, the one who had earnt their loyalty.

They were not sure whether Viras knew more than he dained to tell, or if he was just as in the dark as they were. He had always been of a tricky nature like that. They continued with how the knights had missed her, mourned her and had even held their own funeral rites for her, despite Falon's obvious displeasure at the notion.

"But we believe Mariel could be within his sights." Bersaba uttered. "The King seemed almost placated after Nivres stole you away, but now he appears to grow restless."

"Why target Mariel out of all the knights?" Sabeline questioned, confused. Sure, with her failure to kill Nivres, she had presented the opportunity to remove her on a silver platter, but would it not make more strategic sense to choose Ascilia next? After Falon and his council (of which Ascilia was part of), the Leader of their creed held the most significant power.

"She's been investigating the lower town to honour your memory, just as she swore before the sacrifice. We don't know what she's found or what she's likely to find, but Falon has taken a vested interest in her investigations." Kilyn spat and it was plain for Sabeline to see the disgust in her eyes.

These were her friends. Her fellow knights. Her creed. Her sisters in arms. And as her gaze swept over them all, she could see the things they tried to hide with their body language. The fear. The uncertainty. Never before had such elite warriors been made to feel as such by the very King they had sworn to protect. Nausea curled within her gut. She had hoped it was a moment of insanity when she was led to slaughter, but from what the trio were saying, they were all in grave danger.

"Promise me, all of you, that you will do what it takes to remain safe and away from Falon's attentions." Even to her own ears, her tone sounded begging. It was unbecoming, but she did not care. Not when their lives could be forfeit to Falon's schemes.

"We promise. We have our own plans in place ready for certain potential eventualities. We would not go down without a fight, you know this." Echoris's words were almost reassuring, but the image of her sisters in arms trying to escape High Point as the King picked them off one by one caused the nausea to swirl like a tide.

Banishing the thought from her mind, she uttered a simple "I know."

Nivres, who had been silent for most of the story telling, made a soft noise drawing her attention to him as he slowly pulled his tail from underneath her hand. "Everyone must be hungry. I will go hunt something and bring it back. Stay for the day, the Bringer of Truth has missed you all terribly." His head lowered, nudging her own as he padded once more towards the entrance.

"I need to get me a dragon. Know if there are anymore about Sabeline?" Kilyn grinned at her.

Sabeline smiled back, falling into the familiar jesting, "If I did, I don't know if you could handle it."

Instantly, the mood became lighter and her heart lifted. Nivres had spoken the truth, she had missed them all and mourned them as they had mourned her. For this day, she would enjoy their company and cherish the memories created within this cave.

***

It was close to dusk when her sisters in arms emerged from the cave and said their farewells to her. She had almost insisted they stay till morning, but Bersaba had said they would start to be missed back at High Point soon and with Echoris by their side, travelling through the night was not too much of an issue. But the sight of their retreating, armoured backs tore at her heartstrings. She thought she felt a wetness on her cheeks, but it must have been her imagination. Knights do not cry after all. *You mean like they do not blush?*

Shoving that thought away as Nivres curled around her, Sabeline allowed herself to sink into his scales.

"Your friends are honourable warriors and people." Her dragon murmured as she felt his head come to rest atop of hers, warm breath ruffling the strands of hair.

"Yes." She murmured, disturbed by the hoarse tone of her voice.

"Come back inside, my heart. They are strong, they will make their way back unharmed."

In light of what they'd said over the course of the day, Sabeline was more inclined to believe Kilyn, Bersaba and Echoris would be safer within the forest than back at High Point. Regardless, she allowed Nivres to gently pull her back within the cave. Her bare feet padded against the crevices and sharp rocks, taking little notice of her surroundings as they stepped towards the main chamber.

Stepping over to the fire, she waited for Nivres to make himself comfortable, though surprise flitted across her features as he continued on through another tunnel, motioning for her to follow. Curious, she padded behind him. She did not think they were going back to the spring, nor any such cavern where he kept parts of his hoard. Gazing around, the route seemed vaguely familiar, but then again, she had been to so few places within the dragon's lair that she could easily be mistaken. And yet…she did not think so. The feeling only grew when Nivres slipped through an archway that she recognised.

"Stay outside for a moment Sabeline, I must do something first." He called from what she now knew to be his bed chambers.

"Very well." She affirmed, after realising her dragon could not see her nod of acknowledgement. She heard what sounded like furniture being shifted, along with pained hisses, grunts and almost like bones shifting.

"You may come in now." The words came in much heavier pants than before and with a little caution welling within her, Sabeline stepped through the archway.

The first thing that was impossible not to notice, was a four poster bed that she was certain had not been there the last time she had entered these chambers. It was a grand thing, with silken sheets and carved bed posts in the shape of entwining flowers. Movement to the side drew her attention away from the magnificent bed and her eyes landed on her dragon, though this time, he was in his human form, wearing a shirt and trousers similar to the ones she was still draped in.

"This was not here before." She gestured to the bed, searching for something to say while her heart began to race.

"No, it is a recent acquisition. I thought that perhaps, you would like to sleep in the same bed tonight?" Before she could say anything, he had stepped forward and arms were wrapped around her waist as he muttered into her hair. "I could have lost you. I could have lost you so many times yesterday. And then, when I did not know they were your creed, I thought I would lose you again, that they would think to save you from me and take you away."

Her very soul swelled as it filled with warmth, light and

love. Carefully, she wrapped her arms around his torso and buried her face in his chest, listening to his heartbeat echo against her ear. "I have not felt such fear before in all my years as a knight than I have over the past day. I thought Crysantha would not stop until you were dead and then the thought for my friends murdering you, or you killing them…" A shudder ran through her spine and Nivres tightened his arms around her, indicating he'd felt it too.

Tilting her head up and running her hands over Nivres back until they reached his head, she pulled him down, pressing her lips against his own. They were hesitant at first beneath her own, but as she moulded herself to his body, a grin ghosted across her rather busy lips as Nivres's grew more desperate.

Sabeline pulled away just enough to utter, "You have brought us a bed, take me to it dragon."

He gazed down at her and it was easy to see love swirling within those golden depths. She had every confidence he would look after her, from now until the end of time. Letting her own love for him shine in her eyes, a softer smile decorated her mouth as her dragon did as she asked.

***

Her eyelids fluttered open and Sabeline stretched, awareness creeping in of the very warm, very male body next to her. In this cavern, it was difficult to tell if dawn had broken or not, but she found she did not care. Her body and heart felt sated, reassured and above all else, loved. Her gaze flickered over to Nivres's sleeping face, crimson hair in disarray amongst the pillows. With care, she dragged the back of her fingers over his cheek.

Despite the happiness flowing through her, she needed to talk with him. After the unexpected visit from her sisters in arms, they had discussed more things while he had been hunting and one had struck her, no matter how much she disliked it. It was perhaps the only way to ensure their safety. And time was of the essence, despite her body's protests to enjoy basking in this afterglow with her dragon.

Her fingers dragged over his cheek again with a little more pressure, and finally, Sabeline saw his eyelids flicker before his gaze landed on her and his lips fell into a large, predatory grin, flashing fangs.

"Morning my heart."

"Is it morning?"

"I believe so." He answered, his fingers drifting over her skin.

Refusing to be distracted, she uttered, "Then time is of the essence."

Confusion flickered across his face and she hastily spoke. "I have no regrets about what we have done Nivres. But I have been thinking about our future. In order for us both to remain safe, together, I feel like our only option would be to leave Idrelas."

Her dragon shuffled so he was sitting up. "Leave Idrelas?"

"I do not like the idea any more than you, but from what the knights say, then there may be no choice. If King Falon finds out that I still breathe, I am sure he will send everything at his disposal to ensure I no longer do so. And he will probably ensure your demise as well. I cannot go through seeing your tortured form again." She murmured, glancing away from his unreadable gaze, but running her fingertips over a scar lacing the flesh of his abdomen.

Her dragon was silent for a moment, before murmuring. "I have reason to believe the Chaos Convocation do not solely operate in Idrelas. For some of the things I have seen them acquire, there must be other organisations stationed in other lands. Ones that have not yet felt the wrath of Chaos's Bane."

"If that is the case, it would be remiss of us not to rectify such a thing."

"Indeed, my heart. We can make preparations to leave on the morrow."

"Why the morrow?"

"Because today, today is for us." Her dragon reached for her, enclosing her within his arms and capturing her mouth in a soft kiss.

With an eagerness that had only shown itself before a battle, Sabeline reciprocated his affections. They were together. They were safe. And soon they would be free. Images danced across her mind of lands unseen, of fighting side by side, taking down more settlements and liberating towns controlled by such a foul organisation.

Yes a new kind of adventure was opening up before her and she would experience it all with her beloved dragon by her side.

Sabeline could hardly wait.

Epilogue

Clutching the scroll in his pale fingers, Viras shuffled through the corridors of the palace. He had read the contents of the scroll of course. It was a part of his duties. And that was why sweat was beading across his forehead and the palms of his hands were growing clammy. This one could not be sent to the King later for review. Oh no. This one had to be delivered personally and immediately. Fear flickered across his face as he fought to control his rapid heartbeat.

Ever since the Bringer of Truth had been sacrificed to the dragon, Falon had seemed to be watching and waiting. For what, Viras did not know and was too scared to ask. He just served and if it kept his head on his shoulders, then even better. But he had a terrible feeling that this scroll would be the opportunity Falon had been waiting for.

Drawing in a deep breath and swallowing hard, he brushed one hand over his robes before raising it to knock on the ornate hardwood door of the King's study.

"Enter." The voice of the King echoed and with another swallow, Viras pushed the door open.

Falon was at his desk, quill in hand as he scribbled something down before adorning the paper with the seal of the King. Viras noted a small moon flower terrarium sat on the desk. Strange, he did not think the King moved his terrariums away from their room. Ah well, no matter. He certainly wasn't

EPILOGUE

going to mention it.

Falon's eyes flickered to his own. "What is it Viras?"

"Ah, yes sire. It's erhm, this scroll you see." He raised the hand clutching the parchment.

"And it could not wait?" Falon asked, in a tone that Viras couldn't quite place.

"Not this one Sire, it's from Strix you see. Their royal family in fact." Viras waited, but the King said nothing, so he pressed on. "They want an alliance, something to do with the oceans, well you know Strix." A laugh escaped his lips, but it sounded more like a nervous bark than anything else.

"And how do they propose this alliance?" Falon questioned, placing the quill down on the table and finally giving Viras his full attention. He did not know whether that was a good thing or not.

"Erhm, a marriage. Between their Prince and a Princess of Idrelas. Of course, I know we have no Princesses, but I thought perhaps you would like to know of the offer regardless..." Viras trailed off as Falon reclined in his chair. He wasn't sure he liked the contemplation on the King's face.

"You're right of course, I have no daughters."

"Well yes, so shall I just write back and tell them..."

"But I do have Knights. Fine warriors that any Prince should be glad to have. And I believe one of them is descended from a noble blood line. It is in her title is it not? The Noble Arrow."

"Ah, yes sire. That is correct. Mariel, The Noble Arrow."

"Splendid. Leave the scroll Viras. I shall write back to Strix's King personally. After all, a noble warrior from this legendary creed of ours would make a much finer bride than some pompous princess. Don't you agree Viras?"

"Oh yes sire, yes indeed." He stuttered out. Oh, this had

gone very wrong, very quickly.

"Excellent. Once they accept, we will inform The Noble Arrow." Falon grinned, sending a shudder through Viras that he tried in vain to suppress. "That'll be all then Viras, thank you for bringing such news to me."

"Of course, then by your leave sire." He uttered, stepping forward quickly and dropping the scroll on the table before bowing in haste and attempting to walk with some dignity back through the door. Once it closed behind him with an echoing bang, he rubbed his hands over his face, trying to compose himself.

By the goddess, what had he done?

Acknowledgements

This book wouldn't be before you if it weren't for some very special people helping me along the way, whether they knew it or not.

Many thanks to fellow authors Kindra White, Mana Sol, Maria Warren, Jane Knight, Jenny Fox and H.Latham for general support, advice and author meet up. Writing can be considered a lonely profession and thanks to you lovely ladies, it feels much less so.

To Michelle Cank, who loves books as much as me and Sraddha Khambhayata who listens to me vent about writing from time to time. You two are the best.

To Evie Smith, Ricky Smith and Jamie Colwell for providing much needed fun and good times all year round. The three of you are the best friends a woman could ask for.

To Mum and Dad, who as the dedication says, always believed and supported me in my writing endeavours. And to my brother James, for always being there.

To Joe, the love of my life who is always prepared to answer the strangest questions at the most inconvenient times with no context. Hence Sabeline's dinner of weasel.

And finally to you dear reader, thank you for undertaking Sabeline's journey and joining me in Idrelas.

Coming Soon...

Water's Edge: Book Two of The Knights of Idrelas

The King is desperate to forge an alliance with the dangerous water folk of the Strix Kingdom and with no princesses born to the kingdom, Falon elects to send one of his best knights as a bride.

Mariel is the unlucky one chosen and while tempted to assasinate her future groom, she won't risk a war. However, not long after arriving in Strix, it's clear someone had the same idea and creating a war is on their agenda.

Wedding plans are on hold while Mariel learns the culture of her new land and spends time with the Prince. For knowledge is power and the more she knows, the quicker the hunt for the assassin will be.

Can Mariel find the assassin in time, as well as fending off growing feelings for a Prince? She's nothing if not professional, but the Prince may have beaten the assassin to her still beating heart.

About the Author

Charlotte Townsend is a proud gothic geek who never left the village of her ancestors. She loves fantasy and draws inspiration from obscure mythology, legends, creatures and monsters.

When not writing, she can usually be found playing video games, curled up with a good cup of tea or rolling that D20 for initiative in her latest DnD campaign.

Charlotte lives in Leicester, England with her fiancé and their mischievous cats.

You can connect with me on:
- https://www.instagram.com/charlottetownsendauthor
- https://twitter.com/townsend_char
- https://www.facebook.com/CharlottetownsendAuthor

Subscribe to my newsletter:
- https://mailchi.mp/a512e9bad8cb/charlotte-townsend-author

Also by Charlotte Townsend

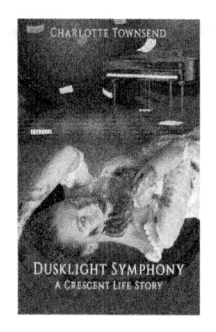

Dusklight Symphony

Welcome to the town of Crescent, where strange is the new normal….

Myra is on the verge of her musical debut. The night before her performance, she returns home to find an inruder in her flat. What follows is a night she'll never forget.

Theodora's Toad

Welcome to the town of Crescent, where strange is the new normal…

Theodora is not having a good day. And that was before the toad started talking to her. Between her overbearing boss, long hours and a surprise visit, will Theodora be able to solve the mystery of the strange amphibian?

The Ichor of Faerie: Tales from the Hollow Grove

Come little mortal, let us take you away...

The Fae realm is a beautiful but dangerous place, with creatures and beings just as likely to kill you than kiss you. Those who wander there must keep their wits about them.

In these tantalizing tales, explore magic and mayhem as Charlotte Townsend and Mana Sol take you to a realm beyond imagination, with inhabitants you'll never forget.